Praise for
Young Lonigan

"A devastating account of the short tragic life of its protagonist and one of the most powerful fictional treatments of the Irish in America."   —James Hurt, *Illinois Authors*

"A masterwork of the Depression years, the *Studs Lonigan* trilogy is a stunning artistic achievement that urgently demands reconsideration by the present generation of readers and scholars. The appearance in 1928 of the first volume, *Young Lonigan,* changed U.S. literature forever in ways that have yet to be fully acknowledged or understood. Farrell, the Proust-toting poet of Chicago's tough Irish South Side, pioneered a unique style that burst asunder the barriers separating 'high art' from 'mass culture.' In the rise and fall of Studs Lonigan, Farrell dramatized the hollowness of the 'cult of masculinity' and the overall malaise of U.S. social institutions in a manner outdistancing by far his more famous contemporaries, such as Dos Passos and Steinbeck."
      —Alan M. Wald, author of *James T. Farrell:*
      The Revolutionary Socialist Years

"I read [Farrell] in my freshman year at Harvard, and it changed my life. . . . I realized you could write books about people who were something like the people you had grown up with. I couldn't get over the discovery. I wanted to write."   —Norman Mailer

"The single literary conversation of my entire Bronx boyhood was about 'the good parts' in *Studs Lonigan*. . . . One summer I read all of the trilogy from beginning to end and enjoyed the other parts even more than 'the good parts.' "
      —*The New York Times Book Review*

continued . . .

Born in the South Side slum section of Chicago, **James T. Farrell** (1904–79) was known for his many novels depicting lower-middle-class Irish-Catholic life; his stories deal with the poverty, bigotry, vices, and frustration he encountered. Farrell's naturalistic style echoed the crudities of his chosen milieu, and it was a source of controversy when his work was originally published; however, the powerful, cumulative effect of his writing helped make *Studs Lonigan* a classic.

Pete Hamill was born in Brooklyn, New York, the oldest of seven children of Irish immigrants from Belfast, Northern Ireland. He has won many awards as a newspaper reporter and columnist and has served as editor-in-chief of both the *New York Post* and the *New York Daily News*. He is currently on the staff of *The New Yorker*. Hamill has also pursued a career as a fiction writer, producing eight novels and two collections of short stories, as well as numerous acclaimed works of nonfiction, including his memoir, *A Drinking Life*, and a biography of the Mexican painter Diego Rivera.

YOUNG
LONIGAN

James T. Farrell

With a New Introduction
by Pete Hamill

SIGNET CLASSICS

SIGNET CLASSICS
Published by New American Library, a division of
Penguin Group (USA) Inc., 375 Hudson Street,
New York, New York 10014, U.S.A.
Penguin Books Ltd, 80 Strand,
London WC2R 0RL, England
Penguin Books Australia Ltd, 250 Camberwell Road,
Camberwell, Victoria 3124, Australia
Penguin Books Canada Ltd, 10 Alcorn Avenue,
Toronto, Ontario, Canada M4V 3B2
Penguin Books (NZ), cnr Airborne and Rosedale Roads,
Albany, Auckland 1310, New Zealand

Penguin Books Ltd, Registered Offices:
80 Strand, London WC2R 0RL, England

Published by Signet Classics, an imprint of New American Library, a division of
Penguin Group (USA) Inc. Published by arrangement with the Vanguard Press.

First Signet Classics Printing, July 2004
10   9   8   7   6   5   4   3   2   1

Library of Congress Catalog Card Number: 2004044982

Printed in the United States of America

East Side, West Side,
All around the town,
The tots sing ring-a-rosie,
London Bridge is falling down.
Boys and girls together,
Me and Mamie O'Rourke,
We tripped the light fantastic
On the sidewalks of New York.

POPULAR SONG.

A literature that cannot be vulgarized is no literature at all and will perish.

FRANK NORRIS.

Except in the case of some rarely gifted nature there never will be a good man who has not from his childhood been used to play amid things of beauty and make of them a joy and a study.

PLATO, "REPUBLIC," Jowett translation.

The poignancy of situations that evoke reflection lies in the fact that we really do not know the meaning of the tendencies that are pressing for action.

JOHN DEWEY, "Human Nature and Conduct."

INTRODUCTION

I first read *Young Lonigan* in 1951, when I was only a few years older than the main character. I was then a high school dropout, working as an apprentice sheet metal worker in the Brooklyn Navy Yard and trying to imagine a way to live my life. Sometimes I thought about becoming a cop. Or a comic book artist. Or some sort of writer. It depended on the day, or the weather, or the counsel of older men. Then I found this novel in a used Signet paperback, for which I paid five cents. It had a decisive impact on my raw, uncertain adolescent consciousness.

The impact was based on obvious affinities. After all, I was the oldest son of Irish immigrants, and lived in a tenement, and had gone to Catholic schools, and knew a lot of tough guys in my neighborhood. This fellow from Chicago, James T. Farrell, told me by example that if I were to become a writer I could draw upon the life I knew in Brooklyn. I didn't need to create colonies on Mars, or ride through an imaginary American West, or follow the lives of bullfighters in Spain. The stuff of fiction was right up the block. I knew at least four guys who could have been Studs Lonigan, and one of them was me. In a mysterious, indirect way, Farrell had given me my own world. I began to look at my neighbors and relatives, the men in bars and those who worked beside me, as parts of a long story. I bought a notebook and

wrote down what they said or how they dressed and what
they did. That notebook was lost many years ago. But for
more than five decades, I've been drawing on those notes.

Reading *Young Lonigan* again, after living a life, has
been an experience full of surprises. The most powerful
surprise was the novel's pervasive innocence.

In memory the saga of Studs Lonigan was a dark narrative, a classic tale of decline and fall, played against a
spiky urban landscape of tenements and empty lots. The
tenements are there, of course, and the lots, and a social
narrowness that could be considered bleak. But this first
volume in James T. Farrell's great trilogy today seems almost sunny. Nobody uses "bad" language, except the ugly
language of bigotry. Nobody shoots anyone. Nobody lives
in grinding poverty. The kids work hard at becoming men,
but what they'll settle for is a double chocolate soda.

This impression of innocence is almost surely driven by
the great changes in American cities since the novel was
published in 1932. That year the Great Depression was rav-
aging the nation, and the cities were heavy with despair,
breadlines, ruined hopes, destroyed certainties. None of that
is in *Young Lonigan*, which is set in Chicago in a year when
the United States was edging closer to entering the Great
War in Europe. Studs has just graduated from grammar
school and as a member of the Irish-American lower middle
class he has options in life that are not available to the poor.
He can go on to high school, which his dull but hardwork-
ing father wants him to do. He can become a priest, which
is the burning desire of his mother. He can go to work. His
inability to make *any* choice is the heart of the novel.

If Studs Lonigan is not living in Depression-era America,
he is even farther away from the American city we've all
come to know. There is plenty of drinking in his slice of
Chicago, but it is not the city where heroin and crack co-
caine have erased so many hopes. He doesn't live in the city
of AIDS. He doesn't live in the city of a million small daily

brutalities and some very large ones; the city of smashed families, of single mothers, of uncertain parentage; the city of welfare and stasis; the city where television plays incessantly, that ultimate mood-altering drug, mindless creator of passivity and the need for conflict; the city of hip-hop, where there's a numbing rhythm but no melody, where women are reduced to bitches and hos, where violence is the core of the lyrics, and where there's almost no presence of love. Studs Lonigan did not live in the modern American city.

Instead, he drifts through the empty streets of a city that now evokes a certain nostalgia. In some ways, it resembles the Brooklyn of my own childhood and youth. There are hard guys around; there are demands made upon boys to be "tough;" there is a conflict between the precepts of Church or family and simple boyish lust. Some of the Chicago language is also the language of my lost Brooklyn. We, too, called softball "indoor," Italian-Americans were called "Guineas," and we used phrases such as "like a bat out of hell."

But Studs is an immobilized teenager. His mind is filled with notions about a personal image, but not of a self. He wants others to think he is tough, a natural desire for a kid who weighs one hundred ten pounds. He poses in front of the bathroom mirror, turning his face into tough-guy masks. He wins some street fights, and achieves something of a reputation, but even this small neighborhood identity doesn't make him happy.

He "likes" a girl named Lucy Scanlan, but he cannot act on his desires. There is a famous scene in the novel where he and Lucy sit on a tree branch in a park and he kisses her. The scene is as sweet and tender as anything in the work of William Saroyan. But Studs cannot follow up. He cannot speak. He cannot express what he feels because he fears that if he did, he would seem soft-to his friends, to himself, to Lucy. He says nothing. And in the summer that follows the moment in the tree, he finds himself in an emotional dead zone of his own making.

This is in contrast to the way Stephen Dedalus roams Dublin in *A Portrait of an Artist as a Young Man*, by James Joyce, one of the two writers Farrell most admired (the other was Marcel Proust). In several insightful essays on Joyce, Farrell goes to the heart of the matter in Ireland, the long national history of defeat and martyrdom and the heartbreaking choice of exile. He reminds us that young Dedalus is intelligent, ambitious to the point of arrogance, consumed by the need to escape the dead zone of Irish life. He has a goal: to escape in order to fully live as an artist.

Studs Lonigan has no such goal, which in his world would have been hootingly dismissed as pretentious. He has no goal at all. That is why, for the contemporary reader, Studs is such an exasperating figure. Instead of planning a return to school, he chooses to be stupid. Instead of getting a job, he chooses to drift through the summer days, cadging money from his mother. He is self-absorbed, and self-conscious, but has no true self. Nothing drives him forward. No ambition. No dream of escape from the platitudes of lower-middle-class life. He has no interior narrative in which he plays the principal part. A vague, inarticulate melancholy rises from him like fog.

In the novel, Farrell offers no explanation for why Studs is Studs. He simply shows his life in impeccably recorded (or remembered) detail. Unlike Joyce's young man, the character of Studs is not autobiographical (it was based on a fellow Farrell knew named William Cunningham). But the world of Studs Lonigan was indeed the product of Farrell's own biography. He was born February 27, 1904, in southwest Chicago. His father was a teamster, his mother a former domestic. James Thomas Farrell would be the second of their seven surviving children, but at two, he was sent to live with his maternal grandparents, both immigrants from Ireland. They were illiterate, but their children contributed enough money for them to live in comfort. If there was true poverty in their world, it was spiritual or emotional. Their influence on the boy was apparently quite strong. And they gave him a childhood. Farrell started going to White Sox games when he was six, got to see some games in the 1913 World Series, and would be a baseball fan all of his life. The character in this novel who most resembles Farrell is Danny O'Neill, who wears glasses, remains in school, learns how to play baseball; Farrell would later write five novels about him. Farrell finished high school (where he played baseball, football and basketball), and after the usual assortment of odd jobs, he started writing stories. In 1925, he enrolled in the University of Chicago and began his life-work. Clearly, Farrell was more Stephen Dedalus than Studs Lonigan. The young Chicago writer wanted to escape into freedom. Studs Lonigan only wants to go swimming.

In this novel, and in later fictions, Farrell would push deeply into the character of Irish-Americans, identifying what they shared with the Irish in Ireland and what made them different. On his own journeys to Ireland, and in his deep reading into Irish history and literature, Farrell saw the paralyzing power of history. As a Marxist and a pragmatist, he rejected most versions of Celtic Ireland and the enduring power of its myths. He also had a certain contempt (mixed with sympathy) for the power of the Catholic Church. But he recognized that hundreds of years of British oppression, and too many defeats, had created a general Irish attitude of passivity, fatalism, acceptance of the Christian dogma that no man or woman could be truly happy until after death, when they would join the company of the Lord in heaven. His Irish heroes were James Connolly and Jim Larkin, men of the left, believers in the possibility of happiness and justice here on earth. But the combination of Irish parochialism and Irish defeatism, along with the bitterness that came with the Irish nationalist Civil War, made any such goal seem impossible. Farrell believed (correctly) that William Butler Yeats was the greatest poet of his time, and surely would have agreed with his line "Too long a sacrifice makes a stone of the heart."

Farrell also knew that Irish-Americans were living in a different narrative, although it was one stained by the Irish past. In America, the Irish immigrants met, lived with, and sometimes married people who were not like them. That cracked the wall of Irish parochialism. The nineteenth-century ghettos were based on class, not race, and so the Irish in New York's notorious Five Points lived in the same streets as African-Americans (and later in the century, Chinese immigrants). For complicated reasons (best described in Noel Ignatiev's 1995 book *How the Irish Became White*) many working-class American Irish became the enemies of blacks. Farrell would deal later with the appalling violence of their enmity, but he foreshadows it in *Young Lonigan*.

Here, too, he depicts the casual anti-Semitism of the world in which Studs lives. Late in the novel, the boys take part in a "gang shag" with a willing young woman. The only kid she rejects is a Jew named Davey Cohen, whose fury at her, and at the Irish, is hard and visceral, although contained in an interior monologue. But another scene is one of the most brutal in the novel. Studs and his boys are walking aimlessly through the day when they spot two young Jews. One of Studs' friends starts the familiar rigmarole about "Christ killers" and they set out to beat up the Jews. Both Jewish kids fight back. Studs takes no part, except to give one of the Jews a kick in the butt, which leaves the boy vulnerable to a sneak punch. One boy escapes the Irish gang. The other is beaten into a moaning heap in an alley. One of Studs' friends, Weary, says, as they walk away, "Now it will be a perfect day, if we can only catch a couple of shines." Studs, being Studs, is silent.

When I was young, in the 1940s, there were still kids like those portrayed by Farrell with such admirable rigor and lack of sentimentality. Out of boredom, or malice, they would go off to Brooklyn's Prospect Park "to beat up Jews." At the time, all of us had already seen the newsreels from Dachau and Bergen-Belsen, and we thought these guys (a few years older than my friends) were sick. But I also had friends who were like Studs Lonigan. They lived in a kind of paralysis. They had no concept of the future. Many of them believed that the deck was stacked against them, that if they were Irish or Italian, there was no point in having too large an ambition. Take the cops' test, they were told. Become a fireman. Try for a clerk's job in an insurance company. Get real. Their parents reinforced this self-imposed limitation. Among the Irish, there was what I once called the "Green Ceiling." If the teenage son of a mechanic said he wanted to be a writer, an actor, a painter, the parents would say, "Who do you think you are?" If a young woman declared such an ambition, she was dismissed with scolding laughter, as if she were committing the sin of pride. Farrell would have known every one of them.

Not all Irish-American parents were like that, of course. And those who established the Green Ceiling usually had decent motives. They had come through the Depression and the war, and they didn't want their children to be hurt. If their kids wanted what they could not get, they could be injured for life. Many of those parents knew that, for too long a time, the deck *was* stacked. They had learned this lesson the hard way.

That all changed very quickly after World War Two, which alas, was too late for the generation of Studs Lonigan. The agent of change was the GI Bill of Rights. For the first time the children of all blue-collar Americans had the chance to go to a university. They had risked everything for their country, and now the country was giving them something back. If they had visions of another kind of life, and they had served in the armed forces, all they had to do was work. In neighborhoods like mine, and neighborhoods filled with the children of people like Studs, the world was turned upside down. It took a while, but it changed everything. The sons and daughters of factory workers, taxi drivers, and longshoremen could study Spinoza and Yeats and, yes, James T. Farrell.

For the GI Bill broke something open in America, the iron barriers of class that Farrell had tried to fight as a Communist, a Trotskyist, and finally a social democrat. As a writer of fiction, he had the great good sense to avoid imposing abstractions on his own fictions, but to insist that the breath of life was the most important component of a true novel. You might want to shake young Studs Lonigan, and tell him to get off his ass and do something; but there is no denying that as a character he is a living human being, even if we readers know him better than he knows himself. We'll never know what Studs might have become if there had been a GI Bill in his time, some hope of a future where the stacked deck had been tossed forever into the air, to be scattered on the wind.

If he were alive today, Farrell surely would be appalled at much of the nonsense about literary theory now being retailed in American universities. Today, as was true in the 1930s, the notion that theory must direct literature can only lead to bad literature. But he would have understood that every Irish-American novel could be discussed with profit in postcolonial studies. The story of the Irish in America is still being unraveled, but as with the story of every other ethnic group, it's invariably connected to the past. As Malachy McCourt once said, "I come from a long line of dead people." With his consciousness of those who came before him, and his fidelity to the truth as he saw it, James T. Farrell led the way for all of us who have tried to tell parts of that larger story. Like Studs, Farrell wasn't *from* Ireland, but he was *of* Ireland.

His work remains alive, a century after he was born. I like to think that some young kid, who isn't even remotely Irish, will pick up this book and discover himself, his friends, and America, too.

—Pete Hamill

SECTION ONE

Chapter One

I

STUDS LONIGAN, on the verge of fifteen, and wearing his first suit of long trousers, stood in the bathroom with a Sweet Caporal pasted in his mug. His hands were jammed in his trouser pockets, and he sneered. He puffed, drew the fag out of his mouth, inhaled and said to himself:

Well, I'm kissin' the old dump goodbye tonight.

Studs was a small, broad-shouldered lad. His face was wide and planed; his hair was a light brown. His long nose was too large for his other features; almost a sheeny's nose. His lips were thick and wide, and they did not seem at home on his otherwise frank and boyish face. He was always twisting them into his familiar tough-guy sneers. He had blue eyes; his mother rightly called them baby-blue eyes.

He took another drag and repeated to himself:

Well, I'm kissin' the old dump goodbye.

The old dump was St. Patrick's grammar school; and St. Patrick's meant a number of things to Studs. It meant school, and school was a jailhouse that might just as well have had barred windows. It meant the long, wide, chalk-smelling room of the seventh- and eighth-grade boys, with its forty or fifty squirming kids. It meant the second floor

of the tan brick, undistinguished parish building on Sixty-
first Street that had swallowed so much of Studs' life for
the past eight years. It meant the black-garbed Sisters of
Providence, with their rattling beads, their swishing
strides, and the funny-looking wooden clappers they used,
which made a dry snapping sound and which hurt like
anything when a guy got hit over the head with one. It
meant Sister Carmel, who used to teach fourth grade, but
was dead now; and who used to hit everybody with the
edge of a ruler because she knew they all called her the
bearded lady. It meant Studs, twisting in his seat, watching
the sun come in the windows to show up the dust on the
floor, twisting and squirming, and letting his mind fly to
all kinds of places that were not like school. It meant Battleaxe Bertha talking and hearing lessons, her thin,
sunken-jawed face white as a ghost, and sometimes looking like a corpse. It meant Bertha yelling in that creaky old
woman's voice of hers. It meant Bertha trying to pound
lessons down your throat, when you weren't interested in
them; church history and all about the Jews and Moses,
and Joseph, and Daniel in the lion's den, and Solomon
who was wiser than any man that ever lived, except
Christ, and maybe the Popes, who had the Holy Ghost to
back up what they said; arithmetic, and square and cube
roots, and percentage that Studs had never been able to get
straight in his bean; cathechism lessons . . . the ten commandments of God, the six commandments of the church,
the seven capital sins, and the seven cardinal virtues and
that lesson about the sixth commandment, which didn't
tell a guy anything at all about it and only had words that
he'd found in the dictionary like adultery which made him
all the more curious; grammar with all its dry rules, and its
sentences that had to be diagrammed and were never diagrammed right; spelling, and words like apothecary that
Studs still couldn't spell; Palmer method writing, that was
supposed to make you less tired and made you more tired,

and the exercises of shaking your arm before each lesson,
and the round and round ▰▰▰▰▰ and straight and
straight ▰▰▰▰▰▰ , and the copy book, all smeared with
ink, that he had gone through, doing exercise after exercise on neat sheets of Palmer paper so that he could get a
Palmer method certificate that his old man kicked about
paying for because he thought it was graft; history lessons
from the dull red history book, but they wouldn't have
been so bad if America had had more wars and if a guy
could talk and think about the battles without having to
memorize their dates, and the dates of when presidents
were elected, and when Fulton invented the steamboat,
and Eli Whitney invented the cotton gin or whatever in
hell he did invent. School meant Bertha, and Bertha
should have been put away long ago, where she could
kneel down and pray herself to death, because she was old
and crabby and always hauling off on somebody; it was a
miracle that a person as old as Bertha could sock as hard
or holler as loud as she could; even Sister Bernadette
Marie, who was the superior and taught the seventh- and
eighth-grade girls in the next room, sometimes had to
come in and ask Bertha to make less noise, because she
couldn't teach with all the racket going on; but telling
Bertha not to shout was like telling a bull that it had no
right to see red. And smart guys, like Jim Clayburn, who
did his homework every night, couldn't learn much from
her. And school meant Dan and Bill Donoghue and Tubby
and all the guys in his bunch, and you couldn't find a better gang of guys to pal with this side of Hell. And it meant
going to mass in the barn-like church on the first floor,
every morning in Lent, and to stations of the cross on Fri-
day afternoons; stations of the cross were always too long
unless Father Doneggan said them; and marching on Holy
Thursday morning in church with a lily in your hand, and
going to communion the third Sunday of every month at
the eight o'clock mass with the boys' sodality. It meant

goofy young Danny O'Neill, the dippy punk who couldn't
be hurt or made cry, no matter how hard he was socked,
because his head was made of hard stuff like iron and
ivory and marble. It meant Vinc Curley, who had water on
the brain, and the doctors must have taken his brains out,
drowned and dead like a dead fish, that time they were
supposed to have taken a quart of water from his oversized
bean. The kids in Vinc's class said that Sister Cyrilla used
to pound him on the bean with her clapper, and he'd sit
there yelling he was going to tell his mother; and it was
funny, and all the kids in the room laughed their guts out.
They didn't have 'em as crazy as Vinc in Studs' class; but
there was TB McCarthy, who was always getting his ears
beat off, and being made to kneel up in front of the room,
or to go in Sister Bernadette's room and sit with all the
girls and let them laugh at him. And there was Reardon
with horses' hoofs for feet. One day in geography in the
fifth grade, Cyrilla called on Reardon and asked him what
the British Isles consisted of. Reardon didn't know so
Studs whispered to him to say iron, and Reardon said iron.
Sister Cyrilla thought it was so funny she marked him
right for the day's lesson. And St. Patrick's meant Weary
Reilley, and Studs hated Weary. He didn't know whether
or not he could lick Weary, and Weary was one tough cus-
tomer, and the guys had been waiting for Studs and Weary
to scrap ever since Weary had come to St. Patrick's in the
third grade. Studs was a little leery about mixing it with
Reilley . . . no, he wasn't . . . it was just . . . well, there
was no use starting fights unless you had to . . . and he'd
never backed out of a scrap with Weary Reilley or any
other guy. And that time he had pasted Weary in the mush
with an icy snowball, well, he hadn't backed out of a fight
when Weary started getting sore. He had just not meant to
hit Weary with it, and in saying so he had only told the
truth.

St. Patrick's meant a lot of things. St. Patrick's meant . . .
Lucy.

Lucy Scanlan would stand on the same stage with him in
a few hours, and she would receive her diploma. She
would wear a white dress, just like his sister Frances, and
Weary's sister Fran, and she would receive her diploma.
Everybody said that Fran Lonigan and Fran Reilley were
the two prettiest girls in the class. Well, if you asked him,
the prettiest girl in the class was black-bobbed-haired
Lucy.

He got soft, and felt like he was all mud and mush inside; he held his hand over his heart, and told himself:

My Lucy!

He flicked some ashes in the sink, and said to himself:

Lucy, I love you!

Once when he had been in the sixth grade, he had
walked home with Lucy. Now, he puffed his cigarette, and
the sneer went off his face. He thought of the March day
when he had walked home with her. He had walked home
with her. All along Indiana Avenue, he had been liking her,
wanting to kiss her. Now, he remembered that day as
clearly as if it had just happened. He remembered it better
than the day when he was just a punk and he had bashed
the living moses out of that smoke who pulled a razor on
him over in Carter Playground, and a gang of guys had carried him around on their shoulders, telling him what a great
guy he was, and how, when he grew up, he would become
the white hope of the world, and lick Jack Johnson for the
heavyweight championship. He remembered the day with
Lucy, and his memory of it was like having an awful thirst
for a drink of clear cold water or a chocolate soda on a hot
day. It had been a windy day in March, without any sun.
The air had seemed black, and the sky blacker, and all the
sun that day had been in his thoughts of her. He had had all
kinds of goofy, dizzy feelings that he liked. They had
walked home from school, along Indiana Avenue, he and

Lucy. They hadn't spoken much, and they had stopped every little while to look at things. They had stopped at the corner of Sixtieth, and he had shown her the basement windows they had broken, just to get even with old Boushwah, the Hunkie janitor, because he always ran them off the grass when they goofed on their way home from school. And she had pretended that it was awful for guys to break windows, when he could see by the look in her eyes that she didn't at all think it so terrible. And they had walked on slow, pigeon-toed slow, slower, so that it would take them a long time to get home. He had carried her books, too, and they had talked about this and that, about the skating season that was just finished, and about the spelling match between the fifth- and sixth-grade boys and girls, where both of them had been spelled down at the first crack of the bat, and they had talked about just talk. When they came to the elevated structure near Fifty-ninth, he had shown her where they played shinny with tin cans, and she said it was a dangerous game, and you were liable to get your shins hurt. Then he had shown her where he had climbed up the girder to the top, just below the elevated tracks, and she had shivered because it was such a dangerous brave thing to do, and he had felt all proud, like a hero, or like Bronco Billy or Eddie Polo in the movies. They had walked home lazy, and he had carried her books, and wished he had the price to buy her candy or a soda, even if it was Lent, and they had stood before the gray brick two-story building where she lived, and he had wanted, as the devil wants souls, to kiss her, and he hadn't wanted to leave her because when he did he knew the day would get blacker, and he would feel like he did when he had been just out of his diapers and he used to be afraid of the night. There had been something about that day. He had gone on in school, wishing and wishing for another one like it to come along. And now he felt it all over again, the goofy, dizzy, flowing feelings it had given him.

He puffed, and told himself:

Well, it's so long to the old dump tonight!

He wanted to stand there, and think about Lucy, wondering if he would ever have days with her like that one, wondering how much he'd see of her after she went to high school. And he goddamned himself, because he was getting soft. He was Studs Lonigan, a guy who didn't have mushy feelings! He was a hard-boiled egg that they had left in the pot a couple of hours too long.

He took another drag of his cigarette.

He wanted that day back again.

He faced the mirror, and stuck the fag in the right-hand corner of his mouth. He looked tough and sneered. Then he let the cigarette hang from the left side. He studied himself with satisfaction. He placed the cigarette in the center of his puss, and put on a weak-kneed expression. He took the cigarette out of his mouth, daintily, barely holding it between his thumb and first finger, and he pretended that he was a grown-up mama's boy, smoking for the first time. He said to himself:

Jesus Christ!

He didn't know that he bowed his head when he muttered the Lord's name, just as Sister Cyrilla had always taught them to do. He took a vicious poke at the air, as if he were letting one fly at a mama's boy.

He stuck the fag back in his mouth and looked like Studs Lonigan was supposed to look. He lowered the lid on the toilet seat, and sat down to think. He puffed at his cigarette, and flicked the ashes in the sink.

He heard Frances talking:

"Get out of my way, Fritzie . . . Get out of my way . . . Please . . . And mother . . . Mother! MOTHER! . . . Will you come here, please . . . I told you the hem was not right on this dress . . . Now, mother, come here and look at the way my skirt hangs . . . If I ever appear on the stage with my skirt like this, I'll be disgraced . . . disgraced . . . Mother!"

He heard his old lady hurrying to Frances's room, saying:

"Yes, Frances darling; only you know I asked you not to call Loretta Fritzie . . . I'm coming, but I tell you, your dress is perfectly even all around. I told you so this afternoon when you tried it on with Mrs. Sankey here."

He could hear their voices as they jabbered away about her dress, but he didn't know what they were saying, and anyway, he didn't give two hoots in hell. Girls had loose screws in their beans. Well, girls like his sister anyway. Girls like Lucy, or Helen Shires, who was just like a guy, were exceptions. But there he was getting soft again. He said to himself:

I'm so tough that you know what happens? Well, bo, when I spit . . . rivers overflow . . . I'm so hard I chew nails . . . See, bo!

He took a last drag at his cigarette, tossed the butt down the toilet, and let the water run in the sink to wash the ashes down. He went to the door, and had his hand on the knob to open it when he noticed that the bathroom was filled with smoke. He opened the small window, and commenced waving his arms around, to drive the smoke out. But why in hell shouldn't they know? What did his graduating and his long jeans mean, then? He was older now, and he could do what he wanted. Now he was growing up. He didn't have to take orders any more, as he used to. He wasn't going to hide it any more, and he was going to tell the old man that he wasn't going to high school.

The bathroom was slow in clearing. He beat the air with his hands.

Frances rapped sharply on the door and asked him to get a move on.

He waved his arms around.

Frances was back in a moment.

"William, will you please . . . will you please . . . will you please hurry!"

She rapped impatiently.

"All right. I'll be right out."

"Well, why don't you then? I have to hurry, I tell you. And I'm in the play tonight, and you're not. When you had your play last May, I didn't delay you like this, and I helped you learn your lines and everything, and now when I have to be there . . . William, *will you please hurry* . . . PLEASE! . . . oh, mother . . . Mother! Won't you come here and tell Studs to hurry up out of the bathroom?"

She furiously pounded on the door.

Studs was winded. He stopped trying to beat the smoke out. The smoke was still thick.

"All right, don't get . . . a . . . don't get so excited!"

He whewed, and wiped his forehead, as if there had been perspiration on it. That was a narrow escape. He'd almost told his sister not to get one on, and then there'd have been sixteen kinds of hell to pay around the house.

Whew!

You'da thought he wanted to stay in there, the way she was acting. Well, he was going to walk out and let 'em see the smoke, and when they blew their gobs off, he would tell them from now on he was his own boss, and he would smoke where and when he damn well pleased; and further-more, he wasn't going to high school.

"William, will you please . . . please . . . . *please* let me in . . . Mother, won't you please . . . please . . . OH, PLEASE, come here and make him get out. He's been in there a half-hour. He's reading. He's always mean and self-ish like that . . . Mother, please . . . PLEASE!"

She banged on the door.

"Aw, I heard you," Studs said.

"Well, if you did, come on out!" she snapped.

He heard his mother coming up to the door, while Frances banged and shouted away. He took a towel . . . why didn't he think of it sooner? . . . and started flapping it around.

His mother said:

"William, won't you hurry now, like a good son? Frances has to go in there, and she has to finish dressing and be up there early because she's going to be in the play. Now, son, hurry!"

"All right. I can't help it. I'll be right out."

"Well, *please* do!" Frances said.

The mother commenced to tell Frances that William was going to let her right in; but Frances interrupted:

"But, mother, he's been in there almost an hour . . . He has no consideration for other people's rights . . . He's selfish and mean . . . and oh, mother, I got to go in there . . . and what will I do if I spoil my graduation dress on his account . . . make him, mother . . . and now I'm getting unnerved, and I'll never be able to act in the play."

The old lady persuaded. And she told Studs that she and his father couldn't go until they had all the children off, and they would be disgraced if they came late for the entertainment on the night their son and daughter graduated.

Frances banged on the door and yelled.

"Aw, don't get so darn crabby," Studs said to her while he fanned the air with his towel.

"See, mother! See! He says I'm insane just because I ask him to hurry after he's been in there all day. He's reading or smoking cigarettes . . . Please, make him hurry!"

"Why, Frances, how dare you accuse him like that!" Mrs. Lonigan commenced to say.

Studs heard his sister dashing away, hollering to the old man to come and do something. He fanned vigorously, and his mother stood at the door urging.

II

Old man Lonigan, his feet planted on the back porch railing, sat tilted back in his chair enjoying his stogy. His red, well-fed-looking face was wrapped in a dreamy expression;

and his innards made slight noises as they diligently furthered the process of digesting a juicy beefsteak. He puffed away, exuding burgher comfort, while from inside the kitchen came the rattle of dishes being washed. Now and then he heard Frances preparing for the evening.

He gazed, with reverie-lost eyes, over the gravel spread of Carter Playground, which was a few doors south of his own building. A six-o'clock sun was imperceptibly burning down over the scene. On the walk, in the shadow of and circling the low, rambling public school building, some noisy little girls, the size and age of his own Loretta, were playing hop-scotch. Lonigan puffed at his cigar, ran his thick paw through his brown-gray hair, and watched the kids. He laughed when he heard one of the little girls shout that the others could go to hell. It was funny and they were tough little ones all right. It sounded damn funny. They must be poor little girls with fathers and mothers who didn't look after them or bring them up in the right home atmosphere; and if they were Catholic girls, they probably weren't sent to the sisters' school; parents ought to send their children to the sisters' school even if it did take some sacrifice; after all, it only cost a dollar a month, and even poor people could afford that when their children's education was at stake. He wouldn't have his Loretta using such rowdy language, and, of course, she wouldn't, because her mother had always taught her to be a little lady. His attention wandered to a boy, no older than his own Martin, but dirty and less well-cared-for, who, with the intent and dreamy seriousness of childhood, played on the ladders and slides which paralleled his own back fence. He watched the youngster scramble up, slide down, scramble up, slide down. It stirred in him a vague series of impulses, wishes and nostalgias. He puffed his stogy and watched. He said to himself:

Golly, it would be great to be a kid again!

He said to himself:

Yes, sir, it would be great to be a kid!

He tried to remember those ragged days when he was only a shaver and his old man was a pauperized green-horn. Golly, them were the days! Often there had not been enough to eat in the house. Many's the winter day he and his brother had to stay home from school because they had no shoes. The old house, it was more like a barn or a shack than a home, was so cold they had to sleep in their clothes; sometimes in those zero Chicago winters his old man had slept in his overcoat. Golly, even with all that privation, them was the days. And now that they were over, there was something missing, something gone from a fellow's life. He'd give anything to live back a day of those times around Blue Island, and Archer Avenue. Old man Dooley always called it Archey Avenue, and Dooley was one comical turkey, funnier than anything you'd find in real life. And then those days when he was a young buck in Canaryville. And things were cheaper in them days. The boys that hung out at Kieley's saloon, and later around the saloon that Padney Flaherty ran, and Luke O'Toole's place on Halsted. Old Luke was some boy. Well, the Lord have mercy on his soul, and on the soul of old Padney Flaherty. Padney was a comical duck, good-hearted as they make them, but crabby. Was he a first-rate crab! And the jokes the boys played on him. They were always calling him names, pigpen Irish, shanty Irish, Pad-ney, ain't you the kind of an Irishman that slept with the pigs back in the old country. Once they told him his house was on fire, and he'd dashed out of the saloon and down the street with a bucket of water in his hand. It was funny watching him go, a skinny little Irishman. And while he was gone, they had all helped themselves to free beers. He came back blazing mad, picked up a hatchet, called them all the choice swear words he could think of, and ran the whole gang out into the street. Then they'd all stood on the other corner, laughing. Yeh, them was the days! And when he was a kid, they would all get sacks, wagons, any old thing, and go over to the tracks. Spike Kennedy, Lord have mercy on his soul, he was bit by a mad dog and died, would get up on one of the cars and throw coal down like sixty, and they'd scramble for it. And many's the fight they'd have with the gangs from other streets. And many's the plunk in the cocoanut that Paddy Lonigan got. It's a wonder some of them weren't killed throwing lumps of coal and ragged rocks at each other like a band of wild Indians. To live some of those old days over again! Golly!

He took a meditative puff on his stogy, and informed himself that time was a funny thing. Old Man Time just walked along, and he didn't even blow a How-do-you-do through his whiskers. He just walked on past you. Things just change. Chicago was nothing like it used to be, when over around St. Ignatius Church and back of the yards were white men's neighborhoods, and Prairie Avenue was a tony street where all the swells lived, like Fields, who had a mansion at Nineteenth and Prairie, and Pullman at Eighteenth and Calumet, and Fairbanks and Potter Palmer and the niggers and whores had not roosted around Twenty-second Street, and Fifty-eighth Street was nothing but a wilderness, and on Sunday afternoons the boulevards were lined with carriages, and there were no automobiles, and living was dirt cheap, and people were friendlier and more neighborly than they now were, and there were high side-walks, *and he and Mary were young.* Mary had been a pretty girl, too, and at picnics she had always won the prizes because she could run like a deer; and he remembered that first picnic he took her to, and she won a loving cup and gave it to him, and then they went off sparking, and he had gotten his first kiss, and they sat under a tree when it was hushed, like the earth was preparing for darkness, and he and Mary had looked at each other, and then he knew he had fallen, and he didn't give a damn. And the bicycle parties.

> *Daisy, Daisy, give me your answer true,*
> *We won't have a stylish marriage,*
> *We can't afford a carriage,*
> *But you'll look sweet,*
> *Upon the seat, of a bicycle built for two.*

And that Sunday he had rented a buggy, even though it cut a terrible hole in his kick, and they had driven way out south. Who would have ever thought he and she would now be living in the same neighborhood they had driven into that Sunday, and that they would have their own home, and graduate their kids from it? Now, who would have thought it? And the time he had taken her to a dance at Hull House, and coming home he had almost gotten into a mixup with some soused mick because the fellow had started to get smartalecky, like he was a kike. Yes sir, them was the days. He hummed, trying first to strike the right tune to *Little Annie Rooney*, then the tune of *My Irish Molly 'O*. He sang to himself:

> *Dear old girl, the robin sings above you!*
> *Dear old girl, it speaks of how I love you,*
> *Dear old girl, it speaks of how I love you . . .*

He couldn't remember the rest of the song, but it was a fine song. It described his Mary to a T. His . . . Dear Old Girl.

And the old gang. They were scattered now, to the very ends of the earth. Many of them were dead, like poor Paddy McCoy, Lord have mercy on his soul, whose ashes rested in a drunkard's grave at Potter's Field. Well, they were a fine gang, and many's the good man they drank under the table, but . . . well, most of them didn't turn out so well. There was Heinie Schmaltz, the boy with glue on his fingers, the original sticky-fingered kid. And poor Mrs. Schmaltz, Lord have mercy on her poor soul. God was merciful to take her away before she could know that her boy went up the road to Joliet on a ten-year jolt for burglary. The poor little woman, how she used to come around and tell of the things her Heinie found. She'd say, in her German dialect, My Heinie, he finds the grandest things. Vy, ony yesterday, I tell you, I tell you, he found a diamond ring, vy, can you himagine hit! And that time she and Mrs. McGoorty got to talking about which of their boys were the luckiest, and about the fine things my Heinie found, and the foine things my Mike is always pickin' up. Good souls they were. And there was Dinny Gorman, the fake silk-hat. When Dinny would tote himself by, they'd all haw-haw because he was like an old woman. He was too bright, if you please, to associate with ordinary fellows. Once a guy from New York came around, and he was damned if High-hat Dinny, who'd never been to the big burg, didn't sit down and try to tell this guy all about New York. Dinny had made a little dough, but he was, after all, only a shyster lawyer and a cheap politician. He had been made ward committeeman because he had licked everybody's boots. And there were his own brothers. Bill had run away to sea at seventeen and nobody had ever heard from him again. Jack, Lord have mercy on his soul, had always been a wild and foolish fellow, and man or devil couldn't persuade him not to join the colors for the war with Spain, and he'd been killed in Cuba, and it had nearly broken their mother's heart in two. Lord have mercy on his and her and the old man's souls. He'd been a fool, all right! Poor Jack! And Mike had run off and married a woman older than himself, and he was now in the east, and not doing so well, and his wife was an old crow, slobbering in a wheel chair. And Joe was a motorman. And Catherine, well, he hadn't even better think of her. Letting a traveling salesman get her like that, and expecting to come home

with her fatherless baby; and then going out and becoming
. . . a scarlet woman. His own sister, too! God! Nope, his
family had not turned out so well. They hadn't had, none of
them, the persistence that he had. He had stuck to his job
and nearly killed himself working. But now he was reaping
his rewards. It had been no soft job when he had started as
a painter's apprentice, and there weren't strong unions then
like there were now, and there was no eight-hour day, neither, and the pay was nothing. In them days, many's the
good man that fell off a scaffold to die or become perma-
nently injured. Well, Pat Lonigan had gone through the
mill, and he had pulled himself up by his own bootstraps,
and while he was not exactly sitting in the plush on Easy
Street, he was a boss painter, and had his own business,
and pretty soon maybe he'd even be worth a cool hundred
thousand berries. But life was a funny thing, all right. It
was like Mr. Dooley said, and he had never forgotten that
remark, because Dooley, that is Finley Peter Dunne, was a
real philosopher. Who'll tell what makes wan man a thief,
and another man a saint?

He took a long puff. He gazed out, and watched a group
of kids, thirteen, fourteen, fifteen, boys like Bill, who sat in
the gravel near the backstop close to the Michigan Avenue
fence. What do kids talk about? He wondered, because a
person's own childhood got so far away from him he forgot
most of it, and sometimes it seemed as if he'd never been a
kid himself, he forgot the way a kid felt, the thoughts of a
kid. He sometimes wondered about Bill. Bill was a fine
boy. You couldn't find a better one up on the graduating
stage at St. Patrick's tonight, no more than you would see a
finer girl than Frances. But sometimes he wondered just
what Bill thought about.

He puffed. It was nice sitting there. He would like to sit
there, and watch it slowly get dark, because when it was
just getting dark things were quiet and soft-like, and a fellow liked to sit in all the quiet and well, just sit, and let any

old thoughts go through his mind; just sit and dream, and realize that life was a funny thing, but that he'd fought his way up to a station where there weren't no real serious problems like poverty, and he sits there, and is comfortable and content and patient, because he knows that he has put his shoulder to the wheel, and he has been a good Catholic, and a good American, a good father, and a good husband. He just sits there with Mary, and smokes his cigar, and has his thoughts, and then, after it gets dark, he can send one of the kids for ice cream, or maybe sneak down to the saloon at Fifty-eighth and State and have a glass of beer. But there was many another evening for that, and tonight he'd have to go and see the kids get a good sendoff; otherwise he wouldn't be much of a father. When you're a father you got duties, and Patrick J. Lonigan well knew that.

While Lonigan's attention had been sunk inwards, the kids had all left the playground. Now he looked about, and the scene was swallowed in a hush, broken only by occasional automobiles and by the noise from the State Street cars that seemed to be more than a block away. Suddenly, he experienced, like an unexpected blow, a sharp fear of growing old and dying, and he knew a moment of terror. Then it slipped away, greased by the thickness of his content. Where in hell should he get the idea that he was getting so old? Sure, he was a little gray in the top story, and a little fat around the belly, but, well, the fat was a healthy fat, and there was lots of stuff left in the old boy. And he was not any fatter than old man O'Brien who owned the coal yards at Sixty-second and Wabash.

He puffed at his stogy and flicked the ashes over the railing. He thought about his own family. Bill would get himself some more education, and then learn the business, starting as a painter's apprentice, and when he got the hang of things and had worked on the job long enough, he would step in and run the works; and then the old man and Mary would take a trip to the old sod and see where John Mc-

Cormack was born, take a squint at the Lakes of Killarney, kiss the blarney stone, and look up all his relatives. He sang to himself, so that no one would hear him:

> *Where the dear old Shannon's flowing,*
> *Where the three-leaved shamrock grows,*
> *Where my heart is I am going,*
> *   To my little Irish Rose.*
> *And the moment that I meet her,*
> *With a hug and kiss I'll greet her,*
> *For there's not a colleen sweeter,*
> *   Where the River Shannon flows.*

He glowed over the fact that his kids were springing up. Martin and Loretta were coming along faster than he could imagine. Frances was going to be a beautiful girl who'd attract some rich and sensible young fellow. He beat up a number of imaginary villains who would try to ruin her. He returned to the thought that his kids were growing up; and he rested in the assurance that they had all gotten the right start; they would turn out A No. 1.

Martin would be a lawyer or professional man of some kind; he might go into politics and become a senator or a . . . you never could tell what a lad with the blood of Paddy Lonigan in him might not become. And Loretta, he just didn't know what she'd be, but there was plenty of time for that. Anyway, there was going to be no hitches in the future of his kids. And the family would have to be moving soon. When he'd bought this building, Wabash Avenue had been a nice, decent, respectable street for a self-respecting man to live with his family. But now, well, the niggers and kikes were getting in, and they were dirty, and you didn't know but what, even in broad daylight, some nigger moron might be attacking his girls. He'd have to get away from the eight balls and tinhorn kikes. And when they got into a neighborhood property values went blooey. He'd sell and get out . . .

and when he did, he was going to get a pretty penny on the sale.

He puffed away. A copy of the *Chicago Evening Journal* was lying at his side. It was the only decent paper in town; the rest were Republican. And he hated the *Questioner*, because it hadn't supported Joe O'Reilley, past grand master of Lonigan's Order of Christopher lodge, that time in 1912 when Joe had run for the Democratic nomination for State's Attorney. Lonigan believed it was the *Questioner* that had beaten Joe; he wouldn't have it in his house. He thought about the Christys, and decided he would have to be taking his fourth degree, and then at functions he could be all dolled up with a plume in his hat and a sword at his side that would be attached to a red band strung across his front. And then he'd get a soup-and-fish outfit and go to the dinners all rigged out so that his own family wouldn't know him. He wasn't a bad-looking guy, and he'd bet he could cut a swath all togged up in soup and fish. And when his two lads grew up, he was going to make good Christys out of them too. And he'd have to be attending meetings regularly. It might even help his business along, and it was only right that one Christy should help another one along. That was what fraternalism meant. He looked down at the paper and noticed the headlines announcing Wilson's nomination at St. Louis. There was a full-length photograph of long-faced Wilson; he was snapped in summery clothes, light shoes and trousers, a dark coat and a straw hat. He held an American flag on a pole about four feet long. Next to him in the photograph was the script of a declaration he had had drafted into the party platform, forecasting the glorious future of the American people and declaring inimical to their progress any movement that was favorable to a foreign government at the expense of the American Nation. The cut was worded, THE PRESIDENT AND THE FLAG.

Now, that was a coincidence. On the day that Bill and

Frances were graduated, Woodrow Wilson was renominated for the presidency. It was a historic day, because Wilson was a great president, and he had kept us out of war. There might be something to coincidences after all. And then the paper carried an account of the day's doings at the Will Orpet trial; Orpet was the bastard who ruined a girl, and when she was in the family way, went and killed her rather than marry her like any decent man would have done. And the baseball scores. The White Sox had lost to Boston, two to one. They were only in fifth place with an average of five hundred, but things looked good and they might win the pennant anyway. Look at what the Boston Braves had done in 1914. The Sox would spend the last month home. He'd have to be going out and seeing the Sox again. He hadn't been to a game since 1911 when he'd seen Ping Bodie break up a seventeen-inning game with the Tigers. Good old Ping. He was back in the minors, but that was Comiskey's mistake. Cicotte and Faber were in form now, and that strengthened the team, and they had Zeb Terry at shortstop playing a whale of a game, with Joe Jackson on the club, and Weaver at third, playing bang-up ball and not making an error a game like he had playing shortstop, and Collins and Schalk, and a better pitching staff, they would get going like a house on fire, and he'd have to be stepping out and seeing them play regular. Well, he could read all about it, and about the food riots in Rotterdam, and the bloody battle in which the Germans had captured Vaux, afterwards. Now, he'd have to be going inside, putting on his tie, and going up with Mary and the kids for the doings. He sat there, comfortable, puffing away. Life was a good thing if you were Patrick J. Lonigan and had worked hard to win out in the grim battle, and God had been good to you. But then, he had earned the good things he had. Yes, sir, let God call him to the Heavenly throne this very minute, and he could look God square in the eye and say he had done his duty, and he had been, and was, a good father. They had given the kids a good home, fed and clothed them, set the right example for them, sent them to Catholic schools to be educated, seen that they performed their religious duties, hustled them off to confession regularly, given them money for the collection, never allowed them to miss mass, even in winter, let them play properly so they'd be healthy, given them money for good clean amusements like the movies because they were also educational, done everything a parent can do for a child.

He puffed his stogy and sat there. The sun was imperceptibly burning low. Old man Lonigan looked about. He puffed on his stogy, and his innards made their customary noises as they diligently furthered the digestive process.

III

Frances rushed up on him, and with excited little-girl madness she asked him to make William get out of the bathroom.

The old man rapped on the bathroom door and told Bill to hurry up.

"Father, he's just a mean old brute. He's been in there an hour. He's reading or smoking cigarettes."

"Why, Frances!" the mother said.

"No, I ain't."

"Bill, tell me . . . are you smoking?"

"Aw, she's all vacant upstairs."

"Why, that is no language for an educated Catholic boy to use," the mother said.

"Father, he's mean and selfish. He's a brute, a beast. He isn't fair, and he doesn't give anyone else the least bit of consideration. I'll be late. I can't go. You'll have to get my diplomas, and they'll have to let someone else act. I can't go. I can't go. He's made me all nervous and unstrung. I'm unstrung, and I can't act now. I can't. And I'm worried because I'm not sure if my dress is even or not and I have to *go* in there. Father, *please* make the brute come out," Frances said melodramatically.

"All right. I'll be right out. I can't help it," Studs said.

"Make him, father!"

"Goddamn it, Bill, hurry!"

"I will."

"He's always like this," Frances said.

"I ain't."

"Every time I'm in a hurry, he's getting in the way. He's selfish, and don't think of anyone but his dirty old self, and he always monopolizes the bathroom . . . he's an ole . . . goat," said Frances.

"Aw, shut up and go to hell," said Studs as he fanned the air.

"Why, William Lonigan! Father, did you hear him insult me, swear at me, like I was one of those roughnecks from Fifty-eighth Street I sometimes see him with?"

"Bill, come right out. I'll not have you cursing in this house. I'm boss here, and as long as I am, you will use gentlemanly language when you address your sister. Where do you learn to speak like that, you, with the education I've given you? You don't hear anyone around here speaking like that," said the old man.

"Aw, heck, she's always blowing off her bazoo," said Studs.

"William, I wish that you wouldn't use such language. After receiving such a fine education . . . I'm shocked," said the mother.

"He doesn't know any better. He couldn't be a gentleman if he tried to," Frances said.

"Now, Frances, don't add fuel to the fire," the mother said.

"All right. I'm coming right out. I couldn't help it. Only it gets me sore to hear her yelling her ears off like that, over nothin'.'"

"Well, it's a good thing I do. Someone ought to expose him, and tell him how mean and selfish and inconsiderate he is, and how he only thinks of himself."

"Now, children, this is your graduation night, and you know your graduation night ought to be one of the happiest of your lives," the mother said.

The smoke had cleared now, so Studs could take a chance. He marched out, leaving the bathroom in perfect order. Frances indignantly brushed by him, her head held proud.

Frances was a very pretty girl of thirteen. Her body had commenced to lose its awkwardness, and she had a trim little girlish figure. Her plain white graduation dress set her off well, with her dark hair and her blackish eyes. She looked older than Studs.

"William, you should be more considerate," the mother said, unheard.

"Bill, you're gettin' at the age where you should be more . . . more chivalrous toward the ladies," the old man said as he chewed away at the remains of his stogy.

"Yeah, but heck, the way she yells over nothing, and starts raisin' all kinds of Cain when there ain't no reason," he said.

Father and mother cautioned him on the use of the word ain't. It was not polite, or good diction.

"Bill, you have to put up with the ladies, and make allowances for their . . . defugalties," the old man said pompously.

He nudged Studs, intimately, and slipped him a buck as a graduation present. Studs felt good over getting the buck, and went to his bedroom to put on the white tie he hated to wear, but had to. He looked at the tie, feeling uncomfortable. He looked out the window, and Goddamned the tie.

He heard his old man and his old lady speaking.

"Well, Mary, we got our children started now. We got Bill and Frances pretty near raised."

"Yes, Patrick, and I'm so happy, because it's been such a hard job, you know."

"Yeah, we done well by 'em, and paid their way, and now it won't be so hard as it was, and when we get 'em all raised, and brought up, and educated, we'll take a trip to Ireland. It will be our second honeymoon . . . And, Mary, you and I'll have to give more time to ourselves and spark about a little. This summer sure, we'll go out to Riverview Park and have a day of our own, like we planned for so long," he said.

"Yes, Patrick . . . And, Patrick, these little spats the children have, they're nothin' at all," she said.

"Nope. They happen in the best regulated families," the old man said; he laughed, as if he had cracked a good joke.

"And nobody can say we ain't done right by our children," he said.

"They certainly can't."

"And we paid their way," he said.

"Yes . . . and Sister Bernadette Marie told me how fine a boy William was, and how grand a girl Frances is," Mrs. Lonigan said.

"Yeah!" the old man said.

Then the old lady started to talk about the high school they would send Studs to. Studs knew what was coming. She was going to suggest that he be sent to study for the priesthood. He got sore, and wanted to yell at her. But the old man dismissed the whole subject. He said they could decide later, adding:

"I got the money, and we can send the lad any place we want to."

"But here, you get your tie on and comb your hair. We have to go, Patrick . . . And, Martin, come here and let me see your fingernails and behind your ears. Did you wash your neck? That's a good boy. And your teeth? Open your

mouth . . . Well, for once you are presentable . . . and
Loretta, is your dress on? Come here. Yes, you look like a
little lady . . ."

She entered Studs' room, retied his tie, and recombed his
hair, much to his discomfort, and made him go over his fingernails again; he felt as if they were trying to make a mollycoddle out of him. She pinned on the long class ribbons
of golden yellow and silvery blue. He sat on the bed, waiting for them, thinking about all kinds of things.

Looking like Sunday, or as if they had just walked out of
a dusty family album, the Lonigan family promenaded
down Michigan Avenue. Studs and Frances marched first.
Studs felt stiff; he told himself he must look like some
queer egg or other. Frances marched along, proud and lady-
like. She did not deign to glance at Studs, but she teased
him in a voice so loud that all heard her. He walked along,
looking straight ahead, his eyes vacant; he thought up all
the curse words he could and silently flung them at her.
Loretta and Martin followed. Loretta was carrying the
beautiful bouquet of white roses and carnations that were
for Frances, and she walked along imitating her sister. She
even teased Martin with the same words that Frances was
using. Martin had to be cautioned by his parents, because
he did not suffer in sulky silence, as Studs did. Father and
mother formed the rear guard; parental pride oozed from
them like healthy perspiration; the lean mother looked fru-
gal, even in the plain but expensive blue dress she had
bought for the occasion. Passers-by glanced at them a second time, and they smiled with satisfaction. The old man
kept repeating that he hoped Father Gilhooley would give
the kids a big send-off.

"Studs's got long pants on," Martin said, to escape the
teasing of Fritzie.

Fritzie giggled.

"Close your beak," Studs turned and said.

"Martin, how many times have I forbade you to call him

that awful name . . . and William, don't talk like that to my baby . . . The two of you cutting up like that in public . . . I'm ashamed of you," the mother said.

"Now, cut it out," the old man said authoritatively.

"I ain't a baby," Martin said.

"I'm walking with the baby," Frances said.

The Lonigans promenaded along Michigan Avenue, looking like Sunday.

Chapter Two

I

FATHER GILHOOLEY floridly faced his audience. He pursed his fat lips, rubbed his fat paws together and suavely caressed his bay front. A fly buzzed momentarily above him, and almost settled on his gray-fringed dome. He stood forward on the crowded little stage, pausing to create a dramatic effect. To his left, and a trifle out of line with him, Father Doneggan and Father Roney, the two parish assistants, stood, their faces expressionless. Back of him the graduating class was phalanxed; the blue-suited boys fidgeted on the left; the white girls stood, like wax models, on the right. All clutched their diplomas, while many also held green-bowed Irish history diplomas and Palmer method certificates.

Every atom of the June heat seemed to be compressed in little cubes that dripped wet discomfort over the heads of the packed audience. Heads constantly turned and switched to gaze at the cool patches of blue sky that were framed in the windows lining the two side walls. The audience had enjoyed the entertainment; at least, it had heartily applauded each number from the very cute little group piece the first-grade girls had spoken to the group dancing of Fritzie's fourth-grade class, the elocution recitation of the sixth-grade girls, the special numbers by prodigies like little Roslyn Hayes and Dorothy Gorman, and the adaptation of a play from *Little Women* that the seventh- and eighth-grade girls had presented. And now the good priest was going to conclude the entertainment with a brief talk . . . at least many hoped that it would be brief.

The good priest blandly commenced:

"This is a *joyous* evening for all of us here at St. Patrick's. We have all enjoyed the skillful and well-acted entertainment to the utmost, just as we enjoyed the similarly well-presented entertainment of the boys of this parish school last May. We could ask nothing more of our children, or of the good sisters who trained them. It has been, and I utter these words without the least iota of doubt in my own mind, an entertainment as amusing and as entertaining as many a professional show. It has also been, my dear friends, an evening which we will carry with us through the years as a golden treasure. And it will be an especially sacred and hallowed memory to you who are the fathers and mothers of the boys and girls in St. Patrick's banner class of 1916. It is you parents who have made this grand evening possible, who have suffered and worried and fretted, sacrificed, stinted yourselves luxuries, in order to send your children off daily to the good sisters where they might receive Catholic training. You have had your fears and your worries sending these sturdy, well-behaved, beloved, and, yes, handsome children to school. But now these fears and worries must be scattering like the fog dissipating before the warming rays of Gawd's golden morning sunlight. Your little ones have been safely steered beyond all the early rocks and shoals and sands in their voyage on the sea of life. The distribution of diplomas, which you have just witnessed on this small stage, symbolizes the arrival of your little ones in the first safe haven on their journey across the stormy and wave-tossed sea of life. It symbolizes the victory and achievement which is the re-

sult of eight hard years of patience and care; a triumph
whose ultimate crown of success will be forged at the very
throne of Gawd Almighty."

He talked on, his language fat with superlatives. Then,
becoming as skittish as a portly and dignified pastor from
the old sod can be, he said that while he was opposed to
gambling, he was still willing to *bet* that there was not a
parish in the great city of Chicago that could have put on a
finer display or have turned out a more stalwart graduating
class than St. Patrick's had on this June evening. He was
interrupted by loud clapping, and he smiled . . . magnificently.

He continued his talk, reminding his dear friends that in
this, their hour of joy, they must not forget the good sisters
who had trained the children, not only in reading and writing and arithmetic, not only for the splendid performance
they had made that evening, but also for the more serious
and important task of . . . saving their immortal souls.

"After all, we are made to love, to serve, and to obey
Gawd in this world, and to be happy with Him in the next,
just as the catechism teaches us," he said profoundly.

And it was the religious training, the daily example and
inspiration provided by the modest, self-sacrificing, holy
virgins who had pointed out the path of salvation for the
children of St. Patrick's parish. The graduates of St.
Patrick's parish all walked in the ways of Gawd, grew up
into sterling-silver specimens of Catholic manhood and
womanhood, because of the teaching, the kind nurturing in
goodness that they met with in the classrooms of St.
Patrick's school. The entire parish owed a heartfelt tribute
to these white-souled women.

In the rear of the hall, left-hand side, were three ex-little
ones of St. Patrick's who had worn out the patience of the
holy women, three naughty little boys who had been
canned from school and who might even end on the gal-
lows. They were kids of Studs' age, Paulie Haggerty and

Tommy Doyle, who were famous not only because they were hard guys but also because they had such fat butts, and tough Red Kelly, whose old man was a police sergeant. Hook-nosed, bow-legged Davey Cohen and Three-Star Hennessey, fourteen, small and considered nothing but a tricky punk, were also with them. They had all snuck in and were having a good time, making trouble. Davey suddenly whisted to Red, Tommy and Paulie. They whispered, and laughed quietly, and Red told Davey to go ahead. Davey goosed Hennessey. Hennessey was goosey anyway, and he jumped; his writhings disturbed a surrounding semicircle of dignity. But Three-Star suddenly saved himself; he pointed out Vinc Curley. Vinc was better goose meat.

The priest spoke on, and the boys on the stage grew more restless. Weary Reilley told Jim Clayburn that he wished old Gilly would pipe down, but Jim didn't answer, because Jim knew how to act in public, and anyway he was almost like a boy scout. TB McCarthy told Gunboats Reardon that it was all a lot of hot air, and Reardon nodded as he shifted his weight from the right to the left gunboat. Father Doneggan heard TB, and gave him a couple of dirty looks. Studs wiped the sweat from his face and fidgeted less than the others. He told himself that he wished Gilly would choke his bull and let it die. Gilly spoke of Catholic education, praising the parents who had possessed the courage, the conscience and the faith to give their children a Catholic schooling. He contrasted them with those careless, miserly and irreligious fathers and mothers who dealt so lightly with the souls of the little ones Gawd had entrusted in their care that they sent them to public schools, where the word of Gawd is not uttered from the beginning to the end of the livelong day. Such parents, he warned, were running grave risks, not only of losing the souls of their children but also their own immortal souls. Of such parents, the good priest said:

"Woe! Woe! Woe!"

And many of the boys and girls on the stage were going on in their schooling. To the parents of these boys and girls he felt it his duty to give warning. The shoals would become more dangerous, the rocks larger. If their souls were to navigate successfully on the stormier seas of life, he commended them to the Catholic high schools of Chicago, where the boys would be trained by holy brothers and consecrated priests and the girls by holy nuns. No sacrifice would be too great to see these fine boys and girls continue in Catholic hands. Let not the parents, after such a fine beginning, fall into the class of those about whom he must monotone:

"Woe! Woe! Woe!"

And his verbal thickets grew thicker and thicker with fat polysyllables. They wallowed off his tongue like luxurious jungle growths as he repeated everything he had said.

II

The Lonigans sat in the rear of the hall. Mrs. Lonigan strained forward in a visible effort to devour every syllable that dropped from the tongue of the noble priest. Patrick Lonigan sat back listening, as comfortable as he could possibly be seated on a camp chair in a hot and crowded hall. Once or twice he yawned, and his wife nudged him. He mopped the perspiration from his brow. At Mama's side the two youngest darlings laughed, squirmed and childishly muttered, much to her annoyance. She nudged Papa, who was just falling into a drowse, and said that William and Frances took the show away from the others; why there wasn't a girl who looked as pretty, or who had acted as well as Frances; and William was a pretty handsome boy, too.

"Uh huh!" the old man said.

"And we don't owe a penny on their education," she said.

"Uh huh!" he grunted.

They listened, and their pastor's words made them feel that they had participated in a great work, that they had done the Will of the Great Man Who sat on the Heavenly throne.

She strained forward again to listen attentively while the priest explained that it would be a shame if St. Patrick's could not dedicate, from among this class on the stage, a few lives to the service of God. Now was the time for the graduates to consider whether or not they had the call, for the mothers and fathers to encourage their children who might have the call, to resolve that they would put all aside and prepare for the consecrated work of the priest and the holy work of the nun. As Mrs. Lonigan listened, a dream of hope lit ecstasy on her thin face. At this moment Loretta said something to Martin, and the two children giggled. Mrs. Lonigan, severely angry, pinched Fritzie and warned her to be quiet. She told Loretta that she acted as if she had not been brought up in a good home and taught politeness and manners. She told Loretta to have respect for the priest and the people listening to him, and she made more disturbance than her daughter.

III

Facing the graduates, the priest gravely said:

"And now comes the painful duty, my dear young friends, of bidding you . . . farewell. It is a duty which I would gladly shirk, if shirk it I could. But . . . *Tempus fugit!* Time flies! Time is sometimes like a thief in the night, or like some lonely bird that comes to the banquet hall of this earth where man is feasting; it comes from a black unknown, flies through while man eats, and is gone out in the black night; and I may add, my dear young friends, the black night is black indeed, unless one has abided by the will of Gawd. Friends, it would be my fondest wish to keep you here with us at St. Patrick's, studying, serving the Lord, playing your happy innocent games of childhood out there in our large playground; but . . .

"*Tempus fugit!* For alas . . . . Time flies!

"Tonight you put aside the joys of childhood to become young men and young women. And just as we, who are older, now recollect the joys and happiness of childhood, so will you one day remember your golden days with us here at St. Patrick's. They will be memories of gold and silver, memories richer than all the treasures of this world. And, my dear young friends, I want you always to remember that, no matter what you may become, no matter if you are rich or poor, famous, as I sincerely trust some of you will be, or just one of the poor, honest workers in the Master's Vineyard, we at St. Patrick's will always remember you as friends, we will always remember the banner class of 1916."

IV

"Vinc, listen to this!" said Three-Star Hennessey.

Vinc listened.

Three-Star made lip-noises.

The others almost strangled themselves checking guffaws. Davey held his nose and whispered to the guys that it was Vinc.

"Ugh!" he muttered.

People near them looked askance.

The guys all told Vinc that he should be ashamed of himself.

"It was him! It was Three-Star, Dave. I didn't do it. I didn't. Hones'! Hones'! Hones'! I didn't. I tell you I didn't. I'll take an oath. Cross my die and hope to heart, I mean, I'll cross my heart and hope to die if I did it. I'm tellin' you that I didn't. Hones'!" pleaded Vinc with pained sincerity.

Three-Star told Vinc to tie his bull to another ash can.

"Why, Three-Star!" Vinc said, shocked.

Someone in the audience told them to shut up.

"Didn't your old lady teach you any better manners?" said Paulie.

"She's better'n' your old lady," said Vinc aloud, but his remark didn't carry up to the stage. People turned, annoyed.

"Yeah!" whispered Paulie to Vinc.

Vinc was open-mouthed and hurt; hurt that he should be treated so unjustly.

V

"Alas, my dear young friends, you must move down the hard and stony paths of life. And at times, it will be a difficult road. It might be a long and lonely journey, unless you take, Gawd forbid, that false path which the great and Catholic-minded William Shakespeare described as the primrose path to the everlasting bonfire; *the primrose path to the everlasting bonfire* sown with the flowers and fruits of the Devil, bounded by beautiful rose bushes behind which hide old Nick and his fallen angels; the foxy, the sly and foxy hordes of hell. You must beware of old Nick, and you must not allow him to snare your souls. Old Nick, the Devil, is tricky, full of the blarney, as they say in the old country. He is like the fox, tricky, cunning, clever. He will always make false promises to you; he will seek to deceive you with all the pomp and gold and glory of this world. He is a master of artifice, and he will pay your price in this . . . if you will pay his price in the next world; *if you pay his price in the next world,* where hell hisses and yawns, and the damned suffer as no earthly being can or has suffered. False friendships, fame, riches, power, success, all will be strewn at your feet by old Nick, if only you sell your soul, like Mephistopheles . . . *if only you deny our Lord, Jesus Christ.*"

From the second row, center, Mr. and Mrs. Reilley listened to the priest. She was a reddish woman, generously
supplied with flesh and bust. He looked like a conventional
cartoon of a henpecked husband.

"Sure, isn't he the walkin' saint of God? And isn't he the
saint?" she said.

Reilley nodded his head from a long-standing habit of
acquiescence.

"And isn't he the grand scholar?"

Reilley nodded.

"And maybe the lad will take all of what he says to
heart."

Reilley nodded.

"And maybe he'll not run around like he does."

"I hope so," Reilley muttered.

"And sure, doesn't the lad and the lass take the cake up
there on the stage?"

"Uh huh!" from Reilley.

VI

The priest described the glee of the Devil when he, Lucifer,
snares a young and innocent soul; and the boy Studs Lonigan on the stage had an imaginative picture of Satan in a
tight-fitting red-horned outfit, like the creature on a Pluto
water bottle, hopping out from behind a bush, clutching the
soul of a young guy or a girl from the stony road of life
and dragging it away as he smiled, showing all his teeth
just like Deadwood Dick in the newspaper cartoons. Father
Gilhooley told how cunning Satan took the Master up to
the mountain tops of the world and offered him all the
pleasures and riches of this life, if He deny His Father, and
Jesus resisted, saying, Get thee behind me, Satan, for He
must be about His Father's work. The priest said that Satan
must have, symbolically, taken the German Kaiser to the
mountain tops and offered him the world and Kaiser Bill

must have accepted, and that was probably why we had the terrible war devastating Europe. Yes, they must beware of old Nick, and they must persevere in the ways of the Master, who died that agonizing death on that terrible cross to redeem mankind. They must always remember that Christ died for them, and they must never put a thorn in His side by sinning. And they must not forgot the advice and example, the teachings of the good sisters. They must say their prayers morning and evening and whenever they were heavily beset with temptations, they must keep the commandments of God and of Holy Mother Church, receive the sacraments regularly, never willfully miss mass, avoid bad companions and all occasions of sin, publicly defend the Church from all enemies and contribute to the support of their pastor. If they did these things, and if they dedicated their lives to God's Holy Mother, and to the good and great patron saint of their parish who had driven the snakes out of Ireland, converting it to the true faith so that it had become the Isle of Saints and Scholars, they would all be among the sheep and not the goats on that grand and final day of judgment, when the God of Love would become the God of Justice. Wishing that they would all go forth to lead holy and happy lives, he gave them one final word of warning. On this very night of their graduation, when they and their parents were so proud, so happy, so righteously gratified, there was many a work-worn father and many a gray-haired mother sitting by the lamplit parlor window, waiting and praying for the return of that prodigal son, that erring daughter, who would, alas . . . never return. He prayed Gawd forbid any graduates of St. Patrick's to cause gray hairs to a father or a mother. Gawd wished that the fourth, above almost all other commandments, be kept . . . *Honor thy father and thy mother; that thy days may be long upon the land which the Lord thy Gawd giveth thee.*

He blessed them, and the ceremonies were closed.

VII

The graduating class shuffled off the stage into the side room on the left. The boys gathered around wrinkled Sister Bertha; the girls giggled about smiling, youngish Sister Bernadette Marie.

Studs stood off by himself, wanting to join the guys and say goodbye to Battleaxe Bertha. He found himself suddenly sad because he wanted to stay in the eighth grade another year and have more fun. He told himself that Bertha was a pretty good sport, all things considered; and anyway, she hadn't treated him so rotten like she had TB McCarthy, or Reardon, whose old man was only a working man and couldn't afford to pay any tuition. Yes, she was a good sport at that. He wanted to go up to her and say goodbye, and say that he felt her to be a pretty good sport at that, but he couldn't, because there was some goofy part of himself telling himself that he couldn't. He couldn't let himself get soft about anything, because, well, just because he wasn't the kind of a bird that got soft. He never let anyone know how he felt. He told himself that anyway he'd join the guys and say goodbye to her. He made several starts to approach the guys, but didn't go up. He stood watching, hoping that someone would recognize him and call him up. But he felt that he didn't belong there. There was Frances, near Bernadette, and there was Lucy Scanlan; but they didn't see him. His old not-belonging feeling had gotten hold of him. He eased out of the door. It was just as well, because he wanted to slip around to the can and have a smoke before he joined the folks out in front to be told he looked so swell and all that boushwah. Inside the damp boys' lavatory on the Indiana Avenue side of the building, he leaned against a sink and puffed away, absorbed in the ascending strands of smoke. He wondered if it was really a sin to smoke, and told himself that was all bunk.

He puffed and looked about the dark and lonely place.

He could hear himself breathing, and his heart beating away, and the queerness of the place seemed to put strange figures in him, and the strange figures just walked right out of his head and moved about the place, leering at him like red-dressed Satan. He felt like he used to feel when he was a young kid, and he would have nightmares, and strange boys, like demons, and as big as his father, would come and lean over his bed, and he would get up and run screaming into the dining room, where he would tear around and around the table until his old man came and shagged them away. Hell, he wasn't afraid of spooks anymore, and all this talk of spirits was a lot of hokum. It was just that he felt a little queer about something. He puffed nervously, and watched the way the rays of moonlight fell into the room and dropped over the damp floor like they were sick things.

Whenever Studs had queer thoughts he had a good trick of getting rid of them. He imagined that his head was a compartment with many shutters in it, like a locker room. He just watched the shutters close on the queer, fruity thoughts, and they were gone, and he'd have a hell of a time bringing them back, even if he wanted to. He saw the shutter close in his mind now, and he puffed away and felt better. He coughed, because he tried to inhale and got too much smoke in his throat and nose. He thought about Gilly's speech, and told himself that, whew, Gilly had talked a leg off of everybody; he talked as much as High-Collars Gorman, the lawyer. He thought of some of the things Gilly had said, and told himself that he didn't care so much about making any long, hard journey, like Gilly had described. He had always wanted to grow up and become a big guy, because a big guy could be more independent than a punk; a big guy could be his own boss. But he felt a little leery about leaving it all behind and going out into the battle of life.

He had long pants, and he wasn't just a grammar school

punk any more, and he could walk down the street feeling he wasn't, but well . . . sometimes he wasn't so glad of it. And now he'd have to go to high school, when he didn't want to, and meet new kids and get in fights all over again to become somebody in a new gang.

He told himself that he'd have to go out now in the battle of life and start socking away. It was fun thinking about it, but that was different from the real thing. And when you had to fight, you got socked in the mush, and a good sock was never any fun. Anyway, he had the summer ahead of him, and he could have fun with the guys around Indiana.

Weary Reilley came in. Weary was carrying his diploma, but he didn't have any Irish history or Palmer method certificates. They were boushwah anyway, and just a lot of extra work.

Studs gave Weary a cigarette, and they stood facing each other. They were a contrast, Weary taller, and with a better build, and looking like a much badder guy. Weary had a mean, hard face, square and dirty-looking.

"I'm glad it's over," Studs said.

"Me, too. This for the works," Weary said, making noises by compressing his lips outward and blowing.

"I'm glad I'm through with Battling Bertha," Studs said.

They laughed in mutual agreement and understanding.

"Wouldn't she get one if she saw us in here smokin'!" said Weary.

"Yeah," said Studs.

They laughed and lit new fags.

"She's too old to teach anyway," said Studs.

"She's a crab," Weary said.

"I never liked the old battleaxe," Studs said.

"Remember when she kept me after school and started to sock me, and I wouldn't let her?" Weary said.

"Yeah. You had to fight with her, didn' cha?" said Studs.

"Well, the old cow went to swing on me, and I told her hands off. No, sir! I'm not lettin' no one take a poke at me and get away with it. Not even Archbishop Mundelein himself," Weary boasted out of the side of his mouth.

"Neither am I!" said Studs.

"Neither am I!" said Weary.

They looked each other in the eye, and kept staring for several long seconds to prove that they were unafraid of each other.

"No one can get away with takin' a poke at me," Studs said.

"Well, I never let anyone get away with takin' a poke at me neither, and I didn't intend to start by lettin' blind Bertha smack me," Weary said.

"After that she never bawled you out, did she?" Studs said.

"She was afraid of me," bragged Weary.

"She used to treat me all right. You see, my old man always gave the nuns a turkey on Thanksgivin' and Christmas," Studs said.

"Say, by the way, did you see Doneggan take a wham at TB?"

"No. Why?"

"Well, Muggsy McCarthy made some crack when Gilly was speakin', and Doneggan didn't like it, so he cracked his puss," Weary said.

"Yeh! Say! You know TB gets it in the neck every shot. I kinda feel sorry for the guy," Studs said.

"He's nuts anyway. I know I wouldn't take what that loogin takes. I don't give a good goddamn who it is, nobody is gettin' away with anything on this gee," said Weary.

"You know, they got a hell of a lotta nerve haulin' off on a guy just because they're priests or nuns," said Studs.

Studs casually shot his butt, just like all tough guys did.

"Well, if a guy stands for it, that's his tough luck," Weary said.

"Yeh, but goofy McCarthy is helpless. Christ, the poor

guy's got one foot in the grave. His brother Red ain't so bad, but he's a sap. I tell you he's fruity," said Studs.

"The loogin's rotting away with TB anyway," said Weary.

"But lemme tell you . . . he's damn smart. Jesus! You know, if he'd a wanted tuh work, he could of had the scholarship to St. Cyril or any of those schools that hold scholarship exams and give scholarships," Studs said.

"But what the hell does that mean?" said Weary.

"Nothin'," said Studs.

"Anyway, I'm glad I'm through with old Bertha, . . . say, gimme another fag?" Weary said.

They lit cigarettes.

"Remember her, how she'd rush down the aisle to hit a guy, and she'd never hit the right one because she's as blind as a bat and she couldn't see enough to take the right aim?" said Studs.

They laughed because Bertha was funny, blind as a bat like she was.

"But she is one lousy crab," said Studs.

"Anyway, I'm damn glad to be out of the dump," said Weary.

"Me, too," affirmed Studs.

"But we had a pretty good time at that," Weary added.

"Yeh, even if we did have Bertha in seventh and eighth grade, and even if we did have guys like Clayburn in the class making it hard for us by always studying," said Studs.

"Clayburn ought to be in the boy scouts," Weary said derisively.

They laughed.

"Say, remember the time we shoved bonehead Vinc Curley through the convent window, and there was a big stink, and Bernadette lammed blazes out of him when he bawled that he didn't do it and she said he did and she would break his head before she let him call her a liar?" said Studs.

"That was funny," Weary said.

"And the time Muggsy hit Bertha with an eraser, and she went sky high, and looked like she'd bust a blood vessel, and she blamed Reardon and nearly put lumps on his head by beaning him with her clapper?" said Studs.

"And the fights we used to have with the Greek kids from the school across the way, and their priest would come over to Gilly, because he and Gilly are friends even if he is a Greek Catholic priest, and Gilly would send Doneggan up to read the riot act to us?" said Weary.

They laughed.

"And remember the time when Bertha fell on the ice?" said Studs.

"That was good because we were off three days," said Weary.

"You know, about the only decent thing about Bertha was that she was always falling on the ice or getting sick so she couldn't teach and we were getting holidays," said Studs.

"Well, Bertha always gave me a pain right here," Weary said, pointing to the proper part of his anatomy.

A pause.

"Are you going to high school?" asked Weary.

"I don't know. I don' wanna," said Studs.

"I'm not goin'," said Weary.

"I don't think I'll go," said Studs.

"Schools are all so much horse apple," said Weary.

"I don't want to go, but the gaffer wants me to, I guess," said Studs.

"Well, I ain't goin', and my old man can lump it if he don't like it," said Weary.

"Gonna work?"

"Maybe," said Weary.

"Maybe I'll get myself a jobber," said Studs.

"Say, by the way, Gilly didn't ask for any dough in his speech, did he? I wonder if the old boy is sick or startin' to get feeble," said Weary.

"Well, he told us all to remember and not forget to contribute to the support of our pastor," said Studs.

"Yeah, that's right. He's never yet made a sermon without askin' for somethin', a coal collection, or a collection for the starvin' chinks, or for Indian missions, or some damn thing," said Weary.

"He's always asking for the shekels. He's as bad as a kike," said Studs.

"And did you hear his crack about the playground?" said Weary.

"Yeah," said Studs.

"Well, I couldn't keep a straight face when he made that crack about our large playground. Boy! a yard full of cinders where you can't play football, or even pompompull-away without tearin' hell out of your clothes and yourself, and they won't let you play ball in it because they're afraid you'll break a window, and he's too damn cheap to put up baskets for basketball. Like the gag he worked on us in winter. We were the snow brigade, and got a lot of praise for shoveling snow off of his sidewalks, and he saved the money he'd of had to pay to have it done . . . and he patted us on the head, said we were good boys, and gave us each a dime," said Weary.

"Well, I gotta go," said Studs.

"Me, too," said Weary.

"Here's some gum to take the fags off your breath," said Studs, sticking some Spearmint in his mouth.

"S . . t, the old man knows I smoke anyway," said Weary.

They walked out to the front to meet their proud, waiting parents.

VIII

Small crowds gathered in front of the parish building, to converse, laugh and reflect the glory of the children and

elders of St. Patrick's parish. The Lonigans stood in one
such small group. Lonigan spied Dennis P. Gorman. Mr.
Dennis P. Gorman was a thin, effeminate man with a dan-
dified mustache, and his nose was sharp. He was exceedingly well tailored in a freshly pressed gray suit; he wore a
clean white shirt, a high stiff collar and a black tie. His
meek, satellite wife was at his side; she was moron-faced,
and looked younger than her thirty-six years. These well-
known parishioners were standing under the arc light, bow-
ing profusely and elegantly to the passers-by. Lonigan
moved from the group he was in, without excusing himself;
his wife followed. He hastened up to Gorman, held out his
hand and said:

"Hello, Dinny!"

Dennis P. Gorman proffered a limp hand. Mrs. Dennis P.
Gorman bowed and offered saccharine compliments for the
Lonigan children.

"Well, Dinny, what did you think of it?" Lonigan asked.

While Dennis P. Gorman paused and cleared his throat
for oratorical delivery, Mrs. Lonigan approached, and she
and Dennis's wife engaged in mothers' talk.

Dennis's effeminate voice was now prepared for action,
and he said in tones of mingled melodrama and sing-song:

"Well, I believe, in fact, I am firmly convinced, that Mr.
Wilson's nomination today was an excellent choice . . . yes,
an excellent choice. I am profoundly gratified that he has
been renominated. I shall be proud to give him my own
humble vote, and believe that it is the positive duty of
every public-spirited citizen to do likewise. I shall en-
deavor, within my own limited power, to assist in his campaign for reelection. There is not one iota, no, not one
slightest crepuscular adumbration of doubt but that Mr.
Wilson is more qualified to wield and sway such power as
resides in the chief executive position of the United States
than his opponent, Mr. Hughes. He has brains, administra-
tive capacity, diplomatic skill, integrity, ability, courage and a

brilliant record. It was due to his efforts that we have, to-day, the Federal Reserve System, which shall, in our own lifetime, render panics impossible. It was his diplomacy that has kept America minding its own business and out of the dreadful militaristic war that now bleeds and devastates Europe, and leads some to believe that we have come to Armageddon. I say, with rich and full conviction, that there is not the slightest doubt, no question whatever, as to the relative merits of the two men. There is absolutely no comparison; it is all contrast, that makes Mr. Wilson's star scintillate with added brilliancy. Were he a Republican, I believe that I would bolt my party to give him my vote. However, I know that a man of Woodrow Wilson's stature, character and all-round ability and integrity could never remain a Republican, because, as every unbiased observer well knows, the G. O. P. is helplessly, hopelessly and irredeemably corrupt. Have I made my opinion clear, sir?"

The keen grayish eyes of Mr. Dennis P. Gorman roamed the spaces of the starry June evening.

"Oh, yeh! I'm for Wilson, too. A brilliant scholar! Wilson's a scholar, the brainiest President we had since Lincoln. And he kept us out of war. I think I'll make a contribution, of course it will be small, a drop in the bucket, but then I'll make my little contribution to the campaign," said Lonigan.

Dennis P. Gorman told Lonigan quickly, but with his customary aloofness and dignity, that every contribution, no matter how small, would be appreciated, and that Wilson was not the President of Wall Street, but of the common people, and the common people were the ones he needed. And the Democratic party, Gorman called it our party, is the voice of the common people, the average, good, honest Americans like those of St. Patrick's parish.

"Yeah, I'll see you later, Dinny, and make a small contribution. But what I meant is how did you like the works tonight, Dinny?"

Lonigan saw Dennis P. Gorman frown at his use of the word Dinny. It was unintentional, a habit carried on from earlier days.

Mr. Dennis P. Gorman paused, and then expostulated:

"Oh! It was excellent. Excellent. Did you hear my daughter rendering a selection from Mozart and a nocturne from *Sho-pan?*"

"She was swell. I liked her," said Lonigan.

"Well, I wouldn't say that she was precisely swell; but I do believe, I do believe, that she interpreted the masters with grace, charm, talent, verve and fire," said Mr. Dennis P. Gorman.

"Yes, Dennis," said Lonigan.

"And your daughter did an excellent piece of acting," said Dennis.

"Yeh, she did pretty well," said Lonigan, his assumed modesty breaking across his face.

The two mothers also talked. They had finished on the superbness of their respective daughters, it was Mrs. Dennis P. Gorman's word, and were now commenting on what a grand speech the pastor had made. Mrs. Gorman used the word new, and she redescribed the entertainment as nice. Mr. Dennis P. Gorman paused from his conversation with Lonigan to inform his wife that nice was not the correct word, and that she had mispronounced *new;* it was not *noo.*

Dorothy Gorman came out with Frances Lonigan; they both received their flowers. Dorothy Gorman was a plain-featured, almost homely girl, and standing beside Fran she looked pathetic. The appearance of the daughters led to gushiness and many cross compliments. When these were duly finished, Mrs. Lonigan invited Mr. and Mrs. Dennis P. Gorman home for a chat and a bit of ice cream. Mrs. Gorman accepted the invitation, but turned to her husband for his consent.

"Well, I'd like to, Mary, but you know that Dorothy here has had a trying time, and I believe that she had better come home, and we had better see that she gets the proper rest . . . But thank you, exceedingly, Mrs. Lonigan. And sometime I should enjoy the company of you and Patrick at our home."

"Yes, do come for tea, but be sure and telephone beforehand to be certain that I'm in, because Dennis and I have a number of social engagements these days," said Mrs. Dennis P. Gorman.

"Yes, May, and thanks," said Mrs. Lonigan.

"Well, so long, Dinny," said Lonigan, again an unintentional slip.

Mr. and Mrs. Dennis P. Gorman and their well-guarded daughter strode magnificently home.

The Lonigans moved over to chat with the Reilleys, who accepted their invitation. Fran Lonigan and Fran Reilley, a very pretty dark-haired girl, rounded up some of the kids. Just then Studs and Weary appeared, and the group trooped down to the Lonigans'.

IX

An extravagance of electricity, with almost every light in the house on, swelled the significance of the evening in the Lonigan household.

"I feel relieved that it's all over," said Mrs. Lonigan as she sat in one of the imitation-walnut dining-room chairs, sipping ice cream.

"It was grand," responded Mrs. Reilley, who sat next to her hostess.

"Well, we did the right thing. I'm glad Father Gilhooley gave it to the people who send their children to the public schools, because the public schools ain't no place for Catholic children, and I say it's the bounden duty of parents to see that their children get the right upbringin' by sending them to Catholic schools. It's only right, and I say, I say, that when you do the right thing, you're happier. You know, when you're not happy, you're worried and nervous, and you worry, and worry causes poisons in your system, and poisons in your system ruin your digestion and harm your liver. Yes, sir, I say that from a hygienic standpoint it pays to do the right thing, like we all done with our children," said Lonigan as he expanded in comfort in the dining-room Morris chair.

He sat there and sucked enjoyment from his stogy.

"And ain't it the truth?" said Mrs. Reilley.

"Yeh," muttered Reilley, who was slumped back in his chair seriously engaged in the effort to enjoy the stogy Lonigan had handed him.

"The Catholic religion is a grand thing," Mrs. Reilley said.

Lonigan told how he had heard two little Catholic girls, no bigger than his own youngest daughter, swearing like troopers. It was because their parents didn't send them to the sisters' school. They all agreed, with many conversational flourishes; and Mrs. Reilley said the girls would sure be chippies.

Mrs. Reilley stated, with swelling maternal pride, that her son, Frank, would attend a Jesuit school and then prepare for the law so that he could some day be a grand Catholic lawyer, like Joe O'Reilley, who had almost been state's attorney.

"The Jesuits are grand men and fine scholars," said Mrs. Lonigan.

"They got these here A. P. A. university professors skinned by a hull city block," Reilley said.

Mrs. Lonigan said that yes the Jesuits were grand men, and she would like to make a Jesuit out of her son William.

"But has he the call?" jealously asked Mrs. Reilley.

"I think so. I say a rosary every night, and I offer up a monthly holy communion, and I make novenas that God will give him the call," Mrs. Lonigan said.

"And wouldn't I give me right arm if me son Frank had the call?" Mrs. Reilley said.

"But, Mary, you know I'm gonna need Bill to help me in my business. Why do you want to start putting things like that in the boy's head?" protested Lonigan.

"Patrick, you know that if God wants a boy or a girl for His work, and that boy or girl turns his back on the Will of Almighty God, he or she won't never be happy and they'll stand in grave danger of losing their immortal souls," said she.

"Isn't it the truth?" said Mrs. Reilley.

"But Mary . . ."

"Patrick, the Will of God is the Will of God, and no mortal can tamper with it or try to thwart it," his wife replied.

Lonigan protested vainly, saying how hard he had worked, and how a father had some right to expect something in return when he did so much for his children.

Mrs. Lonigan opened her mouth to speak, but Mrs. Reilley beat her to the floor and said that when a body gets old, all that a body has is a body's children to be a help and a comfort, and that a body could expect and demand some respect from a body's children. She and her old man had worn their fingers down to the bone working for their children. Reilley had been a poor teamster, and he had gotten up before dawn on mornings when the cold would almost make icicles on your fingers in no time, and she had gotten up and got his breakfast, and fed the horses, and both of them had worked like niggers in those days back of the yards before their children were born. And a mother doesn't have her back near broken with labor pains for nothing. She held up her red, beefy, calloused hands. Then she boasted that she was proud that her children would not have such a hard time. Frank would be educated for the law; Frances would teach school; and maybe she would make a Sister of Mercy out of little June.

Reilley yawned. Lonigan detailed how hard he had worked.

They could hear the young people laughing, having a *harmless* good time in the parlor. Lonigan said it was great to be a kid, and then spoke of the Orpet murder trial. Everybody felt that hanging was too good and too easy a punishment for such a cur. Mrs. Reilley, in a blaze of passion, said that if a boy of hers ever did such a vile thing to an innocent girl, she would fasten the rope around his neck; but her Frank would never be that kind of a cur; her flesh and blood, he couldn't be. Lonigan made a long speech averring that it was a beastly violation of the natural law. June Reilley and Loretta appeared, and Mrs. Lonigan signaled her husband to pause until she shooed the innocent ones off to Loretta's room. They scampered out of the room, and enjoyed their own discussion of forbidden topics. Then the parents joined in a general denunciation of Orpet, adding that no Catholic would ever commit such a foul deed.

"Sure, that's so," Lonigan orated profoundly as if he were shedding the fruit of long and consistent thought.

"And isn't the Catholic Church the grand thing?" Mrs. Reilley said lyrically.

"And just think how awful the world would be without the Church," said Mrs. Lonigan.

"There's nothin' like the Church to keep one straight," said Lonigan.

"It keeps you toeing the mark. That's one thing to say for it," Mrs. Reilley said.

Reilley agreed with a feeble nod of his sleepy head.

"That is the reason we gave our children a Catholic education," Mrs. Lonigan said.

"And isn't it the truth that a mother never need worry when she sends her byes and girls to the good sisters, the holy virgins!" Mrs. Reilley said.

There was a nodding of heads.

"Isn't the Church the grand thing," insisted Mrs. Reilley.

The conversation drifted and dribbled on amidst increasing barrages of yawns.

X

It was the first evening of the official maturity of the young people in the parlor, and after getting seated they wondered what to do; the boys sat stiffly on one side of the room, and gazed furtively at their long trousers; the girls faced them, acting prim and reserved. Growing up had always meant more freedom, and here they were after their graduation, afraid to do anything lest it seem kiddish; afraid, particularly, to play the kids' kissing games they used to play at parties.

"Well, what'll we do?" grumbled Weary, who sat between Studs and sallow-faced TB on the unscratched piano stool.

"Yeah, let's do something," Studs suggested.

Soft-skinned and fattish Bill Donoghue was seated under the floor lamp near them. He said:

"Now that's a bright idea!"

Studs made a face at Bill, as if to say: Go soak yer head!

"Bill's a loogin who always tries to wisecrack," Studs said.

"Studs is a little fruity!" Bill said, and they laughed.

"Such awful slang you boys use!" Helen Borax said.

Studs scowled at Helen and said:

"Bill, I'm going to slap your pretty wrist!"

Helen colored slightly, and elevated her nose.

Bill got limp like a sissy, and tapped his own wrist daintily, and everybody laughed at his comics, because Bill was really very funny.

"Well, anyway, I'm glad I'm through school," said Tubby Connell, a kinky-haired, darkish boy who was plunked, uncomfortably, in the corner easy chair that Mrs.

Lonigan always said must be beautiful, because it had cost over a hundred dollars.

"Ope! Look what the wind blew in!" Bill said, looking at Tubby.

"Another lost country heard from," muttered Studs.

Tubby blushed bashfully.

"Anyway, I'm darn glad to get out of that joint," Weary said.

"Frank, it isn't a joint . . . And you jus' wait. You'll be sorry and wish you were back at St. Patrick's just like Father Gilhooley said we'd all remember our days there," his sister said.

"Weary didn't hear him say that. When Gilly was talking of that, I heard him snoring," Bill said, and they laughed.

Peggy Nugent said you shouldn't speak of a priest like that, or something awful might happen to you. You should always say Father Gilhooley. She smiled, and everybody could see she thought it was thrilling to call him Gilly.

"Well, he has gills like a fish," Bill said.

"How disrespectful," Lucy Scanlan said, twinkling her blue eyes.

Weary made faces at his sister. Tubby reiterated that he was glad to get out of jail because he felt that he had to say something. He was blushing.

They laughed, and TB said he, too, was darn glad to get out of the pen, and they laughed again.

"I'll be glad to get to high school," said well-behaved Dan Donoghue, and just as he did, Bill aimed a peanut at Tubby. Connell told him to cut it out, and Bill asked what in a very innocent voice.

He and Tubby carried on a side-dialogue.

"You will, Dan? Why?" asked Fran Lonigan.

"Oh, I just will," said Dan.

"Well, I don't know if I'm glad or not," said Fran.

"What school do you think you'll go to, Studs?" asked Lucy, smiling with her sweet baby-face.

"None."

"William, you know you're going to high school," his sister said sternly, as if she were an adult scolding him.

"Yeah, I suppose I don't know what I'm gonna do," said Studs.

"You most certainly do not," said she.

"We'll see," said he, trying to save his scattering dignity.

"Father will see!" said she with finality.

He scowled, felt unmanned, felt that Weary was sneering at him as if he was a weak sister. He looked at his meaningless long trousers.

Weary said with great braggadocio he wasn't going to high school and his sister protested. Tall Jim Clayburn said he thought going to school was sensible and necessary if you wanted to get ahead. He said he thought that Sister Bertha had once told them the truth when she said you needed education and stick-to-it-iveness to get ahead in life. Lucy said Jim was so sensible, and she had a devilish look in her eyes. Dan commenced to agree with Jim, but his brother interrupted him:

"Say, did you see High Collars?"

"Yeah, I saw him walkin' with Dorothy and his wife," Tubby said, glad to get back in the conversation.

"He wouldn't let her come to the party. He told Mother that Dorothy needed her proper rest," said Fran Lonigan.

"He's an old mean thing," said Lucy.

"The poor kid! She's all right, and awfully sweet, but she can't ever do anything on account of her father. Sometimes she tells me about it, and cries," exclaimed Fran Reilley.

"I wouldn't want an old man like him," TB said.

They looked at TB, because his old man was nothing to brag about.

"Anyway, he didn't wear his silk hat tonight," Dan said.

"I wonder if he uses perfume?" TB said.

"I'll bet he wears ladies' underwear," contributed Bill Donoghue.

The guys haw-hawed, and the girls giggled modestly after stating that Bill's language was not exactly nice.

They talked on, and wondered what they would do. Bill goofed Tubby, because Connell looked like a smoke, and Bill said that now Tubby was graduated, he shouldn't find no trouble becoming a Pullman porter. TB said that every time he saw Tubby he thought it would rain because of dark clouds all around. Tubby hock-hocked in imitation of Muggsy, and the girls said Tubby was too frightful for words.

Jim Clayburn went to the baby grand, and Bill said that they would now listen to Good Old Stick-To-It-Iveness. Jim played, and they crowded around, singing, but they couldn't get any harmony because Bill bellowed and Tubby and Muggsy tried to be funny. They sang *Alexander's Rag Time Band, The River Shannon Flowing, It's a Long Way to Tipperary, Dear Old Girl, Dance and Grow Thin,* and *Bell Brandon*. Then Jim started *In My Harem*. Bill got in the center of the floor and did a shocking hula-hula that was so funny they nearly split laughing; he sang:

> And the dance they do . . .
> Is enough to kill a Jew . . .
> Da-Da-Dadadada-Da . . .
> In my harem with Pat Malone.

Jim played *When It's Apple Blossom Time in Normandy*, and just as they started the chorus Bill goosed Tubby, and Studs did the same with TB. The two victims jumped, yelling ouch. It broke up the singing and everybody laughed. Bill asked Rastus where the ghosts were, and Tubby replied by calling Bill snake Irish, so low that he crawled in the mud. Studs said that trying to decide which was the worst, an Irishman or a jigg, was like shooting craps for stage money with loaded dice; and he was proud of his crack even if they didn't laugh.

"Let's dance!" Helen said, interrupting all the tomfoolery.

The fellows who knew how foxtrotted with the girls while Lucy played. Studs, TB and Weary stood in a corner whispering dirty jokes. When the others tired of dancing, they sat down; this time the fellows weren't all on one side of the room and the girls on the other. They talked some more, and wondered what they would do, and Bill kept the party going by his clowning. Martin wandered in, looking oh-so-darling, and the girls made a fuss trying to pet him. Tubby finally grabbed him and said:

"Let's fight, you little rascal!"

Martin biffed Tubby, and Bill said:

"The kid takes after his big brother, only he's got it on him with the dukes."

Tubby then grabbed Martin again, and the child said:

"Lemme go, you boob!"

The guys clapped, and the girls were taken by his cuteness. Fran said it was the wrong way for Martin to take after his brother.

Lucy pulled Martin toward her, tied him with her arms, said he was just too darling for words; she kissed him.

"Yeah, he's got it on his brother all around. As a Romeo, he's got Studs backed off the boards," Bill said.

Studs blushed and got exceedingly interested in the stale joke with which Tubby was laboring.

Martin fought free, and as he rushed out of the room he yelled back:

"I wish to hell you'd lemme 'lone!"

They laughed; Fran Lonigan frowned.

The conversation went on; everybody wondered what they would do. Lucy set them at ease by boldly suggesting wink. The girls blushed and giggled while they were getting into their places. But the game went off stiffly because there were too many boys. They changed to kiss-the-pillow. Everyone got into the spirit of the game, even Weary. He found it wasn't so goofy kissing girls. And Helen Borax acted like she might have a crush on him. He'd never thought much of her, except that she was the kind of a chicken who never tried to act her age and who seemed to think she was a queen. But it wasn't hard to kiss her. And Studs got gay because he was getting his chance to kiss Lucy, and he didn't have to keep his liking for her under cover. He told himself he liked her, and repeated this; he liked her around him, liked to look at her, liked her laugh, liked her near him, liked to think of doing things for her, suffering, fighting, playing football, defending her against demons and villains, and anybody.

As they played, Fran Lonigan said: "Gee, what would Sister Bernadette Marie, what would she say if she saw us now?"

"I wonder," smiled Helen Borax.

"Particularly you girls. She'd expect it of me, because she always said I was only a chicken, anyway, and not serious like Helen and you girls," Lucy said.

Helen colored.

Bill smiled broadly, and said that if Bertha knew about it she'd get jealous and wish that she'd been around to play. He said she joined the convent because she'd been disappointed in love, and maybe if she got the chance she'd get a crush on TB or Tubby.

"What do you mean she's been disappointed in love?" asked TB.

"Sure. She acts just like an old maid," Bill said.

"But what I want to know is who'd love her?" asked TB.

They laughed, and the girls thought it was horrid.

Bill kept the floor and said he knew the old battleaxe would like to play. He said he'd show just how she would play. He put on a sour pan, hunched himself a trifle, the way she was hunched, talked shrilly and goofily, and dropped the pillow in front of Muggsy. He kissed Tubby, who blushed with embarrassment, and they nearly all split their sides laughing.

The game went on. Studs dropped the pillow, by accident, in front of Helen. They looked meanly at each other, and neither moved until everybody yelled at them to play the game square, so they knelt down, each at an edge of the pillow, peck-kissed each other, and deepened their mutual hatred.

They changed to post-office. Tubby was suggested as postmaster, but Bill demanded the job, saying he was the logical person to examine all transactions. Fran Lonigan, as hostess, started the ball rolling. As she walked into the bedroom, right off the parlor entrance, Bill grabbed her, and kissed her; it was his tax. She laughed and didn't get angry. Fran called Dan. Dan kissed Bill on the way of entry. It was funny.

Dan called Fran Reilley, and kissed her. She called her brother. She stamped his toe, and ran out saying it was for a special delivery letter. He got sore, but she had gotten away too quickly. He told Bill to call Borax.

Weary kissed her flush on the mouth. He held her there, and when he finally released her, she sighed deeply.

He kissed her again, and she powerlessly tightened against him. He forced her to the bed.

"Stop touching me there. Stop!" she whispered.

When he paused, breathless, she demanded an apology.

"Shut up!" he muttered.

He bent down and kissed her.

"Unhand me, you cur. Take your hands off!" she whispered. "Take your hands off there, or I'll scream!"

He pulled her to him and kissed her. She became limp in his arms. He kissed her again, and she pressed to him. He loosed her. She called him a cur and demanded an apology.

"Shut up!"

She bit her lips, fought back tears, and said in a low, strained voice:

"Apologize!"

"Kiss me!"

She was a girl suddenly baffled by a woman's impulses. She flung herself around him. Then he walked out.

Regaining her composure and rearranging herself, she called in Jim. In the parlor they looked at Weary, surprised and over-curious. There was a tight silence, which Bill broke by saying that Weary had received a delayed letter. They laughed, and Weary's frown broke into a smile.

Jim, in the meantime, had called in Lucy; and she called Studs. She pursed her lips before she kissed him. It was so sudden, and her lips had such a sweet, candy taste that he was pleasantly surprised and stood there, not knowing what to do or say. He had never kissed sweet lips like that before. He faced her, and she was something beautiful and fair, with her white dress vivid in the dark room. She looked beautiful, like a flame. She pursed her lips, moved closer to him, flung her arms around him, kissed him, and said:

"I like you!"

She kissed away his surprise, looked dreamily into his eyes, kissed him again, long, and then dashed out.

Jesus Christ! he said to himself.

The game went on. Studs and Lucy, Helen and Weary kept calling each other into the post office. All the guys except TB and Tubby got their share of kisses. Tubby was called a few times for charity's sake, but TB was left out in the cold. He sat in a corner, wisecracking as if he didn't mind. He knew he didn't belong there anyway. Probably he did have the con, as everybody said and believed.

XI

After all the guests had departed, the Lonigans sat in the parlor talking.

"Well, I'm tired," Lonigan said yawning.

"I'm dead tired," said the mother.

"It was hard work," said Lonigan.

"Isn't Mrs. Reilley common, though?" yawned Mrs. Lonigan.

"But she's a nice, good, wholesome, sincere woman," said Lonigan.

"She's green," the wife said.

"She's ignorant; she's a greenhorn," said Frances.

"Frances!" the mother said.

"Well, she is!"

"But you needn't say so . . . so . . . crudely."

"Anyway, she and her old man are pretty old-fashioned, but they are nice people. They are too nice for that boy of theirs. If he were my son, I'd lambast the stuffings out of him; he's a real bad actor," Lonigan said.

"I'm afraid no good will ever come out of him, and I'm so glad William here is not like he is. Did you hear the way he talked to his mother and father, so disrespectful, saying he'd do what he wanted to, and he wouldn't go right home with them. William, I don't want you to have anything to do with him. He's a bad one. He'll probably end up in the penitentiary," she said.

Studs admired Weary, his enemy. Weary's parents had told him to come home with them, and Weary had wanted to walk home with Helen Borax; there had been a row and he had walked off. Studs was almost impelled to defend Weary, but didn't, because then his old man might have talked all night.

"Well, it's a good thing he isn't my son, or he'd get the stuffings lambasted out of him. I'd knock some good sense in his head," Lonigan said with finality.

"Mrs. Reilley uses awfully bad grammar, too," Mrs. Lonigan said.

"Well, I'd rather have people use bad grammar than have 'em be smart alecks like Dinny Gorman. Why, I knew him when he didn't have a sole on his shoe; and then him stickin' up his nose and actin' like he was highbrow, lace-curtain Irish, born to the purple. And all just because he's got a little booklearnin' and he bootlicked around until he became a ward committeeman. Why, he was nothin' but a starvin' lawyer hangin' around police courts until Joe O'Reilley started sendin' some business his way. What is he now . . . nothin' but a shyster. Maybe he might have a little more booklearnin' than I, but what does that mean? Look here, now: Is he a better and more conscientious father? Does he pay his bills more regularly? Has he got a bigger bank account than I got?" said Lonigan in heated indignation while no one listened to him.

When the old man had finished orating, Studs said:

"All the kids call him High Collars!" The old man laughed.

"And the crust of May! Won't you come to tea, but do call first, as we have so many, oh, so many, social engagements these days!" Mrs. Lonigan said.

"She can't hold a spoon up to you with all her damn society airs," Lonigan said.

"I know her kind. She's just like a cat, all soft and furry, and with claws that would scratch your eyes out," the old lady said.

There was a pause in the conversation; Martin looked mischievously at Studs and said:

"Studs got long pants; Studs got long pants."

"Shut up!"

The old lady reprimanded Martin for using the nickname, and the old man admonished Studs that he shouldn't talk like that to his brother.

"But I do think William looks darling," teased Fran.

"You look pretty slick, Bill. Don't let 'em get your goat," the old man said.

"Yes . . . so cute. Even Lucy Scanlan thought that he looked so . . . cute," said Frances.

Studs gave his sister a dirty look; the old man tried to kid Studs about having a girl; Studs shut up tight as a clam.

"Now, children," the mother conciliated.

"They're not just children any more," the old man said.

"Yes, they are. They are, too. They're my children, my baby blue-eyed boy and my girl. They can't be taken from me, either," the mother said, tenaciously.

The old man looked at Studs as much as to say: What can you do with a woman?

"Now, Mary, you know that people have to grow up," the old man said.

"Dad!" Studs said hesitantly.

"Yes," responded the old man.

"How about my workin' with you now, instead of goin' to school? You'll want me to sooner or later, and I might as well start now," said Studs.

"Well . . . I'll have to think it over."

"Why, William!" protested the mother.

They had a discussion. Mrs. Lonigan kept wondering out loud what the neighbors would think, because it would look like they were too cheap, or else couldn't afford to send their boy to high school. She repeated, several times, that she would be ashamed to put her head in St. Patrick's Church again or to look Father Gilhooley or any of the sisters in the face if their boy were sent out into the cold world to work, with only a grammar school education, when all his classmates went on to high school. Lonigan kept nodding his head in thought, and soliloquizing that he didn't know what to say, because she was right, and yet a lot of this education was nothing but booklearning, nothing but bunk. He had some new thoughts, and these fed further soliloquizing. It was pretty true that in a way knowledge

was power and a person could never know too much, as
long as he was right-thinking. And then he didn't want nobody to think that he wasn't doing the right thing by his
children; and maybe people would misinterpret it if the boy
didn't try high school, at least for a while. And anyway, an
education could never hurt you as long as you were right-
thinking.

Studs tried to dissent, but he was inarticulate.

His incoherent protests were cut short by his mother suggesting that he ought to study for the priesthood. She said
one could always change one's mind, up to the taking of
the vows, and a priest got a wonderful education, and even
if he didn't go on with it, he would be more educated than
most people. She said it was, just as Father Gilhooley said,
the duty of all parents to see if their children had the call.
How would God and his poor Mother, and great St. Patrick,
guardian saint of the parish, feel if Studs turned a deaf ear
on the sacred call? Lonigan opened his mouth to say something, but Studs said decisively he didn't have the call. The
mother said he should pray more, so he would know, and
God would reveal to him if he had. Frances interrupted to
say that Studs should go to Loyola, because everybody of
any consequence was going there and it was the school to
go to. They talked on, and it was decided, against Studs'
wishes, that he go to Loyola.

Then the parents rose to retire, yawning.

Mrs. Lonigan put Martin to bed. She hugged the boy
close to her meager bosom and said:

"Martin, don't you think you'd like to be a priest when
you grow up, and serve God?"

"I want to be a grave digger," Martin answered sleepily.

She left the room, her cheeks slightly wet with tears. She
prayed to God that he would give one of her boys the call.

After they had left the parlor, Studs sat by the window.
He looked out, watching the night strangeness, listening.
The darkness was over everything like a warm bed-cover,

and all the little sounds of night seemed to him as if they belonged to some great mystery. He listened to the wind in the tree by the window. The street was queer, and didn't seem at all like Wabash Avenue. He watched a man pass, his heels beating a monotonous echo. Studs imagined him to be some criminal being pursued by a detective like Maurice Costello, who used to act detective parts for Vitagraph. He watched. He thought of Lucy on the street and himself bravely rescuing her from horrors more terrible than he could imagine. He thought about the fall, and of the arguments for working that he should have sprung on the old man. He thought of himself on a scaffold, wearing a painter's overalls, chewing tobacco, and talking man-talk with the other painters; and of pay days and the independence they would bring him. He thought of Studs Lonigan, a free and independent working man, on his first pay night, plunking down some dough to the old lady for board, putting on his new straw katy, calling for Lucy, and taking her out stepping to White City, having a swell time.

Frances came in. She wore a thin nightgown. He could almost see right through it. He tried to keep looking away, but he had to turn his head back to look at her. She stood before him, and didn't seem to know that he was looking at her. She seemed kind of queer; he thought maybe she was sick.

"Do you like Lucy?"

"Oh, a little," he said.

He was excited, and couldn't talk much, because he didn't want her to notice it.

"Do you like to kiss girls?"

"Not so much," he said.

"You did tonight."

"It was all in the game."

"Helen must like Weary."

"I hate her."

"I don't like her either, but . . . do you think they did anything in the post office?"

"What do you mean?" he asked.

She wasn't going to pump him and get anything out of him.

She seemed to be looking at him, awful queer, all right.

"You know. Do you think they did anything that was fun . . . or that the sisters wouldn't want them to do . . . or that's bad?"

"I don't know."

Dirty thoughts rushed to his head like hot blood. He told himself he was a bastard because . . . she was his sister.

"I don't know," he said, confused.

"You think maybe they did something bad, and it was fun?"

He shrugged his shoulders and looked out the window so she couldn't see his face.

"I feel funny," she said.

He hadn't better say anything to her, because she'd snitch and give him away.

"I want to do something . . . They're all in bed. Let's us play leap frog, you know that game that boys play where one bends down, and the others jump over him?" she said.

"We'll make too much noise."

"Do you really think that Weary and Helen did anything that might be fun?" she asked.

She got up, and walked nervously around the room. She plunked down on the piano stool, and part of her leg showed.

He looked out the window. He looked back. They sat. She fidgeted and couldn't sit still. She got up and ran out of the room. He sat there. He must be a bastard . . . she was his sister.

He looked out the window. He wondered what it was like; he was getting old enough to find out.

He got up. He looked at himself in the mirror. He

shadow-boxed, and thought of Lucy. He thought of Fran. He squinted at himself in the mirror.

He turned the light out and started down the hallway. Fran called him. She was lying in bed without the sheets over her.

"It's hot here. Awful hot. Please put the window up higher."

"It's as high as it'll go."

"I thought it wasn't."

He looked at Fran. He couldn't help it.

"And please get me some real cold water."

He got the water. It wasn't cold enough. She asked him to let the water run more. He did. He handed the water to her. As she rose to drink, she bumped her small breast against him.

She drank the water. He started out of the room. She called him to get her handkerchief.

"I'm not at all tired," she said.

He left, thinking what a bastard he must be.

He went to the bathroom.

Kneeling down at his bedside, he tried to make a perfect act of contrition to wash his soul from sin.

He heard the wind, and was afraid that God might punish him, make him die in the night. He had found out he was old enough, but . . . his soul was black with sin. He lay in bed, worried, suffering, and he tossed into a slow, troubled sleep.

SECTION TWO

Chapter Three

I

STUDS awoke to stare sleepily at a June morning that
crashed through his bedroom window. The world outside
the window was all shine and shimmer. Just looking at it
made Studs glad that he was alive. And it was only the end
of June. He still had July and August. And this was one of
those days when he would feel swell; one of his days. He
drowsed in bed, and glanced out to watch the sun scatter
over the yard. He watched a tomcat slink along the fence
ledge; he stared at the spot he had newly boarded so that
his old man wouldn't yelp about loose boards; he looked
about at the patches in the grass that Martin and his gang
had worn down playing their cowboy and Indian games.
There was something about the things he watched that
seemed to enter Studs as sun entered a field of grass; and as
he watched, he felt that the things he saw were part of himself, and he felt as good as if he were warm sunlight; he
was all glad to be living, and to be Studs Lonigan. Because
when he came to think of it, living had been pretty good
since he had graduated. Every morning he could lie in bed
if he wanted to, or else he could hop up and go over and
goof around Indiana Avenue and see the guys and . . .
Lucy.

He reclined in bed and thought about looking for a job; he did this almost every morning, and usually he had good intentions. Then he would start pretending, as if his good intentions had been carried out and he was working, earning his own living, and independent, so that his old man couldn't boss him. But every morning he would forget his good intentions before he got out of bed. And a morning like this was too nice a one to be wasted going downtown and trying to find a job, and maybe not finding it; and anyway, it was a little late, and most of the jobs for guys like him had been probably grabbed up by other kids.

Studs got up. He thought about saying his morning prayers, but he decided to wait and say them while he was washing; a wise guy could always kill two birds with one stone. He knelt down by the open window and took ten inhales; on colder mornings, when the temperature of the room was not the same as the temperature outside, it was swell and invigorating taking inhales, and Studs liked to do it because it made him feel good, but in summer like now, it was only a physical culture measure that he took, because some day Studs Lonigan was going to become big and strong and . . . tough. He turned and went over to the dresser, thinking about how tough a guy he might become. He studied Studs Lonigan in the mirror, and discovered that he wasn't such a bad-looking guy, and that maybe he even looked older than he was. He took a close-up squint at his mug and decided that it was, after all, a pretty good mug, even if he almost had a sheeny's nose. He twisted his lips in sneers, screwed up his puss, and imagined himself telling some big guy where to get off at. He said, half aloud:

See, bo, I don't take nobody's sass. And get this, bo, the bigger they are, de harder dey fall. See, bo!

He took his pajama top off and gave his chest the double-o. It was broad and solid, all right. He practiced expanding his chest, flexing and unflexing his muscles to feel their hardness, tautening his abdomen to see if he had a cast-iron gut. He told himself that Studs Lonigan was one pretty Goddamn good physical specimen. Scowling like a real bruiser ought to scowl, he shadow-boxed with tip-toed clumsiness, cleaving the air with haymakers, telling himself that he was not only tough and rough, but that he was also a scientific boxer. He swung and swished himself into a good perspiration, knocking out imaginary roughnecks as if they were bowling pins, and then he sat down, saying to himself that he was Young Studs Lonigan, or maybe only Young Lonigan, the Chicago sensation, now in training for the bout when he would kayo Jess Willard for the title.

He snapped out of it, and went to the bathroom. He washed in clear, cold water, snorting with his face lowered in the filled bowl. It felt good, and it also felt good to douse water on his chest. After drying himself with a rough bath towel, he stood up close to the mirror and looked to see if there were any hairs on his upper lip. If he wasn't so light, maybe he'd have to shave now. He imagined himself with the guys, walking, and him saying well, he wouldn't be able to get around so early that night because he had to shave, and shaving was one lousy pain. And maybe girls would be there, and he'd say the same thing, only he wouldn't curse. Himself letting Lucy know he shaved by complaining of it, or by talking about how he cut himself with the razor, or about how it had been hard because the razor was dull. Well, anyway, he could trim a lot of guys who did shave. He was nobody's slouch. And some day he'd be shaving, and have hair on the chest, too. It was like that Uncle Josh piece on the victrola, I'm old but I'm awfully tough. Well, for him it was: I'm small but I'm awfully tough.

Studs left home immediately after breakfast so he could get away from the old lady. She was always pestering him, telling him to pray and ask God if he had a vocation. And maybe she'd have wanted him to go to the store, beat rugs,

or clean the basement out. He didn't feel like being a janitor. He would work, but he wouldn't be a janitor. Janitor's
jobs were for jiggs, and Hunkies, and Polacks, anyway.
He'd asked the old man again to take him to work, but the
old man was the world's champion putter-off. Every year
since Studs could remember, he'd been promising that he
was going to take the old lady to Riverview Park, and he
was still promising. That was just like the old boy. Studs
walked along, glancing about him, feeling what a good
morning it was, walking in the sun that was spinning all
over the street like a crazy top. He could feel the warmness
of the sun; it entered him, became part of himself, part of
his walk, part of his arms swinging along at his side, part
of his smile, his good feelings, his thoughts. It was good.
He walked along, and he thought about the family; families
were goddamn funny things; everybody's old man and old
woman were the same; they didn't want a guy or a girl to
grow up. His mother was always blowing off her bazoo
about him being her blue-eyed baby, and his old man was
always giving advice, bossing, instructing him as if he was
a ten-year-old. Well, he was growing up in spite of them;
and it wouldn't be long now before he had long britches on
every day. Let 'em do their damnedest; Studs Lonigan
would tell the world that he was growing up.

He goofed around for a while in the vacant lot just off
the corner of Fifty-eighth and Indiana. He batted stones. He
walked around kicking a tin can, imagining it was something very important, some sort of thing like an election or
a sporting contest that got on the front page. Then he
thought about Indiana Avenue. It was a better street than
Wabash. It was a good block, too, between Fifty-seventh
and Fifty-eighth. Maybe when his old man sold the building, he'd buy one in this block. It was nearer the stores,
and there were more Catholics on the street, and in the
evening the old man could sit on the front porch talking
with Old Man O'Brien, and his old lady could gossip with

Mrs. O'Brien and Dan's mother, and Mrs. Scanlan. The
house next to Scanlans' would be a nice one to live in.
Some people named Welsh owned it, but they were pretty
old and they'd be kicking the bucket soon. There were
more trees on Indiana, too, and no shines, and only a few
kikes. The building on the right of the lot was the one where
yellowbelly Red O'Connell lived, the big redhead. Studs
wondered if he could fight him. He'd love to paste O'Connell's mush, but Red was big. Maybe the old man would
buy the building and kick the O'Connells out. Down two
doors was the wooden frame house where the O'Callaghans
lived. Old Man O'Callaghan had been one of the first guys
to live in the neighborhood, and he was supposed to be
lousy with dough. And then the apartment buildings where
the Donoghues lived. And then the series of two-story
bricks, where Lucy, Helen Shires and the O'Briens lived.
And then the home where those Jews, the Glasses, lived,
and then the apartment buildings on the corner, where punk
Danny O'Neill, and Helen Borax, and goofy Andy lived,
and they had that bastard of a janitor, George, who was always shagging kids. Some Hallowe'en they were going to
get him, good. If Studs lived on Indiana, he'd see more of
Lucy. He walked down Indiana, thinking he might call for
some of the bunch; but then, he was an independent guy,
the best scrapper of the gang; let 'em call for him. He
stopped at Johnny O'Brien's gangway and checked himself
when he was on the verge of shouting up for Johnny. He
came out on the sidewalk, and looked back toward Fifty-
eighth. He walked backward.

   "Hello, there," sighed Leon.

   "Hello!" said Studs, turning sharply, a little surprised.

   Studs looked at Leon; he almost looked a hole through
him.

   Leon was middle-aged and fat. He had a meaty rump
that always made the guys laugh, and a pair of breastworks
like a woman. His skin was smooth and oily, his eyes dark

and cowy, his lips thick and sensuous, his nose Jewish. Leon was a music teacher, and Studs always felt that he was goofy enough to be . . . just a music teacher.

"I say! Why do boys look backward? I always wanted to know," he said in a half-lisp.

"I was just lookin' to see if any of the guys were down the street."

"Well, you know, it's the funniest thing. It really is. Because I see so many boys looking backward, and I'm always asking myself why they do it. Never for the life of me have I been able to understand," said Leon.

Studs shrugged his shoulders.

Leon placed his hand on Studs' shoulder, and patted his head with the other hand. It made Studs feel a little queer; he felt as if Leon's hands were dirty, or his stomach was going to turn, or something like that. Sometimes his mother tried to hold him and kiss him, and that made him feel goofy. This was a hundred times worse. Once over in the park, an old man sat down by him and asked if he liked the girls, or ever took them over on the wooded island at night, and he tried to feel Studs. The guy had been goofy, and Studs had had an awful feeling that he couldn't describe. He hadn't gone to the park for over a week, and every time he thought of the old guy, and wondered what the bastard had wanted, his thoughts turned sour. He felt the same way with Leon, only Leon was funny and he could laugh at him.

"When are you going to come and see me and let me teach you how to play the piano; you know, you little rascal, that I offered to give you lessons free."

"Oh, some time," Studs said.

"You're missing a wonderful opportunity, my boy. You don't understand now, but you will some day, how fine music can make a life beautiful," persuaded Leon.

What the hell is the damn fool talking about? Where in hell did he get that way? Studs said to himself.

Leon had taken his hands off Studs. Now he patted his head.

Studs stepped back a little.

"You're young now, but I'll bet you're an artist. If you let me teach you, I'll make a musician out of you."

Studs thought he might as well string the guy along a little.

"Then I can play in movie houses?"

"No, not that. I only do that to make a living. I mean a real musician. An artist."

Studs wondered what he meant by artist. He thought an artist was a guy who painted pictures, and always raved like a maniac because nobody liked his pictures.

Holy Jumpin' Jimminy! Studs almost laughed right in the guy's face.

"You must come over now and start those lessons."

"Some time I will," said Studs.

"Don't hesitate. He who hesitates is lost. You have your opportunity now, my boy, and opportunity strikes but once. Now tomorrow morning I'll be free. My mother will be out at eleven, and suppose you come then, and we'll be all alone, and there won't be no one to bother us, and we'll be free . . . for our first lesson."

Leon placed his arm around Studs' shoulder.

"Well, tomorrow, I gotta beat rugs for my mother."

"But mother might let you off if you say it's to take music lessons."

"You don't know my mother."

"But mothers can be convinced. Now, I know. I have a mother who still tries to boss me."

Studs didn't have any answer for Leon. Leon tried to convince Studs. Then he had to rush to get to a lesson. He gave Studs a final pat, and told him to think it over. As he started to wriggle his rump along, he turned and said:

"Well, ta, ta! Now, don't forget the lessons . . . and don't

do anything naughty-nasty . . . like tickling the girlies. Ta!
Ta!"

He waved his arm womanishly, and went on. Studs
watched him. He laughed. He felt a little queer. He wondered why Leon was always placing his hands on a guy.

II

Studs kept futzing around until Helen Shires came out with
her soccer ball. Then they dribbled back and forth on the
paving in front of her place. She lived next door to the
Scanlans. It was a drearily lazy June morning now, and
they played. Helen was a lean, muscular girl, tall and
rangy, with angular Swedish features, blue eyes and yellow-
ish white hair. She was tanned, and wore a blue wash dress,
which was constantly ruffling up, so that her purplish-blue
wash bloomers showed. She looked very healthy.

They played. Helen took the ball to dribble. She strode
down about six yards, turned around, and dribbled forward,
straight and fast, with the form and force of a star basketball player. All the guys used to say she was a natural athlete. Studs stood squat, his hands spread fan-wise, his body
awkwardly tensed for sudden effort. As she approached
him, she feinted toward her right, changed her stroke from
left to right hand, and passed him on his right, making him
look quite sick.

Studs side-glanced up at the Scanlan parlor window.
He'd never before been jealous of Helen's athletic skill, but
now he was. Maybe Lucy had been peeping behind the cur-
tain. He had hoped she was. Now he changed his wish.

"I don't like basketball so well," he said, grinning
weakly.

"You will after you learn the game," she answered, dribbling back.

She dribbled again, and Studs, with a chance swing of
the right arm, batted the ball out into the street. He changed

his wish, and covertly side-glanced at the Scanlan window. Helen complimented him on his good guarding.

It was his turn. He came forward, awkward, clumsier than usual because he tried to show form. He bounced the ball too hard and too high, and he was slowed down. He lost control of the ball before he reached her, and it bounded onto the grass.

It was good he was only pretending that Lucy watched him. They kept dribbling, and she kept making him look sick. She was having a better time than he, because she could do the thing, and she could get the satisfaction one gets out of doing a thing right. But he stuck on.

Once when they paused, she said:

"You ought to make the football team at Loyola."

"I'd like to," he said.

"You will," she said.

They talked for a while, and resumed dribbling. She dribbled and he guarded. He took a turn, and she snatched the ball from him, pivoted gracefully, and dribbled down the other way. They alternated, and he kept side-glancing at the Scanlan window.

After a half-hour, they were both a little fagged, and they sat on Helen's front steps.

"Say, Studs, there's a can house around on Fifty-seventh Street," she said.

"There is?"

"Yeh."

"You sure?"

"Sure! Paulie Haggerty was around the other day, and he told me about it, and I went and looked the other night, and saw a lot of cars parked there and a lot of men enterin' and leavin'. One guy even wore a silk hat."

"Whereabouts was it?"

"The flat building on the other side of the alley on Fifty-seventh. It's on the first floor," said she.

"The red one where we climbed on the front porch that afternoon when it was rainin' and shot craps?" he asked.

"No. Next door to it," she said.

"We'll all go round there some night and look in," said Studs.

"All right," said Helen.

"Say, Weary hasn't been around. I wonder if he's workin'?" said Studs.

"I don't like him," she said.

"I don't care so much for him," Studs said.

"He's too fresh," she said.

"Yeh?"

"Yeh, he's too darn fresh."

"Why?"

"Well, he tries to take liberties with girls. You know what he tried to do to me, don't you?"

"No?"

"Well, one day he asked me to let him see my kid sister's playhouse in the back, and I did. Then he went and tried . . . well, you know what he wanted to do to me, and I wouldn't let him. I don't care to do that sort of thing. I like to play with fellahs because, generally, they're fellahs like you an' Dan and Tubby, and they're square and decent, and not rats like those guys from Fifty-eighth Street, or like Weary Reilley, and they're not fussy and babyish, like girls. Girls are always tattling, and squealing, and snitching, and I can't stand them. With decent guys, you can be . . . well, you can be yourself. Anyway, he tried to do that to me, and I wouldn't let him. He kept arguin' with me, and grabbin' me, and I wouldn't let him fool around and have a feel-day, so he lost his temper like he always does, and he got sore as blazes, and I was afraid, so I rushed out. He tried to get me to come back, and said he was only foolin' and he didn't mean anything, and all that sort of bull. But I didn't fall for it, so he left me, sore as blazes, and sayin' he'd get me some time."

"I never knew that," Studs said.

"Well, he did. I don't like him; I hate him, the skunk; he's a bastard," she said.

"I don't care so much for him, either. But you got to give him credit for being a damn good scrapper. He ain't yellow."

"You can fight him, can't you?"

"I'm not afraid of him," Studs said.

"Sure, you can lick him," she said.

"Well, I never backed out of a fight with him," Studs said.

"Say, let's get a soda," Helen suggested.

"I'm broke," Studs said.

"I'll treat," she said.

They walked down to Levin's drug store at the corner of Fifty-eighth and Indiana and they had double chocolate sodas; they sipped with their spoons, so that the sodas would last longer. Studs told himself that there was something very fine about Helen. She was a square shooter, and she understood things. If he tried to sip a soda with a spoon before anybody else, they would laugh at him. When he and Lucy got to be sweethearts, she'd understand things, like Helen did. A guy couldn't find a pal like Helen every day. They sat, and Studs mentioned Lucy, saying that she was a nice-looking kid. Helen smiled like a person who knew too much. She said she liked Lucy, because she was a sweet kid, and full of fun, and not an old ash can like Helen Borax, who was too stuck up to live on a street like Indiana. She said it served Helen right that she had gotten a crush on a guy like Weary, because Weary would take some of the snootiness out of her and, well, Weary would probably make her do you-know with him, and it would be a good thing for her to be ruined, because she might come down off her high horse, and it would be a swell chance to talk about her, instead of having her talk about everyone else. But Lucy was a good kid for a guy to like, she said; and

Studs said he wasn't so sure how much he liked her. She said, well, a guy like Studs was better off liking a girl like Lucy, and going with the bunch around Indiana Avenue, than he was, say, hanging out with the gang around Fifty-eighth Street. Red Kelly, Tommy Doyle, Davey Cohen and those guys were all louses; the only decent one among them was Paulie Haggerty; and Paulie had been better off when he used to come around Indiana and he was sweet on Cabby Devlin. Studs said he didn't give two whoops in hell for them; but he wasn't afraid of any of 'em.

Finishing their sodas, they returned toward Helen's. They paused before the clapboard frame house of the O'Callaghans. It was set about twenty yards back from the sidewalk, with a well-kept lawn and a large oak in front. Studs and Helen wondered why people lived in such an old-fashioned house, especially when they were rich like the O'Callaghans were. They were stumped by this. Studs tried to think what the neighborhood had been like when Old Man O'Callaghan first settled there and built his house, cutting down trees and living alone just like a pioneer. It must have been like a forest. That must have been good except for the wind at night. Even now, when you lived in a brick house that was all burglar-locked, and there weren't any trees for the wind to blow through, the wind at night was something you almost couldn't stand to hear. What must it have been then? It must have sounded like a horde of ghosts rising from a rainy cemetery, or an army of devils and demons; and he didn't know how Old Man O'Callaghan and his wife stood it. And what about the pioneers? The wind in the trees all around their houses must have sounded like Indians, and they must have jumped out of bed every five minutes and grabbed their guns. He would have liked to be a pioneer and go out to fight Indians and build log cabins. He would have had a swell time, pot-shotting Indians, rescuing girls like Lucy from them, and from smugglers and hold-ups. Or maybe he'd have been an outlaw like Jesse James. That would have been the real stuff, and no outlaw as tough as he would have been would have feared the wind. No, sir!

They played kicking goals between two lampposts. A punt passing over the goal line untouched was a point, and a drop kick was three. They were about even as kickers, and gave each other a good match, and they trusted each other and knew there was no cheating, so they could go ahead and play, not having any squabbles or having to talk and chew the rag a lot. It was swell for Studs to play, kicking, watching the ball soar up and away, and maybe fall in back of the goal line, knowing he had made that good kick and scored that point, or to make a drop kick, or to run back and pick one of Helen's southpaw kicks out of the air. And just to go ahead playing, not bothering to talk or to think of anything, except now and then to imagine that Lucy was in the window watching. They played a long time, and winded themselves; when they quit, Studs was leading thirty to twenty-five.

They sat on Helen's front steps.

"You know, I always used to think I'd feel a little different when I graduated from grammar school, but here it's a couple of weeks ago, and I don't see any difference yet. Everything seems pretty much the same, and well, I don't know. Here I am graduated, and I'm wearin' short pants again, and got to listen to my old man the same as I did before I was graduated, and I come around, and everything and everybody's the same, kidding the punks, playing chase-one-chase-all, and blue-my-blackberry, and baby-in-the-hole, and all that sort of thing, just like before, and, well, in the fall I'll have to go to high school, and, well, things are just not like I imagined they would be after I graduated."

"I feel the same way," Helen said.

"I feel the same; and it's no different when you get confirmed. You are supposed to change, and something that's a mystery called a character is stamped on your soul, that is, if you're a Catholic; but you don't really seem to change any. Anyway, I didn't seem to," Studs pondered.

"Well, I never got confirmation, but I think I know what you mean. But my father and my mother, they don't think so much of confirmation," said Helen.

"Of course we're taught different than you. We're taught that you shouldn't feel that way about the thing. You should believe in God and in the Church, and do all the duties that God and the Church say you should, or else you won't be doin' right and you'll go to Hell. Of course, if a person's not Catholic, but if they're sincere in bein' whatever they are, well, they'll stand a good chance of gettin' into Heaven. That's the way we're taught," said Studs.

"My father and mother say that it's all right what you believe, so long as you live up to that belief and don't do nothin' that's really wrong, or really hurt your neighbor, and if you do that, you ain't got nothin' to worry about from God," Helen said.

"Well, you know, it seems funny. Last night I was thinkin'. I remembered how I thought all the time that I'd feel so different after graduation. But now! Well, I'm just . . . I don't know. When I was a punk in the first grade, I used to look up to the guys ahead of me and feel that eighth-grade kids were so big, and now when I'm graduated I still wish I was bigger, and I don't feel satisfied, like I used to think I would when I was only a punk," Studs said.

"That's just the way I sort of feel."

"Yeh . . . but, oh, well," said Studs.

He felt that there was something else to be said, but he didn't know how to say it; he wondered if he was blowing his gab off too much. Sometimes, with Helen, he could talk more, and say more of what he really meant, than he could with any other person.

"Yeh," said Helen, meaningfully.

He glanced at her; he told himself that she was nice-looking. He felt soft inside, as if his feelings were all fluid, all melting up and running through him like a warm stream of water. He didn't know what he ought to say. He hurriedly glanced across the street. He saw Dennis P. Gorman tote his cane and his dignity down Indiana Avenue on his way to the police court. He laughed at High-Collars; and Helen said her father always called Gorman a mollycoddle who ought to be wearing corsets.

"You know, we'll have to take a look at that can house sometimes," Studs said, because he felt that he had better say something.

"Yeh!"

"I'd like to know what's inside of a can house," said Studs.

He was calmed down again, and he could look at her without feeling strange, and he wasn't in danger of giving his feelings away. He noticed that she, too, had been looking away.

"Well, I suppose one of those places has got a lot of expensive furniture, and the whores all sit around in their underclothes and maybe they drink a lot, and you know," she said.

"I'd sure like to see one some time," he said.

"Me, too," she said.

"Maybe we can sneak up on the porch sometimes," he said.

"Yeah," said Helen.

"We might see someone doin' it, too," he said.

"Yeah," said Helen.

"Sometimes I wonder what it's like," he said.

"So do I," she said.

"I don't think it's so much," said he.

"All the kids act as if they knew, but I'll bet that none of them really do," she said.

"I guess you're right."

She told him of the time that her dog, Billie, had cut its

nose, and had accidentally rubbed a little blood on her nightgown. Her mother had seen the blood spot, and had gotten excited, and had tried to explain to Helen what things were all about, but Helen had known what her mother told her; and her mother hadn't told about the thing that was the real bother; her mother hadn't said a word of what it really felt like. As Helen told this to Studs, he got all excited, and seemed to see her before him, melting and fading. He felt like he'd have to do something, and he was afraid to try.

"Say, wouldn't it be nicer back in the playhouse?" he said, keeping his voice under control as much as he could.

"We can't go back and sit there now. My sister Marion and her girl chums are in it," she said.

"Oh!" he said.

Nothing had seemed wrong in his asking, he guessed. So they sat there and talked. Helen asked him if he knew this Iris who took all kinds of guys up to her house when her mother wasn't home, and let them all have a gang-shag. Studs said he didn't know Iris, but he'd heard of her. Helen said that was going too far; it was like being a whore. Studs said yes.

But he wished he could horn in on one of those gang-shags.

Weary Reilley ambled around, and Helen grumbled a greeting to him. He asked if they'd seen Helen Borax, and they said no. Weary fooled around with the soccer ball, and they barbered about nothing in particular. Then they dribbled, one taking the ball, and the other two standing in a line to block the dribble. Weary had never played basketball, so he was awkward and clumsy and couldn't do the trick right. He went at it rough-and-tumble. He got sore because Helen could make such a monkey out of him. He finally lost his bean and dribbled head on into her, bucking her breasts with his football shoulders. It hurt her. She cried; she knew he had done it meanly and on purpose. She told him so, and he called her a liar. She slammed him in the mush with the ball, and his eyes watered.

"Listen," he said, preparing to rush her and let her have one.

Studs gripped Weary from the rear and held him in a firm clasp.

"Let me go, you sonofabitch," Weary yelled.

Studs flung Weary around and then faced him.

"Who's one?" asked Studs.

"Both of you, and she's a whore," said Weary.

"Why, Goddamn you," said Helen.

"Take that back," said Studs.

"From . . . *you*!" sneered Weary.

Weary socked Studs in the jaw; Studs' jaw flushed, Studs was confused; his breath came fast; maybe he was afraid; he had to fight; he forgot about everything but Weary in front of him. He hauled off and caught Weary on the knob with a wild right haymaker. They rushed into each other and swung. They broke their clinch and circled around. Weary rushed, and a wild uppercut that Studs had started from the ground a trifle before Weary had come in, caught Reilley on the button. Reilley was jogged back; he shook his head, and then walloped Studs with a left and right. But neither of them felt a lot. They fought, absorbed in punching each other. Every time they landed, a feeling of pleasure ran through them, pleasure at having done something physically successful. They fought, slugging, socking away, rushing, swinging with haymakers and wild swishing roundhouses.

Johnny O'Brien, thirteen and fattish, came around and watched. He didn't yell who he was for, and asked Helen how the scrap had started.

"Oh, Weary got snotty and called me an' Studs dirty names. If Studs can't bust hell out of him, I'M GONNA . . . Come on, Studs! Bam him! . . . Attaboy, Studs!"

Helen attaboyed Studs because he had just given Weary

a good bust in the nose. Weary rushed back and made Studs' left ear red from a wallop. Studs missed Weary with a wild haymaker, and almost fell over. Weary jolted him when he was off balance. Studs came back with a rush and caught Weary in the mouth. Weary busted Studs. Studs busted Weary.

A crowd had formed a circle around them, watching, blocking the sidewalks. Women, mothers, yelled unheeded from nearby windows for them to stop. Screwy McGlynn, the fat guy who drove a laundry wagon, and who bragged that he had put the blocks to nearly every K. M. in the neighborhood, climbed down from his wagon and watched the fight with a professional eye. He stood next to Johnny O'Brien, similarly professional, and said the little guy had guts. He rooted for the little guy. Danny O'Neill, twelve, small, curly-haired, four-eyed, joined the mob and yelled for Studs to bust hell out of the bully. Dick Buckford, from Danny's gang, came around and rooted for both of them to win. The mob around had a swell time, shifting, shouting, yelling; it was the fight they had been waiting for. Mrs. Dennis P. Gorman tripped along. She paused and made a vain attempt to tell someone that it was a nasty spectacle which should be stopped. She heard Helen yelling for Studs to slam the cur; she picked up her skirts, crossed the street and tripped on.

Screwy McGlynn chewed on his cigar, grew more professional, and said: "That little guy is sure game . . . Well, he's one of them guys that believes in the old adage . . . the bigger they are, the harder they fall . . . And I always say that a good game little man can lick a good big man."

"Yeah, they're both good boys," said Johnny O'Brien.

Studs fought a boring-in fight. He waved his left arm up and down horizontally, for purposes of defense, so he couldn't do much punching with it, but he kept his right swinging. Weary met Studs and lammed away with both fists. It was anybody's fight.

Studs cracked Weary with a dirty right. They clinched. Weary socked in the clinch.

"HEY! FIGHT FAIR!" young Danny O'Neill yelled.

"DON'T LET 'IM GET AWAY WITH IT, STUDS," yelled Helen.

Lucy Scanlan deserted the carpet sweeper and stood on her front steps watching, rooting for Studs. Helen Borax, on her way to the store, stopped to watch from Lucy's porch. Helen said it was disgusting, and hinted that it would be a roughneck like Studs Lonigan to start such a fight. Lucy was too busy rooting for Studs to hear. She kept yelling:

"BUST HIM, STUDS!"

Helen watched with an aloof expression on her precociously disdainful face.

Weary again socked in a clinch.

"Fight fair," said Studs, a little breathlessly.

"Up your brown!" sneered Weary.

They clinched. Studs swung low, and experienced animal pleasure when the foul punch connected. Weary tried to knee Studs, but it was only a glancing blow off Lonigan's thigh. They clinched again, tumbled onto the grass, rough and tumbled, with first one and then the other on top, socking away. Dan Donoghue and lanky Red O'Connell dragged them apart, and they squared off. O'Connell yelled for Weary. Everybody else cheered Studs. They rushed each other, swinging, fighting dirty, cursing, scratching. Studs connected with Weary's beak, and Reilley got a bloody nose. He asked Weary if he was licked yet; and Weary thumbed his nose at Studs. Weary socked Studs, giving him a shiner. Studs smashed Weary with rights on three successive rushes. Studs seemed to be winning, although he lumbered tiredly. Weary was bleeding, breathing almost in pants, and his shirt was torn; his shoulder was scratched; and there were scratches on Studs' arms. They fought, and Studs kept connecting with Weary's mush, hitting twice for every one he took.

Diamond-Tooth, tough, red-faced, big-mouthed, hairy-handed, looking as much ape as man, came around; he separated them with his crane-like paws.

"Now, you fools, shake hands," he commanded.

Weary refused. He told Diamond-Tooth to mind his own Goddamn business and go to hell.

"Oh, you're tough! I see! Thanks for the tip! You're a tough punk, not afraid of nothin'. Huh! You want your snotty puss bashed in a little more. Huh? Didn't this little squirt here give you enough?"

Most of the kids laughed.

Weary retreated a few paces and picked up a boulder.

"PUT THAT BRICK DOWN!"

Weary didn't reply.

"I see! I GOTTA SLAP YOUR PUSS, and run the gang of you in, give you a nice little ride in the wagon and let your old ladies come down to the station bawlin' to get you out."

The kids drew back nervously. Screwy McGlynn, who had moved forward to remonstrate with the stranger, retreated, hopped onto his wagon, and was gone. Diamond-Tooth cowed the gang with his detective's star.

"Gee, he's a real bull," Danny O'Neill whispered too loudly.

Profound silence!

"Yeh, he's a real bull, punk; and you better clamp that trap of yours tight!"

"Come on, you guys. Maybe you'll change your minds."

He dragged them along. Studs was meek and afraid; Weary was sullen, glowering. The others started to follow them toward Fifty-seventh, and he turned and snottily told them to blow, before they were hauled in.

He asked, after the three of them had turned the corner:

"What were you punks scrappin' over? Huh?"

"He called my mother a name," Studs said.

"He called me one, too," Weary said.

"Maybe you were both right," Diamond-Tooth said.

They stood there.

"Now, shut up and shake hands; if you don't, I'll fight the two of you," said the dick.

They shook hands, insincerely. Weary walked east along Fifty-seventh, toward Prairie Avenue. His pride was even more bruised than his face. He walked determining revenge, entertaining extravagant schemes of cold-blooded murder, of framing Studs on some stunt or other, of getting him from the back sometimes with a rock or a beebe gun or a knife, or maybe a twenty-two, of some day walking up to him and renewing the fight, taking an advantage by busting him right square between the eyes before he knew what was coming, or maybe cracking him in the neck and choking his windpipe, or in the solar plexus. He was angry. He sensed his own weakness. He could get little satisfaction out of planning revenge. He hated Studs, hated him with the face Studs had punched, with the body he'd battered; and that face and body told Weary he was licked when his mind refused to believe it. He was interrupted by Helen Borax, who called him from behind. She said that she was sorry, and that Studs was a beast, and she knew that Studs must have hurt him, and she was awfully sorry. Her pity made him see white. He drained off his hatred by glaring at her, calling her a bitch, and telling her he had gotten all he wanted from her under her back porch on the night they had graduated.

Studs, the conquering hero, returned to the gang. As he walked back, he thought up a brave story, about how he had told the gum-shoe to lump it, which he would tell the gang. But when he was sitting in the center of the adulatory group, he couldn't tell it. Damn it, he couldn't spread the bull on thick; he didn't know how to string people along and tell lies like some people did. He told them what had happened, and they had fun talking it over. They talked about the battle, showering Studs with praise, telling him how great he was and how he was the champ of the neighborhood. Johnny O'Brien had been going around telling everybody how thick he was with Red Kelly, and every time he got in dutch with anybody bigger than he was he would always threaten to get Red Kelly after him. Now he told Studs that he could clean up Kelly. Studs was tired, sick in his stomach, aching all over. And he kept feeling his swollen eye. Johnny O'Brien ran home and copped a piece of beefsteak from his old lady. Helen and Lucy applied it. Studs was happy, even though he felt rotten. He was now the cock of the walk, and the battering he had gotten from Weary was worth this; but he'd hate to have to fight him again; his jaw was all cut on the inside; well, Weary was probably worse off. Weary Reilley had been licked; he, Studs Lonigan, had pounded the stuffings out of him. Now, that was something to be proud of.

He listened to the sycophantic comments; they purred sweetly on his ears. Helen gave a vigorous redescription of how the fight started. Red O'Connell, who hated Studs, and was kowtowing to him only because he had cleaned up Reilley, kept saying it had been a bear of a fight. Dan Donoghue said there hadn't been a fight like it in the whole history of the neighborhood. Dick Buckford told Studs he could fight like blazes until they all told the punk to keep quiet. And Lucy said it showed Studs was brave.

Studs told himself he had been waiting for things like this to happen a long time; now they were happening, and life was going to be a whole lot more . . . more fun, and it was going to make everything just jake; and he was going to be an important guy, and all the punks would look up to him and brag to other punks that they knew him; and he would be . . . well, in the limelight. Maybe it would set things happening as he always knew they would; and he would keep on getting more and more important.

It was all swell; and it made him feel good, even if he was tired and aching. After they had all talked themselves almost blue in the face, they decided that it would be cooler in the Shires' playhouse. They went back there, and Helen chased away her kid sister's gang. The guys all chipped in to buy lunch, with Johnny O'Brien putting up most of the money. Red, Dan and Johnny went to the delicatessen store for grub; coming back, they copped a couple of bottles of milk from ice boxes. It was a fine lunch, and afterward they played post office, and Lucy gave her hero plenty of kisses. Life was fine and dandy for Studs, all right, and the only thing bothering him, besides his headache, was that he would have a heck of a time explaining his shiner to the old lady.

Chapter Four

I

STUDS couldn't stay in one place, and he kept walking up and down Indiana Avenue, wishing that the guys would come around. As he passed Young Horn Buckford and some punk he didn't know, Young Horn said hello to him. He gruffed a reply. He heard Young Horn say, as he walked on:

"You know who that is? That's STUDS LONIGAN. He's the champ fighter of the block."

Studs laughed to himself, proud.

He came back to Fifty-seventh, and sat on the curb, watching two kids race each other up and down the street with barrel hoops. They pretended they were auto-racers. A little kid in a blue shirt kept saying he was Dario Resta; and the other called himself Ralph De Palma. Resta and De Palma raced back and forth, and at the conclusion of every race there was an argument between the two winners. He would have liked to play in such a game, but it was too young for him. He smoked a butt.

"H'lo, Studs!"

"Hello, Half-Wit," said Studs to snotty-nosed, Jew-faced, thick-bodied, thirteen-year-old Andy Le Gare.

"Studs, can I feel your muscle?"

"I will if you will show me how you can bat your head against a brick wall."

"Gwan," said Andy.

"Say, Wilson's gonna get skunked," Studs said.

"He won't. My father said so; and he knows," said Andy.

"Listen! Wilson's a morphidite," Studs said.

"What's that?"

"A guy that's both a man and a woman at the same time, like fat Leon," said Studs.

Andy looked at Studs, hurt, puzzled, betrayed.

"I don't believe it. I'll bet you ten bucks," said Andy.

"Where'd you get the ten bucks," sneered Studs.

"Never mind, I'll get ten bucks," said Andy.

"Boushwah!"

A pause. Andy again asked Studs if he could feel his muscle. Studs consented if Andy would show his stuff. Andy said it was a bargain. Andy felt Studs' muscle, and said: Gee! He again gripped Studs' hard-fibered right arm, and repeated his exclamation of admiration. Studs then made Andy carry out his part of the bargain; so Andy went over to the corner building, and laughing idiotically, he snapped his head against the brick wall six times. Studs watched him open-mouthed, and said:

"Your bean must be made of iron. Watch out they don't take it some day to use on the elevated structures."

Andy went off. Studs watched him, laughing and muttering exclamations of surprise.

Studs hung around until the gang dribbled along. They sat on the grass in front of the apartment building on Indiana, where Danny lived. They whiled away the time with kid trivialities.

Danny O'Neill said that he had a good one on Three-Star Hennessey.

"Spill it," said Dan Donoghue.

"Well, it's funny; it's a good one," said Danny. Danny laughed like the goofy punk that he was.

"Well, for Christ sake, out with it before we take your pants down," said Johnny O'Brien, who acted as if he were a big guy like Studs and Dan.

"Well, Hennessey was under the Fifty-eighth Street elevated station . . . and gee, it's funny . . . !"

"Well, then, shoot it while you're all together," said Studs.

"Well, he was under the Fifty-eighth Street elevated station . . ."

"Yeh, we heard that," said Johnny O'Brien.

". . . lookin' up through the cracks to see if he could get an eyeful when the women walked up and down stairs . . ."

"Yeh, and we know what he was doing. That's nothing new," said Johnny.

"He once had a race with Paulie, and they both claimed the other had fouled," said Studs, and they laughed.

"But this time it's funny . . . You see, a dick caught him and shagged him down the alley. Three-Star got away, because nobody could catch him anyway, but the guys told me it was funny, him legging it, with his stockings hanging . . . and he didn't even have time to button up," said Danny.

They gabbed and laughed. Bill Donoghue interrupted the discussion on this latest of Hennessey's exploits to say:

"That's a warnin' for you, TB."

"Say . . . I don't do that," said TB.

"No!" said Studs ironically.

"What you got them pimples on your forehead from?" asked Johnny O'Brien.

"Why, you're gettin' so weak that young O'Neill here can toss you," Studs said.

TB and Danny were made to wrestle. O'Neill dumped McCarthy with a crotch hold. TB squirmed, and O'Neill tried to turn and pin him with another crotch and a half-nelson, but Muggsy slid free. He was just getting behind O'Neill, when he was shoved by Bill and Studs. He squawked about dirty work being done him, and called

Danny names, threatening to get him alone some time. The guys told Muggsy that just for that he would get the clouts. They held him from behind, and encouraged Danny to sock him in the puss. Then they made Danny jerk open his buttons. It was fun.

"Jiggers!" yelled Johnny O'Brien.

Across the street, where Johnny pointed, they saw TB's old man, a tough, red-mustached, Irish police sergeant. They legged it to O'Brien's basement by a circuitous route and peered up from the basement window in time to see the old man finish slapping TB around. He bawled out Monk, kicked him in the slats, and told him to go on home.

When the coast was clear, they came out and sprawled on the grass, laughing over Muggsy's punishment. He was a goop, anyway.

They gassed. Studs suddenly reflected:

"You know, Hennessey must have some screws loose."

"Just some? That loogin is all loose, his bean is all screwy," said Johnny O'Brien.

"He's a sap. The squirrels call him brother," said Bill.

"He's got bats in the belfry," said Dan.

A banana man lazily shoved his cart across Fifty-seventh Street, shouting, droning, sing-songing: Bannano-oe!

The guys had great fun listening to Bill mimic the dago.

They sat around and chewed the fat. Studs said:

"You know, even my old lady warns me to keep away from Three-Star."

"Hell, so does mine," O'Brien said.

"Is Hennessey the bull artist?" said Danny O'Neill.

"But you know, sometimes he's good-hearted," said Tubby.

"Say, he'd steal your stockings without touching your shoes if he had half a chance. He'd even steal 'em if they were stiff and full of holes," Johnny O'Brien said.

"He's cookoo," said O'Neill.

"Well, Tubby, you're older and he thought you'd make a

good friend and maybe stick up for him some time, that's why he treated you. He needs someone to protect him because there's gangs of guys always out to get him, and nearly every guy his size in the neighborhood has cleaned on him," said O'Brien.

"Sometimes he will get the livin' hell pounded out of him," Dan Donoghue said.

"Yeh," said Studs.

"He deserves all he gets, though, the little degenerate," said Dan.

"He should have been a nigger or a hebe instead of Irish," said O'Brien. Johnny added that Hennessey had even been caught in a basement with his half-wit sister.

"Yeah!"

"Speak of the devil and he's sure to appear," said Tubby.

"Yeh, Rastus!" said Bill.

They spied Hennessey and Haggerty dragging themselves along Indiana toward them. They came closer. Both were chewing tobacco, expectorating the juice like dyed-in-the-wool hard guys. Three-Star's face was smeary, framing his innocent blue eyes; he had a cherubic dimpled chin. He wore an old, dirty blue shirt and filthy khaki pants that were falling down. He had holes in his stockings, and no garters.

"Hello, Falling Socks!" said Studs.

"Hey, Hennessey, don't you believe in baths?" asked Johnny O'Brien.

"Hello, Nuts and Bolts!" said Bill.

Three-Star thumbed his nose at them.

"Hey, punk!" said Bill.

Hennessey won forgiveness by passing out wads of Tip-Top for the older guys to chew.

They goofed Three-Star about the elevated incident, but he only laughed and gave them the low-down on it; he was quite proud of the way he had given Johnny Law the slip. He told some dirty jokes he had just collected. Then he looked at Danny O'Neill, who was his own size, and said he'd like to start mooning punks. He said he was fed up on the dago chickens around State Street anyway. The guys all thought that was a new word. Studs tried to talk Hennessey into going down in O'Brien's basement and doing his stuff, but Hennessey wouldn't. They hung around and gassed. They got to shouting and talking loud. Studs tried to promote a fight between Danny and Hennessey, and got them to tip-tapping with open hands. George, the cranky janitor, came out and told them to make less noise. After he turned his back, Hennessey made faces at him and the guys laughed. George turned around and caught Three-Star. He came back, and told Hennessey that if he caught him on the premises again, he'd break his dirty neck. When George had gone, they all talked of what a crab he was. Then the older guys got Hennessey and O'Neill tipper-tapping again. Studs got in back of Danny, and Bill stood behind Hennessey. They shoved simultaneously. The two punks batted their domes together and got sore. They started fighting. Hennessey lowered his head, and rushed, swinging wildly. Danny stood off and met each rush with a stiff left uppercut. He was cleaning on Three-Star for fair, much to the delight of the gang. They all yelled too loudly. George appeared on the roof and doused a pail of water on them; everybody but Studs and Johnny O'Brien got wet. They stood there, cursing up at George. He stood on the roof and laughed down at them. Then he got sore again and yelled for them to beat it while the beating was good. They knew George, so they straggled away. They went back in the alley, and the fight was resumed. Danny cut Hennessey up some more. Three-Star quit. He went off bawling that he'd get O'Neill alone some day. When he was a good distance away, he swore at them. They didn't shag him, because he was too hard to catch.

The next day, when they came around Indiana, they found themselves all roundly cursed in chalked markings

that extended the whole length of the block. And they met
George with a policeman. They were shown the mail boxes
in George's two buildings on the corner. Every one of them
had been smashed with a hammer or a hatchet. They all got
leery, but they had alibis, and the cop only took their names
and went around to their homes to find out what time they
had come in.

They knew who did it, but they didn't want to be snitch-
ers. They went back to Johnny's yard and noticed that two
side windows of the basement had been broken. They
armed themselves with clubs and sticks and marched forth
like an army going to war. But Hennessey was nowhere to
be found.

II

When the guys were out looking for Hennessey, Johnny
O'Brien told Studs to come along with him, so they ditched
the gang. They returned to Indiana, and met old man
O'Brien. He took them with him in his Chalmers. He was a
husky, grayish man, starting to get a goodly paunch. They
went first to the O'Brien coal yards at Sixty-second and
Wabash, and then they toured the south side while O'Brien
checked up on coal deliveries.

As they were driving east on Sixty-third, old man
O'Brien said, his voice exaggeratedly rough:

"Who's the hardest guy in the gang?"

"Studs," said Johnny.

Studs blushed a little, and wanted to say something to
make it appear like he wasn't so awful tough after all, but
he was secretly pleased. He sat there, trying to think of
something to say, and he couldn't get hold of a word.

"Well, some day, Studs, let's you and I mix. I'm not so
young as I used to be, and maybe I'll be a little bit slow
and will get winded, but just let's you and I mix. I'll tell
you what I'll do. I'll tie my knees together, have one arm

tied behind my back, and throw a gunny sack over my head. Now is that square?" old man O'Brien said.

They laughed. Studs thought that old man O'Brien was a pretty tough one when he got going. He remembered that night when they had all been standing at the corner of Fifty-eighth and Indiana. They had just been talking there, not doing a thing out of the way. And MacNamara, the lousy cop, came around. He blew his bazoo off, and told them to get a move on, and not be hanging around corners molesting the peace. They said they weren't doing anything. He blew his bazoo off again, and told them not to talk back to him or he'd run the whole damn bunch of them in. He said they weren't no good anyhow, and wanted to know what kind of fathers they had that would let them be out on the streets at night, molesting decent people and disturbing the peace. He told them to get a move on, and he grabbed Johnny's arm and started to shove him. Old Man O'Brien had been in the drug store, and he'd taken the whole show in. He got sore as a boil and stepped up to the lousy flatfoot. He told him where to get off at in regular he-man's language. He said he was the kind of a father these boys had, and what was there to say about it? And he told MacNamara that those boys would stand on the corner as long as they pleased, and as long as they were behaving, as they had been then, no one would try and bully them . . . not while he was around. And no cop could think that he was going to get away with pushing his son. And he told the damn bluecoat that if he would take off the star, he'd punch him all over the corner, and when he got through, wipe the street with him. MacNamara had walked away like a whipped dog, mumbling apologies. If he had cracked a wise one, old man O'Brien would have socked him. And if he had run old man O'Brien in, with Mr. O'Brien being in the right like he was, well, he would have been in a jam, because old man O'Brien had money and a pull. Studs and all the guys had wished they had an old man like Johnny had. Now, riding in the car, Studs thought what a swell old man he was. He remembered Johnny saying his dad never once hit him. And he gave Johnny plenty of spending money. He was a real old man, all right.

They drove down South Park Avenue. Old man O'Brien said he'd take Studs and Johnny to White City some time. He and his wife had been there only last week, and had had a dandy time. Studs felt that Mr. O'Brien was different from his own gaffer. He wasn't a putter-off, but when he said he'd do something, he did it. Old man O'Brien turned, and said:

"Hell, you kids ain't as tough as kids used to be in my days. When we fought then, we fought. And we all had to use brass knuckles."

"You wouldn't fool us, Gov'nor, would you?" kidded Johnny.

Studs thought it wasn't every guy who could kid with his old man, like Johnny could. Most old men were, like his own, always serious, and always demanding that you show them respect and listen to everything they said, and never contradict them or think they were in the wrong. And they never understood a kid.

Johnny had some old man, all right.

"Yeh, and when I was a kid, we used to fight Indians, and if we made a slip then, well, we'd have been tommy-hawked."

"No!" Studs exclaimed with surprise. He knew what old man O'Brien said couldn't be true, and yet he half-believed it was. He had an imaginary picture of Mr. O'Brien wading through a field of Indians, throwing a whole tribe of them up for grabs.

"Yeah, I was once near tommy-hawked at the place where White City now stands."

"He's always trying to bunk a guy," Johnny said.

"That's the trouble with this kid of mine. He never believes anything I say," Mr. O'Brien said.

He turned and smiled good-naturedly at them. In the moment that he turned, the car had swerved, and he had a narrow escape from hitting a rattling Ford.

He got sore, and cursed after the other driver, telling him to take his junk in the alley where it belonged, and to try riding a bicycle until he learned how to drive.

"They ought to prohibit those goddamn Fords from being driven in the streets. They are nothing but a pile of junk."

"They are automobile fleas," Johnny said.

Studs told a joke he had read in a Ford joke book. A rag man was going down the alley one day, and he was called in a back yard. The man who had called him said how much will you give me for this, and he pointed to a Ford. The rag man looked, and looked, and he looked some more. Then he said vel if you give me fife dollair, I'll take it avay for you. They laughed at the joke. Old Man O'Brien said it was a pretty good one.

Old man O'Brien spoke of the good old days, gone by, of the Washington Park racetrack, with its Derby day in the middle of June and the huge crowds it attracted, its eighty acres, its race course with a gentle slope from east and north that made it a faster track than a dead level one, its artificial lakes and garden works on the inner sides of the main track, its triple deck stands, its bandstand at one end of the stand, why, it was a dream. And all the color and noise and foment, and the crowds shouting, the betting and the excitement, when Burns, or Turner, or Burnett would lead a horse into the home stretch. And some of them horses, too, they were beauts, Hurley Burley, Enchanter, Imp, and them two horses that were goddamn good nags, Ben Hadad and Saint Cataline. Johnny's mother knew how good them horses were, because she had had a good time more than once on their winnings, right after she got married, and yes, sir, them horses had bought Johnny's sister Mary something when she was learning to walk. Yes, sir. And he told them of Garrison. Garrison, he said, was the jockey who was such a good man in the home stretch that they took the word, Garrison-finish, from the way he rode a horse. He'd seen Garrison ride, and Sloan, too. And he spoke of the trolley parties and picnics of yore, and the dances and prize fights at Tattersalls. All the kids used to sneak in, the way kids always sneak in. They had a million ways of crashing the gate. One of their tricks was to bribe a stable man to let them in through the stables. Well, one night during a big fight, all the lights in the place went out and the management had to give tickets for the next night. Well, you should have seen the crowd that came. Every newsboy and teamster in town must have had a five-dollar ringside seat. And of all the old fighters he'd seen in action, Bob Fitzsimmons, Jimmy Britt, Jim Jeffries, Gentleman Jim Corbett, who could wiggle a mean tongue, and don't think old Gentleman Jim didn't know how to curse. Terrible Terry McGovern, ah, there was a sweet fighting harp for you, a real fighting turkey with dynamite in each mitt and a fighting heart that only an Irishman could own. Young Corbett, who was born with a horse shoe in his hands and a four leaf clover in his hair, and who put a jinx on Terrible Terry; Benny Yanger; the Tipton Slasher whom old man O'Brien knew personally; Stanley Ketchell who didn't know when to quit fighting even when he had a gun jammed against him; Joe Wolcott, Dixon, Joe Gans, Young Griffo, the most scientific fighter of all times with maybe the exception of Nonpareil Jack Dempsey, who came before Mr. O'Brien's time; Tom Sharkey—all of them old boys. They didn't have fighters like that nowadays. None of 'em were no-fight champions like Jess Willard, and most of them were real Irish, lads who'd bless themselves before they fought; they weren't fake Irish like most of the present-day dagoes and wops and sheenies who took Hibernian names. None of them were no-fight champions like Jess Willard, the big elephant. Why, an old timer like Philadelphia Jack O'Brien or Kid McCoy could have spotted the big elephant all his blubber and laid him low in a round. Now, McCoy was the trickiest fighter that ever lived. He had a brain and a corkscrew punch that made the big boys see stars once it landed. Once he was fighting some big bloke, and he suddenly pointed down and told the big ham his shoe laces were untied. The ham looked down, and the old corkscrew snapped across, and the big bum was rolling in the resin; and another time, McCoy pointed to the gallery, and the big dummy he was fighting looked up, and the old corkscrew right went over and the dummy started trilling to the daisies. And the baseball games in the old days of Spike Shannon, Mike Donlin, Fred Tenney, Jimmy Collins, Cy Young, Pat Dougherty, Fielder Jones of the Hitless Wonders, and even earlier when he was a kid, and they had the Baltimore Orioles, and he used to see Kid Gleason pitch, and there was Hit-Em-Where-They-Ain't Willie Keeler, Eh Yah Hughie Jennings, Muggsy McGraw, old Robby, Pop Anson, Brothers and the Delehantys. Hell, even Ty Cobb wasn't as good as Willie Keeler.

"And you know who was the greatest of them all?" asked old man O'Brien.

"Who?" asked Studs.

Studs usually didn't give a damn about baseball. Danny O'Neill was the one who knew all about it. But when old man O'Brien talked of baseball, it was as exciting as going to see a movie serial, like that one a long time ago, *The Adventures of Kathleen.* And the ball players he named were like heroes, as great as generals.

"Well, old Rube Waddell. Rube was a guy. He was a left-hander, and all left-handers are cracked."

Old man O'Brien paused. Then he said:

"Studs, you ain't left-handed, are you?"

"No, sir!"

"Don't call me sir . . . Well, my kid there ain't either . . . but he ought to be."

"YEAH!" kidded Johnny.

He told them all the familiar Rube Waddell stories. Then he said that poor Rube ruined his health, and practically killed himself because he was left-handed. It was Rube's left-handedness that made him always want to run after a fire like a kid. Well, Rube was always leaving Connie Mack and joining up with some hick fire department, and Connie'd have to send his scouts out to find the southpaw. Once Rube got himself in with the hook and ladder crew in St. Louis or somewhere, and went to a fire. When Rube was in fighting the fire, a door caved in on him and he got lost with some others under the wreckage, and they turned the hose on him. It was funny, but that was what put the kibosh on poor Rube's lungs. Studs sat listening, enchanted, imagining himself a great guy like Rube Waddell.

Old Man O'Brien talked on:

"But I ain't so much interested in sports as I used to be. Baseball's the only clean game we got left. The Jews killed all the other games. The kikes dirty up everything. I say the kikes ain't square. There never was a white Jew, or a Jew that wasn't yellow. And there'll never be one. Why, they even killed their own God. . . . And now I'll be damned if they ain't comin' in spoiling our neighborhood. It used to be a good Irish neighborhood, but pretty soon a man will be afraid to wear a shamrock on St. Patrick's day, because there are so many noodle-soup drinkers around. We got them on our block. I even got one next door to me. I'd never have bought my property if I knew I'd have to live next door to that Jew, Glass's his name. But I don't speak to him anyway. And he's tryin' to make a gentleman of that four-eyed kid of his . . . as if a Jew could be a gentleman."

Johnny and Studs laughed, and told him that the Glass kid was nothing but a sissy. They had nothing to do with him.

"Well, don't . . . unless it's maybe to paste him one."

A pause.

"And say, Studs, you got 'em over your way, too. What does your old man think of 'em?"

"Well, he's always talking of selling. My father thinks they are ruining the neighborhood."

"They are . . . only, say . . . listen . . . can that my father stuff. Both of you kids know damn well that when you're alone you say . . . my old man . . . come on, act natural . . ."

Studs told himself that Johnny's old man was like a regular pal to a kid.

They stopped in an alley at Fifty-second and Prairie. Old man O'Brien bawled hell out of a sweating Negro who was putting in a load of coal. The Negro was grimed with coal dust, and perspiration came out of him in rivers. He worked slowly but steadily, shoveling the coal into a wheelbarrow, pushing it down a board and emptying it down a chute through a basement window.

They drove on, and Mr. O'Brien said:

"You got to put pepper on the tails of these eight-balls. They're lazy as you make 'em. A Jew and a nigger. Never trust 'em farther than you can see 'em. But some niggers are all right. These southern ones that know their place are only lazy. But these northern bucks are dangerous. They are getting too spry here in Chicago, and one of these days we're gonna have a race riot, and then all the Irish from back of the yards will go into the black belt, and there'll be a lot of niggers strung up on lampposts with their gizzards cut out . . . My kid here wanted to wrestle in that tournament over at Carter Playground last winter, and I'da let him, but he'd of had to wrestle with niggers. So I made him stay out. You got to keep these smokes in their place and not let 'em get gay."

They stopped for sodas, and Mr. O'Brien bought them each two. Studs could have caught his old man buying a kid two sodas like that. While they were sitting with their sodas, Old Man O'Brien told them of the things of yesteryear, and of plays he'd taken Johnny's mother to. One was called *Soudan*, given way back in about 1903, and was it a humdinger! They killed forty-five men in the first act. Was it a play! They had shipwrecks at sea, and what not, and when the shooting started half of the audience held their heads under the seats until it ended, and when the villain came on the stage everyone kept going ss! ss! And the dime novels, and Nick Carter! But times had changed. Times had changed. Even kids weren't like they used to be, they had none of the old feeling of other times, they didn't have that old barefoot-boy attitude, and they weren't as tough, either, and they didn't hang around knotholes at the ball park to see the great players, not the ones around Indiana anyway. Times had changed.

They drove around. At one place, Mr. O'Brien had to see a sheeny and explain why the coal delivery had been late. The fellow talked like a regular Oi Yoi Yoi, waving his arms in front of him like he was in the signal corps of the U.S. Army. He protested, but Old Man O'Brien gave him a long spiel, and as they were leaving, the guy all but kissed Johnny's father. When they drove on, O'Brien said to the kids:

"You got to soft soap some of these Abie Kabbibles."

He winked at them and they laughed. Studs kept thinking of his old man and Johnny's, and dreaming of being a kid like Mr. O'Brien had been and wishing that his gaffer was more like Mr. O'Brien. . . . Well, anyway, he wasn't as bad as High Collars.

It had been a great afternoon, though.

III

That night when Studs was ready to go out, he walked into the parlor. The old man and the old lady were sitting there, and the old boy was in his slippers sucking on a stogy; and the two of them were enjoying a conversation about the latest rape case in the newspapers in which the rapist was named Gogarty. Studs noticed that when he entered they shut up. He wondered what the hell did they think he was. Did they think he was born yesterday, and still believed in Santa Claus, the Easter Rabbit and storks? He wanted to tell them so, tell them in words that would show how much of a pain they gave him when they treated him as if he was only a baby. But the words wouldn't come; they almost never came to him when he wanted them to. He stood swallowing his resentment.

The old man said:

"You know, Bill, a fellow ought to come home some time. Now when I was your age, when I was your age, I know I liked to get out with the fellows, and that's why I can understand how you feel about bein' a regular guy, and bein' with the bunch, and I don't want you to think I'm always pickin' on you, or preachin' to you, or tryin' to make you into a mollycoddle, because I ain't. I know a kid wants a little liberty, because I was your age once . . . BUT . . ."

Studs got Goddamn sore. He knew what was coming. The old man always worked the same damn gag.

"You see, Bill, you're stayin' out pretty late, and you know, well, it's as your mother says, the neighbors will be thinkin' things, wonderin' if we, the landlords here, set a good example for our children, and live decently, an' if we are takin' the right sort of care of our children. I'm the owner of this here building, you see, and I got to have a family that sets the right kind of an example. Now what do you think they'll think if they see you comin' in so late every evenin', comin' in night after night after most respectable people have gone to bed?"

"But what is it their business?" asked Studs.

"And, William, you know you have to look out for your health. Now what will you do if you go on getting little sleep like you do? You know you should get to bed early. Why, this very day in the newspapers, there was an article saying that sleep gotten before twelve o'clock was better and healthier sleep than sleep gotten after midnight. You're wearing yourself out, and you're wearin' out me, your mother, because I worry over you, because I can't let my baby get tuberculosis," the mother said.

"I'm all right; I'm healthy," Studs said.

"Well, I think, Bill, I think a fellow could get enough play all day and until ten o'clock at night. You always want to remember that there'll be another day," the old man said oracularly.

Studs said that all kids stayed out, sitting on someone's porch, or in the grass in front of someone's house, talking, and there wasn't anything wrong with it, because it was so nice in the evening. And the other kids' fathers didn't care. Mr. O'Brien never kicked about Johnny being out, and Johnny O'Brien was younger than he was.

"If Johnny O'Brien jumps in the river, do you have to?"

That was the way his old man always was!

Studs just stood there. The old man told him to save something for another day. Studs sulked, and told himself there wasn't any use arguing with his old man and old lady. They just didn't understand.

The old man brought out a Lefty Locke baseball book, which he had bought for Studs and forgotten to give him. He said it would be a good thing if Studs stayed in and read it. Studs ought to do more reading anyway, because reading always improved a person's mind. Studs sat down, pouted, and read the book for about ten minutes. But Lefty Locke wasn't anything at all like Rube Waddell; it was a goofy book. He fidgeted. Then he said hesitantly that he'd like to take a little walk, and the old man, disappointed, said all right.

When Studs met the guys, he told them that he'd won a scrap with the old man. That evening they played tin-tin with the girls, and Studs kissed Lucy. It made him forget that his old man and his old lady and home weren't what sisters and priests made them out to be at school and at mass on Sundays.

IV

It was a hot early July afternoon, and life, along Indiana Avenue, was crawlingly lazy. A brilliant sun scorched the impoverished trees and sucked energy from the frail breezes that simpered off a distant Lake Michigan.

The gang had all gone swimming, and Studs had not felt like going home for his suit. Danny O'Neill was at the corner of Fifty-eighth, playing a baseball game by himself with a golf ball. He threw the ball at the ledge on the side of Levin's tiled wall. Every time it struck the ledge, and the rebound was caught, a run was counted. Every throw was a time at bat. Danny played away, happy and contented by himself. Studs stood across the street, hands on hips, watching, shaking his head because he couldn't make out goofy O'Neill. He could have such a swell time by himself, playing some goofy baseball game or other or just sitting down playing knife. Danny was such a crack knife player that no one would play pull the peg with him. He was goofy, though. Studs crossed the street and said:

"Hello, Goof!"

They played the baseball game, and Danny beat Studs four times. Studs didn't like to get beat at anything, so he quit playing. He pulled Danny's cap over his eyes, almost bending the punk's glasses, and said:

"You're dizzy!"

He started tip-tapping with the kid, telling him that he was a good young battler but needed training. Studs said he was going to train Danny so he could lick any punk in the neighborhood. They tip-tapped. Studs let loose a rough slap, telling Danny he had to learn to take it. The slap hurt, but Danny bit his lip and didn't cry. They sparred, tapping easily. Danny stepped around Studs and slapped him with lefts. Studs hauled off, and let Danny have a pretty stiff one. Danny bit his lip. He was the kid who could take punishment, so he didn't cry. Studs put his hands on his hips, and looked surprised at the shrimp, as if to say, Christ, but you're goofy. They sparred on, and Studs kept hauling off on Danny, training him to take punishment. Then Studs told O'Neill he'd show him some tricks in scientific fighting. Studs got on tip-toe, danced and lumbered around, and almost fell over his own feet. So he gave the punk a vicious slap in the puss. Breathless, they paused.

"You're good! you kin clean up any of the punks around here, even ivory-domed Andy Le Gare. None of them can hurt you," Studs said.

"It's because I know how to breathe. You see, when the kids fight, they breathe out of their mouths, and they lose their wind, quick; while I breathe out of my nose and save my wind, and we fight until they are winded, and I win. That's the way I beat Andy," Danny said.

Studs said Danny was a goof. The reason he could fight was that he was so goofy that he couldn't be hurt. They sparred a little more, but Studs had lost interest in training Danny. They talked.

"Say, did you ever hear of Rube Waddell?"

"Sure, I got an autographed ball from him."

"Don't goof me. You're too young to have got it."

"Well, he gave it to my uncle for me when he was playing in the American Association, and I got it at home. He was the greatest left-hander in the game, and I know Stuffy McInnis, the greatest first baseman in the game. He gives me balls when the Athletics are here," said Danny.

Studs said the Rube was no good. Danny didn't have any right to have a ball from Rube Waddell. Studs walked away, sore. He walked down to Fifty-seventh Street, furtively looked around to see if anyone saw him, and when the coast was clear he sniped a butt from the street. He walked back, smoking it. Then he met Lucy, returning from the store with an armful of groceries. He carted them for her. As they walked slowly back toward her house, Studs had some of the old feeling he had had on that March day. She asked him what he was going to do, and he said he didn't know, but he thought he might take a walk over to the Washington Park playground, and fool around if that old crab Mr. Hall didn't kick him out. She told him it was a good idea, because she thought she'd go to the park, and they could walk over together. She said Mr. Hall was a mean old frog. Studs told himself that it was swell, and he was in luck. He told Lucy that he guessed they could walk together at that. He became suddenly leery and uncertain, because a guy could never be sure when he was, and when he wasn't, saying the right thing to a girl; he felt that he should have said something different to her; he hoped that he hadn't said anything that would make her sore and change her mind so she wouldn't go to the park with him. He waited and worried while she went into the house, and it took a long time, so that he got nervous and was afraid she wasn't coming, but he waited anyway. He heard some young kids in the Shires' gangway, Helen's kid sister, a couple of her girl friends, and a ten-year-old punk named Norman something or other. They were talking about having a show party in one of the basements across the street. They enthusiastically agreed to, and they ran across the street, looking quite cute and innocent. Studs watched them skip, and said to himself with a quizzical look on his face:

Jesus Christ!

He scowled, scratched his head and asked himself if he should tell Helen Shires. He decided not to, because he hated any kind of a snitcher. He laughed to himself, thinking how funny it was, and what a knockout of a story it would be for Dan and the guys if they would promise not to pass it on. He thought of his kid sister, Fritzie, telling himself that she wouldn't never do a thing like that. If he ever found her doing it, he'd certainly boot her tail around the

block until she couldn't walk straight. But then, he guessed
there was something in Catholic girls that made them different from other girls. Now, there was Helen Shires; she was
fine, just like a pal or a guy's best friend; but then, there was
something different and purer in a girl like Lucy which
stopped her from talking about the things he and Helen
talked about. Yes, sir, he was pretty certain about that something purer in Catholic girls. He laughed, because the little
kids had been so funny. He thought about going over and
peeking in on their party, but just then he saw Lucy.

She came out wearing a reddish-orange wash dress
which looked nice on her, because she was dark, curly-
haired, with red-fair skin, and the dress set her off just
right. And she had on a little powder and lipstick, but it
didn't make her look like a sinful woman or anything of
that sort. Studs didn't usually pay attention to how girls
looked, except to notice the shape of their legs, because if
they had good legs they were supposed to be good for you-
know, and if they didn't they weren't; and to notice their
boobs, if they were big enough to bounce. He looked at
Lucy. She was cute, all right. He told himself that she was
cute. He told himself that he liked her. He repeated to himself that he liked her, and she was cute. His heart beat
faster, and he scarcely knew what he was doing.

They strolled east on Fifty-seventh Street. A Negro
nursemaid came along with a bow-legged baby, and Lucy
made a fuss over it; Studs thought it was a pain, but he decided that girls were girls, and if they were like Lucy, they
must be higher creatures that a guy just couldn't understand, no matter how much he tried. He pretended that he
was interested in the darling tot, but it gave him a pain.
They strolled on, and Studs kept side-glancing at angelic
Lucy, straining his mind to think of something to say. He
said that it was a nice day, all right. She agreed. He said
that it was the kind of a day that made a fellow want to do
nothing, and she said yes. She said she liked doing nothing.

Studs said that usually he didn't like doing nothing, but now he felt different from the way he felt on most days. He said that there was too much for a guy to do to want to do just nothing; he told her some of the things a kid could do, instead of doing nothing; he told her how he, Red O'Connell, and the gang had gotten Red's beebe gun, and had stood on Red's porch, shooting pigeons, and he had killed the most, three; and how Red had shot Muggsy McCarthy in the pa . . . . the back, and Muggsy didn't know who shot him, and it was funny, and then Red had gotten his old man's Chalmers, and they had gone riding, and Red had stepped on it, and they had gone down South Park Avenue fifty miles an hour, and they had kept shooting away, trying to break windows, and they had broken five or six of them. She said it was just horrid, and that boys just wanted to make mischief; as Sister Bernadette Marie always said, boys had the germ of destruction in them, and they did perfectly awful, horrid things; but she said it just like a girl, meaning the exact opposite.

They came to the park, where it was cooler. She walked more slowly, and they gazed idly about them. Everything was sun-colored, and people walked around as if they had nothing to do. It was nice out, all right, with the sky all so blue and the clouds all puffed and white, and floating as if they were icebergs in a sea that didn't have any waves. And he thought it would be fine if he and Lucy could have wings and fly away past the sky; he thought about their flying away, flying right through clouds, and way past the other side of the sky, where there was nothing, and they flew through nothing until they came to some kind of a place with a palace, and servants, and everything they wanted to make them happy, and all Studs had to do to get the place, for himself and Lucy, was to clean up on a couple of big boloneys that owned it. But he called a stop to these thoughts, and told himself that Studs Lonigan was not the kind of a gee to have goofy thoughts like that. She said

that it was awfully nice. Studs said that it was cooler in the
park than it was outside. They glanced off at their left, and
saw the playground, surrounded by shrubbery and an iron
picket fence. From inside they could hear the shouts of
playing children. They saw the swings, with the colored
shirts and dresses of kids flashing, disappearing, flashing
above the shrubbery, a momentary rhythm in the sunlight.
It all sounded and seemed as if it belonged to the park.
Lucy said that she thought it would be nicer to walk around
than to go into the playground, because anyway, it was for
little kids, and if they went in they'd get all hot and dirty,
playing. Studs thought, too, that if old skin-and-bones
crabby Hall kicked him out for being too old right in front
of Lucy, he would be so ashamed he could never look her
in the face again. Studs deeply pondered the idea of not going to the playground, and said that it was a good idea; yes,
he repeated, it was a good idea. As they crossed, their feet
sank in the asphalt drive that was gooey on account of the
heat, and they moved onto grass that was like velvet and
bright with many colors from the sun. She took his hand;
they walked, swinging hands, heads lowered, not saying
anything to each other.

As they walked over to the wooded island, Studs felt,
knew, that it was going to be a great afternoon, different
from every other afternoon in his whole life. They walked
on, not talking, but the way she held his hand made him
feel good, and he repeated to himself that it was one of his
days. They crossed the log bridge over onto the island . . .
a spread of irregularly wooded and slightly hilly ground
with the sheep pen at one end of it. They walked on until
they came to a full-leaved large oak that stood near the
bank. It looked nice and they decided to climb it, and sit on
one of the large branches. Studs helped her, and saw her
clean wash bloomers. He was tempted, and wondered if he
ought to try feeling her up. He remembered Marion Shires,
and the other little kids, and wondered if he ought to, and

how he might ask Lucy to have a show party with him. He got excited. But when they were up in the tree, and Lucy was laughing about her dirtied dress and the little scratch on her hand, he forgot all about these temptations. They sat, not having much to say, and he held her hand.

Below them, a man and wife moved, watching their baby stumble and giggle ahead of them. Lucy watched the kid, a piggish-faced child, and told Studs that it was awfully cute. She suddenly lowered her head, muttered shyly that she would probably never get married and have children. Studs was a little surprised, because girls like Lucy weren't supposed to think about such things. He told himself that if she was like that Iris from Carter School it would be different, and he could understand it. But Lucy! He wondered if he ought to try feeling her up, and he tried to think up an answer for her; but his mouth was dry, and all he could think of was the lump in his throat. Three times he asked himself what he ought to say. He watched the group below disappear. He finally said that it had been a cute kid. Lucy said yes. Lucy said that she was never going to marry and become a mother, because she was going to join a convent and be a nun. She talked as if she was mad about something. Studs wondered what was the matter. He looked at her, and her face seemed to melt in a misty sort of asking expression. He asked her if she thought she had the call to be a nun, and she said yes, she was going to become a nun. Studs said that she ought to think it over first; he told himself that he loved her, and wanted her not to become a nun, and knew that she wouldn't if he could only tell her the way he loved her, but he didn't know what he wanted to say, because it wasn't words but a feeling he had for her, a feeling that seemed to flow through him like nice, warm water. She told him yes, she had definitely made up her mind. Her voice sounded angry, and he wondered what was the matter.

The breeze playing upon them through the tree-leaves

was fine. Studs just sat there and let it play upon him, let it
sift through his hair. He said that it was nice and cool; he
said that it was cooler in the trees than it was on the
ground. Lucy said yes it was, and she didn't seem interested, and it made him still wonder what was the matter.
The wind seemed to Studs like the fingers of a girl, of
Lucy, and when it moved through the leaves it was like a
girl, like Lucy, running her hand over very expensive silk,
like the silk movie actresses wore in the pictures. The wind
was Lucy's hand caressing his hair. It was a funny thought
to have, and Studs felt goofy and fruity about having it, and
felt that he hadn't better let anyone know he had thoughts
like that; he wouldn't tell her. But he did; he told her the
wind was like the hand of a pretty girl, and when it touched
the leaves, it was like that pretty girl stroking very fine silk.
She laughed, and said that it was a very funny and a very
silly thought for a person like Studs Lonigan to have. It
made him ashamed of himself, and very silent, and he
wished that he was somewhere else and Lucy was not with
him, probably laughing at him like she was in her mind.

They sat. There seemed to be a silence on the park.
Nothing but the wind. Studs could hear his heart beating
like it was a noisy clock. He felt as if he was not in Washington Park, but that he and Lucy were in some place else,
a some place else that was just not Washington Park, but
was better and prettier, and no one else knew of it. He
glanced about him. He looked at the grass which slid down
to the bank, and at the shrubbery along parts of the lagoon
edge. He gazed out at the silver-blue lagoon that was so
alive, like it was dancing with the sun. He watched the
rowboats, the passing people. He took squints at everything
from different angles, and watched how their appearances
would change, and they would look entirely different. He
listened to the sounds of the park, and it seemed as if they
were all, somehow, part of himself, and he was part of
them, and them and himself were free from the drag of his

body that had aches and dirty thoughts, and got sick, and could only be in one place at a time. He listened. He heard the wind. Far away, kids were playing, and it was nice to hear the echoes of their shouts, like music was sometimes nice to hear; and birds whistled, and caroled, and chirped, and hummed. It was all new-strange, and he liked it. He told Lucy it was swell, sitting in the park, way up in a tree. Lucy said yes, it was perfectly grand. Studs said: YEAH!

"It's so lovely here," she said, leaning toward him, puckering her lips.

Studs looked at her. Without knowing what he was doing, he kissed her. It was all-swell to kiss Lucy, and it was different from a game where she had to kiss him, and everybody was kissing everybody else. And she kissed with her red lips in a queer sweet way; and he kept telling himself that it was fine to kiss her. In the movies, and in the magazines, which he sometimes read, the fellow always kissed the girl at the end of the story or the picture, and the kiss always seemed to mean so much, and to be so much nicer, and to have so much more to it than ordinary kisses. Kissing Lucy was getting a kiss like that. And it made him feel . . . all-swell.

And everything just kept on being perfectly jake, not spoiling it there with him and Lucy. They sat. There he was, and there was Lucy, swinging her legs, singing *The Blue Ridge Mountains of Virginia*, and it was nice, and he told himself that no afternoon in his whole life had been like this one, not even the afternoon after he had licked the stuffings out of Weary Reilley. He had felt sick from the fight then, and the gang had all been around and made things a lot different from now, with himself and Lucy sharing and owning all the niceness themselves. And he had a feeling that this was a turning point in his life, and from now on everything was going to be jake. He had always felt that some time something would happen to him, and it was the thing that was going to make his whole life

different; and this afternoon was just what was going to
turn the trick; it was Lucy. Living was going to be swell
now, and different from and nicer than it had ever been before. The only thing the matter with it all was that it couldn't
last forever. That was the way things were; they ended, just
when they began to be most jake.

A bird cooed above them. He usually thought it was sis-
sified to listen or pay attention to such things as birds
singing; it was crazy, like being a guy who studied music,
or read too many books, or wrote poems and painted pictures. But now he listened; it was nice; he told himself how
nice it was.

If some of the kids knew what he was doing and thinking, they'd laugh their ears off at him. Well, if they did, let
'em; he could kick a lot of mustard out of the whole bunch
of 'em. He gazed up at the bird. Some white stuff dropped
on him, and somehow, seeing the bird that sang like this
one doing that, well, it kind of hurt him, and told him how
all living things were, well, they weren't perfect; just like
the sisters had said they weren't in catechism. He was glad
Lucy hadn't noticed it. They sat. Lucy touched his sleeve,
and told him to listen to the bird music. He listened. But
Lucy was suddenly distracted by an oh-so-cute-and-so-
darling baby, being led below them by a nursemaid.

They sat. Studs swinging his legs, and Lucy swinging
hers, she chattering, himself not listening to it, only knowing that it was nice, and that she laughed and talked and
was like an angel, and she was an angel playing in the sun.
Suddenly, he thought of feeling her up, and he told himself
that he was a bastard for having such thoughts. He wasn't
worthy of her, even of her fingernail, and he side-glanced
at her, and he loved her, he loved her with his hands, and
his lips, and his eyes, and his heart, and he loved everything about her, her dress, and voice, and the way she
smiled, and her eyes, and her hair, and Lucy, all of her. He
sat, swinging his legs, restless, happy, and yet not so happy,

because he was afraid that he might be acting like a droop, or he might be saying or doing something to make her mad. He wanted the afternoon never to end, so that he and Lucy could sit there forever; her hands stole timidly into his, and he forgot everything in the world but Lucy.

"Isn't it awfully nice here?" she said.

"Yeah!" gruffed he.

He wanted to say more, and he couldn't. He wanted to let her know about all the dissolving, tingling feelings he was having, and how he felt like he might be the lagoon, and the feelings she made inside of him were like the dancing feelings and the little waves the sun and wind made on it; but those were things he didn't know how to tell her, and he was afraid to, because maybe he would spoil them if he did. He couldn't even say a damn thing about how it all made him want to feel strong and good, and made him want to do things and be big and brave for her.

His tongue stuck in his mouth.

They sat swinging their legs.

And Time passed through their afternoon like a gentle, tender wind, and like death that was silent and cruel. They knew they ought to go, and they sat. Accumulating shadows raked the scene which commenced to blur beneath them. They sat, and about them their beautiful afternoon evaporated, split up and died like the sun that was dying a red death in the calm sky. Lucy said that it was getting late, and she had better be going. Studs told her to wait just a little while longer. She insisted that she had to go. They sat, and Lucy puckered her lips. Studs kissed her. She stroked his hair, and it was even nicer than the wind, and she said that she liked him bushels and bushels. She said that she had to go, and she sat swinging her legs so that he could notice them; and they had a nice shape, too. She pointed to another baby. Studs thought of how babies were born, and he blushed. She asked him what he was doing, and offered a penny for his thoughts. He said he wasn't doing nothing,

only looking, not thinking. He again thought of feeling her
up, and again it made him feel like he was a dirty bastard.

They sat, and more precious minutes were squeezed,
drained dry. When they finally climbed down, the sun was
dead in the sky. They hurried home, half-running, not
speaking. Leaving the park at Fifty-seventh, they saw
Sunny Green and Shorty Leach playing tennis, lamming
the ball at each other in the half-darkness, playing and vol-
leying better than most men could. Lucy asked him if he
could play tennis better than the two kids, and he said yes.
He was sorry he told her such a lie, almost before the
words were out of his mouth, just like he felt pretty lousy
because he had exaggerated the story about how he and the
guys had gone riding in Red O'Connell's car, shooting
beebes. He promised to teach her how to play tennis. They
parted in front of her house at a quarter to eight. She stood
a moment on the porch, smiling at him through the summer
dusk; and the spray from the sprinkler on her lawn tapped
his cheeks; the boy, Studs, saw and felt something beautiful
and vague, something like a prayer sprung into flesh. She
threw him a kiss and fled inside. He walked home, pretending that he was carrying her blown kiss in his handkerchief.
As soon as he arrived home, he rushed to his bedroom and
kissed his handkerchief. He brought out his tennis racket
and gestured before the mirror like a star tennis player, and
resolved to practice his game, and some day for Lucy he
might make himself as good as McLaughlin. He was proud
of his form, too. Then he shadow-boxed, and imagined that
he was beating up some hard guy to protect Lucy's character. Soon he was beating up a whole gang of them. He
imagined her rewarding his heroism with a kiss, and fold-
ing his arms around the bed-pillow, tenderly, he kissed it.
He sat on his bed, and contemplated the fact of Lucy. He
told himself that he was one hell of a goddamn goof; he sat
on the bed, thinking of her and becoming more and more
of a hell of a goddamn goof.

V

STUDS LOVES LUCY . . . LUCY IS CRAZY ABOUT STUDS . . .
I LIKE TO KISS LUCY—STUDS . . . STUDS KISSED LUCY
A MILLION TIMES . . .

Studs saw chalked writings like these all over Indiana
Avenue, on sidewalks, fences, buildings. It was two mornings after he and Lucy had been in the park. On the previ-
ous day, he had cleaned out the basement for his old man,
and he had been too tired at night to wash up and come
around. When he read the scrawlings all over, his face got
red as a tomato, and he got so sore he cursed everybody
and everything. He promised himself that a lot of guys
were going to get smacked. He was so sore that he didn't
take the trouble to examine the childish writings, a scrawl
quite like that of his sister Loretta and her girl-chum, June
Reilley.

Danny O'Neill came along, and stopped at Studs' side.
He read the words aloud, and laughed. Studs socked him.
Danny, in a temper, stuck his tongue out at Studs, called
him a bully, and said, mimicking:

"I'm gonna tell Lucy!"

Studs cracked Danny in the jaw with all his might, and
the punk, holding his mush in his hands, bawled.

Most of the guys saw Danny's swollen jaw, so they didn't
try to kid Studs. The older guys sat on the grass, talking,
blaming the punks, planning how they would swoop down
on them and get even by taking their pants off and hanging
them on trees, making them eat dirt, giving them a dose of
it that they wouldn't forget until kingdom come. But the
punks had all smelled trouble, and they were gone. The
bunch sat around and talked about revenges. Studs didn't
say much; he didn't even look anybody in the eye. Suddenly, he got up and left, and the guys said that when Studs
walked away from his friends like that, without saying a
word, he was pretty Goddamn sore, and when he was pretty

goddamn sore, he wasn't the kind of a guy you'd want to meet in a dark alley. He walked for blocks, not recognizing where he was going, feeling disgraced, feeling that everybody was against him, blaming everybody, blaming that little runt, Danny O'Neill. He felt that he was a goddamn clown. He blamed himself for getting soft and goofy about a skirt. He planned how he would get even, and kept telling himself that no matter what happened, it couldn't really affect him, because STUDS LONIGAN was an iron man, and when anybody laughed at the iron man, well, the iron man would knock the laugh off the face of Mr. Anybody with the sweetest paste in the mush that Mr. Anybody ever got. He vowed this, and felt his iron muscle for assurance. But he didn't really feel like an iron man. He felt like a clown that the world was laughing at. He walked, getting sorer and sorer and filling his mind with the determination to get back at . . . Indiana Avenue, the whole damn street. As far as he was concerned, it could go plumb to hell. He was through hanging around with the Indiana Avenue mopes, and as for O'Neill, well, Studs Lonigan hadn't even begun to pay that little droopy-drawers back yet.

When Studs got home, Martin, speaking like he had been coached, said:

"How's Lucy?"

"I seen Lucy today; she looked nice, like she was looking for someone . . . and she had paint on her lips," Fritzie said.

Frances asked him if he was going over to see Lucy after supper. If he was, she'd walk over with him . . . and she said if he was he had better wash himself clean and shine his shoes.

The old man sang monotonously:

> *Goodbye, boys . . .*
> *For I . . . get . . . married . . . tomorrow . . .*

Mrs. Lonigan seriously warned him that he was still a little young and he would have plenty of time later on for girls, and girls would make a fool of him, and he should not be thinking of them, but he should be praying and meditating to see if he had a vocation or not.

Studs walked out of the room, saying that they could all go to hell.

He heard them laughing after him. Even the walls and the furniture seemed to laugh, to jibe and jeer. He went out for a walk without eating, and he met Helen Borax on Fifty-eighth Street. She asked him how Lucy's gentleman was, and said that she heard he was a specialist in osculation; she said she would never have believed it, but she couldn't doubt all the proof she had seen around the neighborhood in the last few days. And she would never be able to understand how Lucy mistook him for Francis X. Bushman; but then everyone had his or her right to like people. She said she knew Lucy needed a sort of roughneck to carry her books when she went to high school, because Lucy was going to St. Elizabeth's, and it was in a nigger neighborhood, and he could protect her, and walk home with her through the nigger neighborhood. Helen spoke so swiftly and cattishly that Studs couldn't get in a word edgewise. She didn't stop for over five minutes, and then she only paused for breath. After she had talked a blue streak, they stood making faces at each other.

He said, sore as a boil:

"Kiss my . . ."

She blushed, gulped, swallowed, looked shocked and horror-stricken. He turned his back on her, and walked away.

"Lucy's gentleman!" Helen called after him.

He turned and thumbed his nose.

VI

The next day he wandered forlorn streets, wishing that he would meet Dan, or Helen Shires, or someone, and not

having the nerve to go around Indiana, where he might find
them. At Fifty-eighth and Prairie, he met Lucy. She was
with some girl he didn't know, and she said hello booby to
him, winking at her friend. He got sore, and stuttered goofy
things to her, like she needn't think she was so much. She
said she was a lady, and only cared to associate with gentlemen. He said that girls were a pain. She said that girls
wouldn't think much of him after the awful thing he had
said to Helen Borax; she said her mother would certainly
forbid her to associate with such a person. He stood looking at her. She asked him if he saw anything green. He
didn't have any comeback.

They walked away, their heads stuck up, laughing at
him. He stood there, trying to figure out why girls were so
un-understandable, and why they changed and were flighty
like the weather. He walked on in a trance, thinking about
this and about things in general. He told himself again and
again that the world was lousy and he was going to give it
one Goddamn run for its lousy money, all right. It was rotten, all right. Just when things were jake, they blew up like
they had a stick of dynamite under them. Well, Goddamn
everybody, let them lump it. He walked, thinking, dream-
planning heroic revenge, telling himself how he would become something daring and famous like an aviator, a lone
wolf bandit, an Asiatic pirate, a German submarine com-
mander.

He walked. The day was fine. The wind was cool. It
would have been so nice to walk with Lucy. He went over
to the park, and found their tree and sat up there, imagining
that Lucy was by his side swinging her legs and kissing
him. He forgot where he was, and everything else. He only
thought of Lucy. Then he thought he was some place else,
and this time, some place else was sad, and he didn't want
to be in it, and there was no place else for him to go. The
wind again waved through his hair, but now it was only the
wind.

He cursed.

He finally grew lonely and needed to find someone, anyone, to be with. He climbed down and walked snappily, so people seeing him would think he had some place to go and that he wasn't just drooping around like a damn mope. He found himself over near the playground. He went in. Johnny O'Brien, Danny O'Neill and a number of other younger kids were playing indoors, and Miss Tyson, the pretty director, was umpiring. Miss Tyson was a pretty chicken, all right, and a good sport, and whenever she played with the guys, and had to run bases, she slid, and then they could all see her legs. Studs stood and watched them for a minute, and he was just going to ask them to let him in the game, when Old Man Hall, in his tan uniform and looking like he was on his last legs, came up. He looked at Studs, sour and crabby, as if it was Studs' fault that he was an old man ready to go west.

"Come on, now. Get out of here, and don't be plaguin' them that are smaller'n you are. This is no hangout for fellows like you. You ought to be ashamed of yourself, hanging around here, a big fellow like you that ought to be working and earning a living. Come on, get out!" he said in a creaky voice, starting to shove Studs.

"Don't go shoving me!" Studs said.

"I told you to get out, and if you don't, I'll call the police," Hall said.

"Well, just watch who you're shovin'."

The indoor game stopped, and everybody collected around Studs and Old Man Hall. It made Studs feel like an even bigger clown.

Miss Tyson tried to intercede and explain to Hall that Studs was all right, but the old codger made a long speech, telling everybody that he ran the playground, and as long as he did toughs would stay out even if he had to have the police to put them out.

Miss Tyson smiled sweetly at Studs, and apologized. But

she couldn't do anything. To save his pride, he said he didn't
want to come in anyway, and they could all go to the devil
before he'd play on their indoor team in the playground
tournament, like he'd said he would when he'd been asked
to. He left, Hall hobbling along beside him, and almost
every kid in the playground witnessing his humiliation. At
the gate Hall said:

"Now if you come back, I'll have you run in. Good rid-
dance to bad rubbish!"

An old guy, who was so feeble he couldn't probably
hold a spoon of soup without spilling it all over himself,
doing a thing like that to Studs! It made him Goddamn
sore. He told himself: I'm riled sure, now.

He sat outside the playground, brooding, wondering how
he'd get even with Hall. Then he walked on and sat near
the sun-blue lagoon, down past the boathouse. He sat. He
watched the people flood over the park. He wished he was
somebody else. He watched the sky roll down back of the
apartment buildings that stood above the trees lining the
South Park edge of the park. He watched a familiar looking
airedale dog shag about, snapping at the heels of the park
sheep, until Coady, the flat-footed, red-faced park cop,
hoofed it after the dog, probably sweating and cursing his
ears off. The dog scampered away from the cop, ran down
to the lagoon, and took a swim. The cop sought the shadow
of the boathouse. The dog came out, shook the water from
its back, and ran. Studs noticed it more closely. It was
goofy Danny O'Neill's dog, Lib, and it ran away every day
to come over to the park and take a swim. The dog was a
damn sight smarter than Danny. He told himself that
airedales were peachy dogs, they were fighters, they could
swim and liked the water, and they were smart; an airedale
was too smart a dog for O'Neill to have. Studs thought of
getting even with Danny by doing something to the dog,
but when he watched it run, its movements so graceful, its
body so alert, its ears cocked the way he liked to see a

dog's ears cocked, he couldn't think of hurting it. He called: "Here, Lib!" The dog came up. Studs patted its head, softly stroked its forehead the way dogs like to be stroked, rubbed his cheek against the dog, liked it even if it did smell like a livery stable.

"Good dog!" he said.

He stood up, grabbed a piece of branch and threw it. The dog chased the branch, grabbed it, returned, dropped the branch at Studs' feet, and spread out on all fours, waiting to be patted. Studs kept throwing the branch until it was ugly wet with saliva. He rubbed his hand in the grass and patted the dog. He told the dog to stand up, and it obeyed. Then to play dead dog. Then to roll on its back in the grass and speak. He ran, and the dog legged it with him, and rapidly left him behind.

Lib spied the park sheep and was after them. The sheep milled and bleated, and Lib tore circles around them, running like an efficient sheep dog. The cop again appeared, waddling on his defective feet. The dog ran at the sound of the cop's voice. It was too wise for the cop, Studs thought, and laughed. Coady yelled at Studs, complaining, in his Irish brogue, that he wished he'd keep that dog of his away. It was a disturbance of the peace, with it always scaring the sheep, jumping up and getting ladies' dresses muddy, and running around without a leash and muzzle, all against the law. Suppose the dog went mad and bit a baby. The next time he saw the dog, he would shoot it. It was too damn troublesome, and too damn wise.

"Sure it knows I'm after it, and runs when I come," Coady said in an Irish brogue.

Studs said it wasn't his dog.

"Well, then, bejesus, whose dog is it?"

"I don't know."

"Well, keep it away from here, or sure it'll be a dead dog."

The sun was too much for Coady. He flatfooted it back

to the shade. Studs laughed. It was always fun to see a cop-per stumped. The dog was gone now, on its way home. Studs walked, wishing he had a dog of his own, because you could have fun with a dog, particularly when you were lonesome. A dog was almost human, and a guy was always wishing he could get closer to it, speak to it, understand what it meant when it barked. It was pretty the way the dog looked at you, the way it ran and cocked its ears. It got a guy. A dog was a real friend, all right. But his old man wouldn't have a dog, because he said dogs were dirty, and his mother said they brought bad luck into the house, be-cause sometimes dogs were the souls of people, who had put a curse on you, come back to life.

He walked around the park, and didn't meet anyone he knew.

Chapter Five

IN SUMMER, the days went too fast. They raced. In June, right after his graduation, Studs had had no sense of the passing days. And now July was almost gone, and the days were racing toward September and school. He remembered the Fourth; he had spent it with the Indiana gang, lighting firecrackers under tin cans to watch them pop.

It had promised to be a great summer for him and it was turning out pretty punk. And now it was one of those days, like the ones that came so often in mid-August. It was hot, but there was no sun; and the wind sounded like there were devils in it; and the leaves were all a solid, deep green. It was just that kind of a day. It made him feel different, glum; and his thoughts were queer and foggy, and he didn't have the right words for them. There was the feeling that he wanted something, and he didn't know what it was. He couldn't stay put in one place, and he kept shifting about, doing all sorts of awkward things, looking far away, and not being satisfied with anything he did.

He didn't go around Indiana any more, so he had walked up and down other streets and had ended up in the Carter Playground. He fooled around. He batted out stones. He climbed up the ladders and slid down, and didn't mind doing that, but canned it, because the ladders were for young squirts. He sat on the edge of the slide and thought of Lucy,

and of how he had scarcely seen her since that day. He
liked Lucy. He liked her. He loved her, but after what had
happened he was even ashamed to admit it to himself. He
was a hard-boiled guy, and he had learned his lesson. He'd
keep himself roped in tight after this when it came to girls.
He wasn't going to show his cards to nobody again. He sat
on the slide. He got up and climbed the ladder. He slid
down. He picked up pebbles and shot them as a guy shot
marbles. He went to the fountain for a drink. He wished he
could think of something he'd like to do.

He thought about how he had licked Weary Reilley and
become such a big cheese around Indiana, and well, he
had turned out to be a different kind of a big cheese now.
He walked down to Cannon's confectionery store near
State and bought an ice cream cone. He licked the ice
cream with his tongue so that it would last longer. When
he returned to the playground, Red Kelly, Davey Cohen
and Paulie were there. Guys had always wondered what
sort of a showing Studs would make in a scrap with the
lads from Fifty-eighth and Prairie, but none of them had
ever bothered Studs. As he walked across the playground
toward them, he suddenly wondered if any of them, if
Red, would start something now. He saw Davey Cohen
talking to Red, and pointing at him. When he got up to
them, Red asked him if he thought he was tough. He asked
Red why. Red said he just wanted to know if Studs
thought he was tough, because if he was, well, he, Red
Kelly, would knock a little of it out of him. He and Red
looked at each other. Red spat. Studs spat. Davey said put
a stick on Studs' shoulders. Davey picked up a stick, and
handed it to Paulie. After hesitating, Paulie placed it on
Studs' shoulder. Red glowered at Studs. Studs made faces
back. Red spat from the corner of his mouth. Red knocked
the stick off and said that he didn't even bury his dead; he
let them lie. They fought. Studs gave Red a bloody nose,
and Red showed a yellow streak and quit; he walked off

and said he'd square matters later. Davey and Paulie sidled around Studs. They asked him why he never hung out with their gang.

"We have a swell time all the time, better than the St. Patrick's guys from Indiana," Paulie said.

"Hell, they're all mopes," Studs said.

"Yeh, well, then come on around with us," Davey said.

Studs said that he would.

Some young punks, Joe Coady and Denny Dennis, came around. Joe got the ball and bat from the instructor's office, and they played move-up piggy.

Studs batted. Paulie pitched. He served one up to Studs. Studs leaned on it, and it went out to center field on the fly. Davey caught it.

Paulie batted, and Coady pitched. Studs went out to right field.

Coady twirled the ball.

Paulie didn't hit it.

"Come on and pitch 'em right," said Paulie.

"I'm pitchin' right. What's a matter?" asked Coady.

"Pitch 'em and cut it out," Paulie said.

Studs told them to play and quit dynamitin'.

"Hey! Hey! can the goofin'," he added.

Coady twirled the ball, and Paulie sizzled one along the ground.

"Goddamn you! Pitch right!" Paulie snarled.

"I'm pitchin' it all right. Can't you hit it?" answered Coady.

"You ain't. Come on, you Goddamn punk, or I'll fling the bat at you!" Paulie said.

"You better not. He's Tommy Doyle's cousin," young Dennis said.

"All right, punk. No one asked you tuh put your two cents in," Paulie said to Dennis.

"Hey, can it!" Studs said.

Coady made an elaborate pitching gesture, and under-handed a floater straight over the pan. Paulie let it go by.

"Damn you, pitch right," Paulie said.

Studs walked in and out. He picked up stones, and threw them aimlessly.

"I'm pitchin' all right. Why don't you hit it?" asked Coady.

"You lousy punk, pitch right!" Paulie said.

Coady twirled the next pitch, and Paulie lashed, hitting a mean, twisting foul by first base. Coady ran after it, and got his hands on the ball but muffed it.

"Come on, Joe! Let 'im hit it," Davey yelled.

"Pitch it right, you little bitch," said Paulie.

Coady did, an easy floater, and Paulie popped a fly to Denny. He threw the bat at Coady, but Joe dodged and laughed. He moved toward him. Coady ran, Paulie wriggling his tomato after Joe. Joe was too swift for Haggerty.

"If I catch you, I'll bust your neck," yelled Paulie.

"Hey, cut it out," Studs yelled.

"Aw, come on, you guys," pleaded Denny.

Paulie kept shagging Coady. Joe would slow down until Paulie got near him, then he would dodge, twist and dart off, laughing at Paulie. Joe had won medals in grammar school track meets, and he was fast. He had Paulie puffing like a balloon, and Haggerty had to give it up. Joe laughed at him.

Studs got sore and threw pebbles at both of them. Paulie lined rocks at Joe.

Studs asked Paulie if he wanted to keep on playing.

"Yeh, but I'd like to kill the lousy punk and bust his freckled neck," said Paulie.

He shook his fist at Joe.

"Can't you hit? . . . You couldn't hit the flat side of a barn . . . you couldn't hit one if it had crutches on it," Joe yelled.

"Lemme get my hands on you, and I'll hit all right," Paulie said.

"Come on, Paulie, can it! You'll get another bat," said Davey.

Paulie took his place out in center field. Denny pitched. Coady batted. He hit the first one on a line past third. No one was near it. Davey shagged after the ball.

Denny pitched again.

Coady did not swing.

"Come on! Hit it!" yelled Paulie.

"I will," said Joe.

Denny pitched.

Joe smacked another one over third.

He hit another one over third.

They all got sore and yelled at him.

Studs went over and leaned against the ladders in foul territory.

Coady lined one to right field. Studs would have had it, if he had been in position. He got sore and cursed, running after the ball.

Coady kept on placing his hits, chopping them, hitting down and lining out grounders, cutting them over third, drawing them in back of first base.

"What the hell you think you're doin'?" raged Paulie.

"I'm batting, ain't I?"

"What you think you are?" asked Studs.

Joe accidentally hit one on first bounce to Denny, and his turn would have been up, but Denny fumbled.

"Christ sake! You're all thumbs," said Paulie.

"Come on, you punks," said Studs.

Coady placed one over Davey's head in deep short. The ball rolled way out in left field. Davey watched it roll. So did Paulie. They looked at each other.

"You're the outfield," said Davey.

"I'm center field," Paulie said.

"I'm playin' infield," Davey said.

"I'm not gonna get it. It wasn't my field," Paulie said.

"Well, I'm not neither," Davey said.

Paulie sat down.

Davey sat down.

Studs went over and leaned against the slide bars.

"You get it, Denny," Davey said.

"I don't have to get it. It ain't my ball. I was pitchin'," Denny said defensively.

"One of you guys gotta get it," Studs said.

"It ain't mine," Paulie said.

"It ain't mine," Davey said.

"Come on and quit dynamitin'," Studs said.

"I ain't dynamitin'," said Davey.

"Commere, Denny," Studs said.

"No, I won't. I'm pitchin'. I don't have to get it," yelped Denny.

"Come on, you guys. I want my bats," Coady said.

"Hell, you got 'em," Paulie said.

"I want mine, too," Denny said.

"Well, you get the pill then," Paulie said.

"Come on and give me my bats," Coady said.

Paulie threw some stones around.

"Commere, Denny," Studs said.

Denny reluctantly went over to Studs.

"Go and get the ball, and we'll get you your bats," said Studs.

"No, I don't have to," said Denny.

"Go ahead! I'll do you a favor some time," said Studs.

"Heck! Why should I? I didn't hit it or miss it. I was pitchin'. If it was my position, I would, but it wasn't," said Denny.

"Go on, get it," persuaded Studs.

"I won't."

Studs grabbed Denny, and twisted his arm back in a hammer lock.

"Ouch! UUUUU! Damn you! You big bully! Let me go!

I'll get my brother after you, and he'll kill you for this. Let me go! Ouch! UUUUUU!"

"Well, will you get the ball?"

"Owwww! Let me go, you bully! Let me alone!"

"Now will you get it?"

"Make 'im get it," said Davey.

Studs twisted again. Denny yelled. He promised he would get the ball. Studs relaxed his hold. Denny started walking away. He bawled. He called Studs a big bully. Suddenly, he turned and thumbed his nose at Studs.

"You bastard," he yelled.

Studs shagged him, and Davey and Paulie took up the chase. Denny was caught. Studs twisted his arm again. He called Studs a big bully. Davey suggested taking his pants off. Paulie ripped his buttons open.

"Let me go, you bullies. Let me alone! I didn't do nothin' to you. I didn't bother you. Pick on someone your own size. I'll tell my brother. He'll kick the crap out of you," yelled Denny, frantically.

Studs twisted his arm again.

Denny shrieked that they were sbs.

Studs twisted. Paulie slapped Denny's face. Denny bawled, large tears rolling down his dirty face. Paulie goosed him. Denny squirmed, and yelled.

"Take it all back," demanded Studs.

"No."

Studs twisted.

An agonized yes.

Studs loosed his hold.

Paulie snatched Denny's cap.

Denny begged for it.

They laughed at him. They threatened to hang his pants on the picket fence. Denny cried for his cap.

Paulie handed the cap to Studs. Denny ran toward Studs. Studs tossed it to Davey. Denny ran toward Davey. Davey passed it to Paulie. Denny picked up some boulders and moved toward Paulie. Paulie told the punk to drop the rocks while he knew he was well off. He passed the hat to Studs.

Studs wrapped some stones in it. He said to Denny: "Here it is!"

When Denny came to Studs, Studs threw the cap on the roof of Carter school.

Denny bawled, and yelled that his brother would get the whole bunch of them, and he got a kick in the slats for his mouthiness.

Studs, Paulie and Davey left the playground.

"You'll get it like that," Paulie yelled at Joe.

"Got to catch me first."

"Let's get him," said Davey.

"Hell, we'd never catch him," said Studs.

"We hadn't better. He's Tommy Doyle's cousin," said Davey.

"Listen, Studs, you ought to hang around with us guys at Fifty-eighth and Prairie. You'll have more fun," said Paulie.

Studs said he might. They told him how swell a scrapper he was.

"You're as good as anyone on Fifty-eighth. You're as good as Tommy Doyle," said Davey.

Studs felt pretty good again. He felt powerful. Life was still opening up for him, as he'd expected it to, and it was still going to be a great summer. And it was a better day than he imagined. A sun was busting the sky open, like Studs Lonigan busted guys in the puss. It was a good day.

They walked on down toward the Fifty-eighth Street corner. Davey sniped a butt and lit it. Paulie jawed a hunk off of his plug of tobacco. He offered some to Studs but Studs didn't take it; chewing tobacco made him sick. Paulie's pan was stuffed with tobacco. They walked along, all feeling pretty good.

Studs heard his mother calling him, and they hurried around the corner as if he didn't hear her.

"What'll we do?" asked Davey.

"What'll we do?" asked Paulie.

"Let's do something," said Studs.

"Let's," said Davey.

They walked along. Studs took a drag on Davey's butt. Paulie got between them, putting an arm around each of their shoulders. They were a picture, walking along, Paulie with his fat hips, Davey with his bow legs, and small, broad Studs.

"We'll find something to do," said Davey.

"Sure," said Paulie.

They walked along, looking for something to do.

SECTION THREE

Chapter Six

I

STUDS LONIGAN, looking tough, sat on the fireplug before the drug store on the northeast corner of Fifty-eighth and Prairie. Since cleaning up Red Kelly, he, along with Tommy Doyle, had become a leading member of the Fifty-eighth Street bunch. Studs and Tommy were figured a good draw. Studs sat. His jaw was swollen with tobacco. The tobacco tasted bitter, and he didn't like it, but he sat, squirting juice from the corner of his mouth, rolling the chewed wad from jaw to jaw. His cap was pulled over his right eye in hard-boiled fashion. He had a piece of cardboard in the back of his cap to make it square, just like all the tough Irish from Wentworth Avenue, and he had a bushy Regan haircut. He sat. He had a competition with himself in tobacco juice spitting to determine whether he could do better plopping it from the right or the left side of his mouth. The right-hand side was Studs; the left-hand side was a series of rivals, challenging him for the championship. The contests were important ones, like heavyweight championship fights, and they put Studs Lonigan in the public eye, like Jess Willard and Freddy Welsh. Seriously, cautiously, concernedly, he let the brown juice fly, first from the left, then from the right side of his mouth. Now and then the

juice slobbered down his chin, and that made Studs feel as
goofy as if he was a young punk with falling socks.

People paraded to and fro along Fifty-eighth, and many
turned on and off of Prairie Avenue. It was a typically
warm summer day. Studs vaguely saw the people pass, and
he was, in a distant way, aware of them as his audience.
They saw him, looked at him, envied and admired him, noticed him, and thought that he must be a pretty tough
young guy. The ugliest guy in the world passed. He was all
out of joint. His face was colorless, and the jaws were
sunken. He had the most Jewish nose in the world, and his
lips were like a baboon's. He was round-shouldered, bow-
legged and knock-kneed. His hands were too long, and as
he walked he looked like a parabola from the side, and
from the front like an approaching series of cubistic planes.
And he wore colored glasses. Studs looked at him, laughed,
even half-admired a guy who could be so twisted, and
wondered who old plug-ugly was, and what he did. Then
Leon ta-taed along, pausing to ask Studs about taking music lessons. He put his hands on Studs' shoulders, and
Studs felt uncomfortable, as if maybe Leon had horse ap-
ples in his hands. Leon wanted Studs to take a walk, but
Studs said he couldn't because he was waiting for some
guys to come along. Leon shook himself along, and Studs
felt as if he needed a bath. Old Fox-in-the-Bush, the priest
or minister or whatever he was of the Greek Catholic
Church across from St. Patrick's, walked by, carrying a
cane. Studs told himself the guy was funny all right; he
was Gilly's bosom friend. Studs laughed, because it must
be funny, even to Gilly, listening to a guy talk through
whiskers like that. Mrs. O'Brien came down the street,
loaded with groceries, and Studs snapped his head around,
like he was dodging something, and became interested in
the sky, so that she wouldn't see him, not only because he
was chewing, but also because if he saw her, he'd have to
ask her if he could carry her groceries home for her. Hell,

he was no errand boy, or a do-a-good-deed-a-day boy
scout. And there was old Abraham Isidorivitch, or whatever
his name was, the batty old half-blind Jew who was eighty,
or ninety or maybe one hundred and thirty years old, and
who was always talking loud on the corners. Abraham, or
whatever his name was, did repair work for Davey Cohen's
old man sometimes, and the two of them must be a circus
when they're together. Mothers passed with their babies,
some of them brats that squawled all over the place. Helen
Borax, with her nose in the air, like she was trying to avoid
an ugly smell. Mrs. Dennis P. Gorman, with a young kid
carrying a package of her groceries that was too heavy for
him. Studs got the gob of tobacco out just in the nick of
time. She stopped and asked him how his dear mother was.
She said he should be sure and tell her and his father to
telephone them sometimes, and to come over for tea. And
she asked him how he was enjoying the summer. Dorothy
was just doing fine. She was very busy with her music, and
she was going to summer school at Englewood, because she
wanted to do the four years high school in three. And she
said that Mr. Robinson, head master of the troop of boy
scouts in the neighborhood, had been over to her house the
other evening, and he talked about getting more boys in his
organization, because that kept them out of mischief. The
boy scouts, she explained, were an excellent organization,
which made gentlemen out of boys, gave them opportuni-
ties for clean, organized fun and sport, and they taught
boys to do all sorts of kind deeds like helping blind ladies
across the street. The little boy helping her with groceries
was a boy scout, and his good deed every day was to carry
her groceries home; and he wouldn't take a penny for it.
And her husband said that the boy scouts gave boys pre-
liminary military training and discipline so that it would be
easier for them later on in the army, if they were called to
defend their country, as they might have to with that old
Kaiser trying to conquer the world. She expected to see

Studs and all the other boys on Indiana Avenue join the boy scouts. She started to move on, and said in parting:

"Now, do tell your dear mother and your father to come and see us, and now don't you forget to, like little boys often do."

The boy scout struggled after her with the bundle that was too heavy for him. Studs watched them, and thought unprintable things about old lady Gorman.

He stacked some more tobacco in his mug. He sat there. He put on a show to please himself, and imagined that everybody noticed him. He tired of his tobacco juice spitting contest, and quit. He watched snot-nosed Phil Rolfe, the twelve-year-old little pest, tear after a motor truck heading north. The runt got his hitch, even though Studs yelled after him to confuse him, and wished that he'd break his kike neck. Old man Cohen, dirty, bearded, paused and accusingly asked Studs if he had seen Davey. Studs said no. Studs felt sorry for Davey, with an old man like that. He sat there.

Nate shuffled by, and, seeing Studs, came over. Nate was a toothless, graying little man, with an insane stare in his smallish black eyes. He wore a faded and unpressed green suit that had cobwebs on it and a thick, winter cap of the kind that teamsters wore.

"What's on your mind, Nate?" Studs asked, using the same tone and manner that the older guys around Bathcellar's pool room used with him.

Nate said he was getting some new French post cards, and told Studs that he'd sell them for a dime apiece. They were *some* pictures. Oh, boy! They showed everything. Studs said that he'd take a dozen or two when Nate brought them around. Nate tried to collect in advance, but Studs was no soap for that. Nate started to shuffle away and Studs asked him where the fire was.

"Work, my boy! I was jus' tellin' myself about the chicken I made lay eggs today. I was deliverin' some gro-

ceries over on South Park Avenoo, and this chicken was
the maid. See! Well! Well, I delivers my groceries, and she
says the missus ain't in, and she looks at me, you know
the way a chicken looks at a guy!"

Nate winked, leered and poked Studs in the ribs expres-
sively. He continued:

"She says I should leave the groceries, and you know
that ain't good business, so I calls ole man Hirschfield, but
he says it's o. k. So I leaves the groceries. She tanks me,
and she says she has jus' made a cup of tea, an' I should
siddown and have one wid her. She was a looker, so I takes
the tea wid her, and we gets to barbering about one ting an'
anoder, about one ting and anoder . . ."

Nate paused to wipe the slobber off his whiskery chin.

"We gasses about one ting an' anoder, and soon she ups
and walks by me to go to the sink, so I pinches her, and it
was de nicest I ever pinched, an', my boy, I pinched many
in my day, because I'm old enough to be yer grandaddy.
Well, first ting you know . . ."

Nate leered.

"The first ting you know . . . why . . . I schlipt her a little luck."

"Yeh?"

Nate poked Studs confidentially, leered, and said:

"Yeh, I schlipt her a little luck."

"Yeh?"

"Yeh!"

Nate turned to gape at a passing chicken, and Studs
goosed him. Nate jumped.

He shuffled away, furious, telling himself about the
damn brats who got too wise before their diapers were
changed.

Studs laughed.

He took out another chew, and resumed his competition.
The right hand side of his mouth won easily. He thought of
Lucy who was probably still sore at him. The old feeling

for Lucy flowed through him, warm. She seemed to him
like a . . . like a saint or a beautiful queen, or a goddess.
But the tough outside part of Studs told the tender inside
part of him that nobody really knew, that he had better forget all that bull. He tried to, and it wasn't very easy. He let
fly a juicy gob that landed square on a line, three cracks
from him. Perfect! He saw Lucy, and acted very busy with
his tobacco juice squirting. He let fly another gob that was
a perfect hit. She laughed aloud at him, and said:

"Think you're funny, Mr. Smarty!"

Studs let fly another gob. She laughed again, and walked
on. Studs sat, not looking nor feeling so much like a tough
guy. He didn't turn and see Lucy twist around to glance at
him. He threw his wad away. He sat, heedless of the noisy
street. A dago peddler parked his fruit wagon in back of
Studs, and he was there calling his wares for some time before Studs laughed, like he laughed at all batty foreigners.
He thought of Lucy. Lucy . . . she could go plum to . . .
LUCY! He shoved another thumb of tobacco in his puss,
but didn't chew it with the same concentration. He almost
swallowed the damn stuff. Mr. Dennis P. Gorman passed,
after his trying day at the police court. Studs coughed from
the bad taste in his mouth.

Kenny Killarney appeared, and Studs smiled to see him.
Kenny was thin, taller than Studs, Irish, blue-eyed, dizzy-
faced, untidy, darkish, quick, and he had a nervous, original
walk.

"Hi!" said Studs.

"Hi!" said Kenny, raising his palms, hands outward.

"Hi!" said Studs.

"Hi!" said Kenny; he salaamed in oriental fashion.

"Hi!" laughed Studs.

"Hi!" said Kenny.

"Hi!" said Studs. "Jesus Christ!" said Studs.

"Hi, Low, Jack, and the Game," said goofy Kenny.

They laughed and stuffed chews in their faces. Studs

marveled at Kenny's skill in chewing. Juice rolled down his own chin, and he had to spit the tobacco out again.

Kenny gave a rambling talk. Studs didn't listen, and only heard the end, when Kenny said:

"And I said I'm from Tirty-turd and de tracks, see, an' I lives on de top floor ob de las' house on de left-hand side of de street, and deres a skull an' crossbones on de chimney, and blood on de door, and my back yard's de grave-yard for my dead."

Studs laughed, because you had to laugh when Kenny pulled his gags. Kenny was a funny guy. He ought to be in vaudeville, even if he was still young.

"Well, Lonigan, you old so-and-so, what's happening?"

"It's dead as a doornail, you old sonofabitch," Studs said.

Kenny looked at Studs; he told him not to say that; he cried:

"Take that back!"

"What's eatin' you?"

"Nothin'. But I don't care if you're kiddin' or not. I love my mother, and she's the only friend I got, and if I was hung tomorrow, she'd still be my mother, and be at my side forgivin' me, and I can't stand and let anybody call her names, even if it's kiddin'; and I don't care if you are Studs Lonigan and can fight, you can't say anything about my mother," Kenny said. He drew back a step, wiped the tears from his face with his shirt sleeve, and picked up a wooden slab that lay on the sidewalk.

Studs looked questioningly at Kenny, who stood there nervously clenching and unclenching his free fist, determined, his face ready to break into tears at any moment.

"Hell, Kenny! I was only kiddin'. I take it all back," said Studs.

They faced each other, and in a minute or two the incident was forgotten. Kenny became his old self.

"It's too hot, or we could go raidin' ice boxes. But I don't feel like much effort today," Kenny said.

"Let's go swimmin'," suggested Studs.

"O.K.," said Kenny.

"All right. I'll get my suit and meet you here in twenty minutes," said Studs.

"But I'll have to get a suit. I ain't got none," said Kenny.

"Whose will you borrow?" asked Studs.

Kenny winked.

"What beach'll we go to?" asked Studs.

"Fifty-first Street," said Kenny.

"Ain't there a lot of Jews there?" asked Studs.

"Where ain't there kikes? They're all over. You watch. First it's the hebes, and then it's the niggers that's gonna overrun the south side," Kenny said.

"And then where ull a white man go to?" asked Studs.

"He'll have to go to Africa or . . . Jew-rusalem," said Kenny.

Kenny sang Solomon Levi with all the sheeny motions, and it was funny, because Kenny was funny, all right, and could always make a guy laugh.

Afterward Studs said:

"If we go to Jackson Park, it might be better."

"There's Polacks there," said Killarney.

"Well, how about Seventy-fifth Street beach?" asked Studs.

"It's O.K. But listen, sometimes Iris is at Fifty-first."

"That's a different story. I got to meet this here Iris," said Studs.

"Yeh," said Kenny.

"I hope she's there."

"She's sweet. Boy, she's just UMMMMMMMMMM-MMMMMMM," said Kenny.

"Is she really good?" asked Studs.

"Best I ever had," said Kenny like he was an older guy with much experience.

"Well, I'm going to be a disappointed guy if she ain't," said Studs.

"But listen! Don't work so fast. Suppose she don't give you a tumble. Sometimes she gets temperament, and then she's no soap until some guy she gets a grudge against beats it . . . She's like a primadonna," said Kenny.

"I thought she was like a sweetheart of the navy," Studs said.

"Well, sometimes she is and sometimes she isn't."

"Yeah. But anyway, you just lead me to her," boasted Studs.

"Well, at that, you're talkin' horse sense," said Kenny.

"Horsey sense," said Studs.

"Well, anyway, I got to get my suit," said Kenny.

Kenny told Studs to walk down Fifty-eighth toward Indiana.

"And when I come tearin' along, you run, too, and cut through the lot on Indiana, and down the alley, and through that trick gangway to Michigan," he added.

Studs did. In a moment, Kenny came running along, and they carried out their plan of escaping, though no one was chasing them. On Michigan, Kenny pulled out the two-piece bathing suit he had copped; the trunks were blue, the top white.

"If it only fits now," he said.

They laughed together, and Studs said that Kenny had real style. Kenny laughed, and said it was nothing to cop things from drug stores. Studs told himself that Killarney was a guy, all right.

They put their suits on under their clothes at Studs'. The suit fitted Kenny. They went over to South Park and bummed rides to Fifty-first, and did the same thing along Fifty-first and Hyde Park Boulevard. They had fun on Hyde Park Boulevard. It was a ritzy neighborhood where everybody had the kale and all the men wore knickers and played tennis and golf, and all the guys were sissies. Kenny

had chalked his K.K. initials all over the Fifty-eighth Street
neighborhood, so he started putting mysterious K.K. signs
on the Boulevard. And he kept walking on the grass, making fun of the footmen and wriggling his ears at the well-
dressed women. They saw one hot dame, in clothes that
must have cost a million bucks, and Kenny commented on
the large breastworks she had. He spoke too loud, and she
heard him. She went up in the air like a kite, and talked
very indignantly about ragamuffins from the slums. When
they got out of her hearing, they laughed.

The lake was very calm, and way out it was as blue as
the sky on a swell summer evening. And the sun came
down over it like a blessing. And they were tanned, so they
didn't have to worry about getting sunburned and blistered.
They ran out from the lockers with feelings of animal glee.
The first touch of the water was cold, and they experienced
sharp sensations. But they dove under water, and then it
was warm. The lake was just right. They went out, splash-
ing, diving under water, trying to duck each other, laughing
and shouting. The diving board was crowded but they
climbed up and took some dives. Kenny did all kinds of
dippy dives, back flaps and rolls. The people about the diving board watched them and thought Kenny was pretty
good. He started a stump-the-leader game on the board but
he was too good for them, so they all lost interest.

Kenny and Studs swam out where it was cold and deep,
and there was no one around them. They dove, splashed,
floated, splashed, swam, snorted. They were like happy
seals. Studs got off by himself and wheeled and turned
over in the water like a rolling barrel. He called over to
Kenny that it was the nuts. Kenny yelled back that boy it
was jake. They swam breast-stroke, and it was nice and
easy; then they did the crawl. They went out further. Only
the lake was ahead of them, vast and blue-gray and nice
with the sun on it; and it gave them feelings they couldn't
describe. Studs floated, and looked up at the round sky, his

head resting easy on the water line, himself just drifting, the sun firing away at his legs. It was too nice for anything. He just floated and didn't have anything to think about. He looked up at the drifting clouds. He felt just like a cloud that didn't have any bothers and just sailed across the sky. He told himself: Gee, it was a big sky. He asked himself: I wonder why God made the sky? He floated. He floated, and suddenly he liked himself a lot. Sometimes he was ashamed of his body, like when the old man came in to use the bathroom when he was taking a bath and didn't have anything on, or like on the night he graduated, when he was in bed and had a time trying to sleep. Now he liked his body, and wasn't at all ashamed of it. It moved through the water like a slow ship that just went along and didn't have any place in particular to go and just sailed. About ten yards away he heard Kenny wahooing and singing about Captain Decker who sailed on the bounding main, and lost his . . . and Kenny seemed almost as far away as if he was on the other side of the lake. He splashed with his hands. Then he held his toes up and tried to wiggle them, but he got a mouthful. He turned and swam a little way, taking in a mouthful of water and holding it. He turned over and floated, spouting the water, pretending he was the most powerful whale in all the seas and oceans, floating along, minding its business, because all the sharks were leery of attacking it. He had a sudden fear that he might get cramps and drown, and he was afraid of drowning and dying, so he turned over and swam. But he wasn't afraid for long. Then he and Kenny tried to see who could stay under water the longest, and they waved in to attract attention, so people on the diving board might think they were drowning and get all excited. He dove down, imagining he was a submarine, and the water kept getting cooler, and he kept his eyes open but could only see the water, clear, all around him. He felt far away from all the world now, and he didn't care. He came up, choking for air, and it was like coming to out of a

goofy dream where you are falling or dying or something.
Kenny was up before him, and Studs, after he had gotten a
good breath, told Kenny he wasn't so good.

"Drowning ain't my specialty. That's not my trick!"
Kenny yelled back.

They swam slowly in.

When they got on the beach, they gazed about and ran
all around, looking for Iris and eyeing all the women to get
some good squints. Kenny said it would be swell, like
heaven, if all women wore the same kinds of swimming
suits that Annette Kellerman did. Studs said it would be
better if they didn't wear anything. Kenny said women
sometimes did go swimming without anything on. Studs
said he'd give his ear to see them.

Finally, they sprawled face downward in the sand, the
sun fine and warm on their backs, evaporating all the wet.
They didn't talk. They just sprawled there. It was too good
to talk. Studs forgot everything, and felt almost as good as
when he had been by himself way out in the deep water.
He just lay there and pretended that he wasn't Studs or
anybody at all, and he let his thoughts take care of themselves. He was far away from himself, and the slap of the
waves on the shore, the splash of people in the water, all
the noise and shouts of the beach were not in the same
world with him. They were like echoes in the night coming
from a long way off. He was snapped out of it by Kenny
cursing the goddamn flies and the kids who ran scuffing
sand all over everybody. Studs looked up. Then he looked
out over the lake where the water and sky seemed to meet
and become just nothing. He thought of swimming far, far
out, farther than he and Kenny had, swimming out into the
nothingness, and just floating, floating with nothing there,
and no noises, no fights, no old men, no girls, no thinking
of Lucy, no nothing but floating, floating. Kenny broke off
his thoughts. He talked about swimming across the lake,
arguing that a good life guard could swim all the way to

Michigan City or Benton Harbor. Studs said that Kenny was nuts, but then he couldn't talk as fast as Killarney, so he lost the argument. Kenny just talked anyway, and it didn't matter what he talked about or make him less funny.

At six they went home, and moving along Hyde Park Boulevard, trying to bum rides and cursing everybody who passed them by, Kenny said:

"It was swell today."

"Yeh! it was swell," Studs said.

"Only I wish Iris had been there," said Kenny.

"Yeh," said Studs.

"I'm so hungry, I could eat a horse," said Kenny.

"Wouldn't it have been nice to have had her there and have her let us lay our heads in her lap, and have a feel-day, or go out with her way out, or swim around to the breakwater, where nobody was, and out there get our ashes hauled," said Studs.

"Almost as nice as eating a steak would be this very minute," said Kenny.

"Sure," said Studs.

They walked on. When Studs had been lying in the sand, he had been at peace, almost like some happy guy in a story, and he hadn't thought that way about girls, and it hadn't bothered him like it did other times, or made him do things he was ashamed of way deep down inside himself. Now his peace was all gone like a scrap of burned-up paper. He was nervous again, and girls kept coming into his mind, bothering all hell out of him. And that made him feel queer, and he got ashamed of the thoughts he had . . . because of Lucy. And he couldn't think of anything else.

At home they had steak, and Studs, like a healthy boy, forgot everything but the steak put before him.

II

The July night leaked heat all over Fifty-eighth Street, and the fitful death of the sun shed softening colors that spread gauze-like and glamorous over the street, stilling those harshnesses and commercial uglinesses that were emphasized by the brighter revelations of day. About the street there seemed to be a supervening beauty of reflected life. The dust, the scraps of paper, the piled-up store windows, the first electric lights sizzling into brightness. Sammie Schmaltz, the paper man, yelling his final box-score editions, a boy's broken hoop left forgotten against the elevated girder, the people hurrying out of the elevated station and others walking lazily about, all bespoke the life of a community, the tang and sorrow and joy of a people that lived, worked, suffered, procreated, aspired, filled out their little days, and died.

And the flower of this community, its young men, were grouped about the pool room, choking the few squares of sidewalk outside it. The pool room was two doors east of the elevated station, which was midway between Calumet and Prairie Avenues. It had barber poles in front, and its windows bore the scratched legend, Bathcellar's Billiard Parlor and Barber Shop. The entrance was a narrow slit, filled with the forms of young men, while from inside came the click of billiard balls and the talk of other young men.

Old toothless Nate shuffled along home from his day's work.

"Hello, Nate!" said Swan, the slicker, who wore a tout's gray checked suit with narrow-cuffed trousers, a pink silk shirt with soft collar, and a loud purplish tie; his bright-banded straw hat was rakishly angled on his blond head.

"Hello, Moneybags!" said Jew Percentage, a middle-aged, vaguely corpulent, brown-suited, purple-shirted guy with a cigar stuck in his tan, prosperous-looking mug.

"Hello, Nate! How's the answer to a K. M.'s prayer on

this fine evenin'?" asked Pat Coady, a young guy dressed like a race-track follower.

"How're the house maids?" asked young Studs Lonigan, who stood with the big guys, proud of knowing them, ashamed of his size, age and short breeches.

The older guys all laughed at Young Lonigan's wise-crack. Slew Weber, the blond guy with the size-eleven shoes, looked up from his newspaper and asked Nate if he was still on the trail of the house maids.

Nate had been holding a dialogue with himself. He interrupted it to tell them that he was getting his.

Slew Weber went back to his newspaper. He said:

"Say, I see there's six suicides in the paper tonight."

"Jesus, I knew it," said Swan.

"This guy Weber is a guy, all right. All he needs to do is smell a paper, and he can tell you how many birds has croaked themselves. He's got an eagle eye fur suicides," said Pat Coady.

Nate started to talk; he said:

"Say, goddamnit, I'm tired. I'm tired. I'm gonna quit this goddamn wurk. Jesus Christ! the things people wancha tuh do. Now, today I was hikin' an order, and some old bitch without a stitch on . . ."

"Naughty! Naughty! Naughty Nate!" interrupted Percentage, crossing his fingers in a child's gesture of shame.

"She was without a stitch on, and she wants me to go an get her a pack of cigarettes, an I looks at her, and I said, I said . . . but Jesus, it was funny, because I coulda killed her with the look I gave her; but I said, I said, Lady I'm workin' since seven this mornin', and I still gotta store full of orders to deliver. Now Lady how do you expect me ever to get finished, and Lady if I go runnin' for Turkish Trophies for every one that wants 'em . . . Well, sir! Ha! Ha! She shuts up like a clam. And then I always gotta deal with these nigger maids dat keep yellin' for you tuh wipe yer feet. I said, give uh nigger an inch, and dey wants a hull mile. And my rheumatism is botherin' me again. But say you oughta see the chicken I got today . . ."

Saliva and browned tobacco juice trickled down Nate's chin.

"Well Nate, the first hundred years is the hardest," said Percentage.

"Yeh, Nate, it's a tough life if you don't weaken," said Swan.

"Say, Nate, did you ever buy a tin lizzie?" said Studs, trying to be funny like the older guys.

"Think yuh'll ever amount to much, Nate?" asked Pat Coady.

"Say, listen, when you guys is as old as me you'll be in the ground," said Nate.

"Say, I'll bet Nate's got the first dollar he ever earned," said Slew.

"And a lot more," said Pat.

Nate told them never to mind; then he started to talk of the Swedish maid he had on the string. He poked Slew confidentially, and said that every Thursday afternoon, you know. Then he said he was getting in a new stock of French picture cards, and tried to collect in advance, but they told him to bring them around first.

A girl passed, and they told Nate there was something for him. Nate turned and gaped at her with a moron's excited eyes.

Percentage told Nate he had a swell new tobacco which he was going to let him try. Nate asked the name and price. Percentage said it was a secret he couldn't reveal, because it was not on the market yet, but he was going to give him a pipeful. He asked Nate for his pipe, and Nate handed him the corncob. Percentage held the pipe and started to thumb through his pockets. He winked to Swan, who poked the other guys. They crowded around Nate so he couldn't see, and got him interested in telling about all the chickens he made while he delivered groceries. Percentage slipped the pipe to Studs, and pointed to the street. Studs caught on, and quickly filled the pipe with dry manure. Percentage made a long funny spiel, and gave the pipe to Nate. The guys had a hell of a time not laughing, and nearly all of them pulled out handkerchiefs. Studs felt good, because he'd been let in on a practical joke they played on someone else; it sort of stamped him as an equal. Nate fumbled about, wasting six matches trying to light the pipe. He cursed. Percentage said it was swell tobacco, but a little difficult to light, and again their faces went a-chewing into their handkerchiefs. Nate said they must all have colds. Nate said that whenever he had a cold he took lemon and honey. Percentage said that once you got this tobacco going, it was a swell smoke, and all the colds got suddenly worse.

Nate shuffled on, trying to light his pipe and talking to himself.

Percentage took Studs through the barber shop and back into the pool room to wash his hands. Studs said hello, casually, to Frank who always cut his hair; Frank was cutting the hair of some new guy in the neighborhood, who was reading the *Police Gazette* while Frank worked. The pool room was long and narrow; it was like a furnace, and its air was weighted with smoke. Three of the six tables were in use, and in the rear a group of lads sat around a card table, playing poker. The scene thrilled Studs, and he thought of the time he could come in and play pool and call Charley Bathcellar by his first name. He was elated as he washed his hands in the filthy lavatory.

He came out and saw that Barney was around. Barney was a bubble-bellied, dark-haired, middle-aged guy. He looked like a politician, or something similarly important.

"Say, Barney, you think you'll ever amount to much?" asked Barlowe.

"Sure, he's something already," said Swan.

"What?"

"He's a hoisting engineer," said Swan, who accompanied his statement with the appropriate drinking gesture.

"Yeh, he's a first-class hoistin' engineer," said Emmet Kelly, one of Red's brothers.

"He hoists down a barrel of beer a week, don't you, Barney?" said Mickey O'Callaghan.

They laughed. Studs told himself that, goddamn it, they were funny all right.

"You two-bit wiseacres can mind your own business," said Barney.

They all laughed.

"But, Barney, no foolin' . . . I want to ask you a question in all sincerity," said Percentage.

"Save the effort and don't get a brainstorm, hebe," said Barney.

"Why don't you go to work?" asked Percentage.

"Times are hard, jobs are scarce and good men is plentiful," said Barney.

They all laughed.

"Well, anyway, Barney, did you get yer beers last Sunday?" asked Weber.

"Listen, brother! Them Sunday blue laws don't mean nothin' to me," said Barney.

"Nope, I guess you'd get your beer even if the Suffragettes put Prohibition down our necks," said Pat Coady.

"Why, hell! I seen him over in Duffy's saloon last Sunday, soppin' up the beers like there was no law against buyin' drinks on Sunday. He was drinkin' so much, I thought he was gonna get his false teeth drowned in beer," Barlowe said, and they all laughed.

Studs noticed the people passing. Some of them were fat guys and they had the same sleepy look his old man always had when he went for a walk. . . . Those old dopey-looking guys must envy the gang here, young and free like they were. Old Izzy Hersch, the consumptive, went by. He looked yellow and almost like a ghost; he ran the delicatessen-bakery down next to Morty Ascher's tailor shop near the corner of Calumet, but nobody bought anything from him because he had the con, and anyway you were liable to get cockroaches or mice in anything you bought. Izzy looked like he was going to have a funeral in his honor any one of these days. Studs felt that Izzy must envy these guys. They were young and strong, and they were the real stuff; and it wouldn't be long before he'd be one of them and then he'd be the real stuff.

Suddenly he thought of death. He didn't know why. Death just came into his thoughts, dripping black night-gloom. Death put you in a black coffin, like it was going to put Izzy Hersch. It gave you to the gravediggers, and they dumped you in the ground. They shoveled dirt on you, and it thudded, plunked, plump-plumped over you. It would be swell if people didn't have to die; if he, anyway, didn't have to; if he could grow up and be big and strong and tough and the real stuff, like Barlowe was there, and never change. Well, anyway, he had a long time to go.

People kept dribbling by and the guys stood there, barbering in that funny way of theirs.

Lee came along, and the guys asked him why he was getting around so late.

"Oh, my wife invited me to stay home for supper, just for a change, and I thought I'd surprise her and accept the invitation," Lee said.

"Hey, you guys! did you get that? Did you? Lee here said his old woman asked him to come to supper, just to vary the monotony a little, and he did. He actually . . . dined with his old woman," Percentage said.

"Next thing you know he'll be going to work and supportin' her," said Pat Coady.

"Jesus, that's a good one. Hey, Lee, tell me some more . . . I got lots of Irish . . . credulity," said Barney.

They laughed.

"That's a better one," said Lee, pointing to a girl whom

everybody marveled at because they said she was built like a brick out-house.

"She has legs, boy," said Studs, trying to horn back into the conversation.

They didn't pay any attention to him.

"Well, I object!" said Percentage.

"Why?"

"I OBJECT!"

"Why?"

"Goddamnit, it ain't right! I tell you it ain't right that stuff like that moll be wasted, with such good men and true around here . . . I say that it is damn wanton extravagance," said Percentage.

"Hey, Percentage, you shoulda been a Philadelphia lawyer, with them there words you use," said Barlowe.

The guys laughed, and Percentage said he saw the objection was sustained.

Swan, Percentage and Coady had a kidding match about who was the best man. It was interrupted by Barney. An ugly-looking, old-maidish female passed, and Barney said to the three kidders:

"That's your speed!"

They trained their guns on Barney, and told him how dried up he was.

Another dame ambled by, and Percentage repeated his objection, and they kidded each other.

A third dame went by, and Percentage again objected.

"Them's my sentiments," said Fitz, the corner pest.

A good-looking Negress passed.

"Barney, how'd you like that?" Studs asked.

"Never mind, punk! . . . And listen, the niggers ain't as bad as the Irish," said Barney.

"Where's there a difference?" asked Percentage.

"Well, if you ask me, Barney is a combination of eight ball, mick, and shonicker," said McArdle, one of the corner topers.

"And the Irish part is pig-Irish," said Studs.

"The kid's got your number," said Percentage as they all gave Barney some more merry ha-ha's.

Studs felt grown up, all right.

Barney called Studs a goofy young punk. But they all laughed at him. Studs laughed weakly, and hated bloated-belly Barney. He told himself he'd been a damn fool for not having put on his long pants before he came out.

They hung around and talked about the heat and the passing gals. It grew dark, and more lights flashed on. Andy Le Gare came along. He spoke to Studs, but Studs didn't answer him; Studs turned to Barlowe, and said the punk had wheels in his head. Barlowe said yeh; he remembered him in his diaper days down around Forty-seventh; but his brother George was a nice guy, and a scrapper. Studs again felt good, because Barlowe had talked to him like one equal to another. Andy stopped before Hirschfield's grocery store, and started erasing the chalked announcement. He rubbed out the lower part of the B on the brick butter announcement, and stood off to laugh in that idiotic way of his. The guys encouraged the punk. They talked about baseball. Swan spilled some gab about the races. Then he told of what he had seen at the Johnson-Willard and Willard-Moran fights. He said that Willard was a ham, and that Fred Fulton would mow him down if they ever got yellow Willard in the same ring with the Minnesotan. Studs said the Irishman Jim Coffey was pretty good. Swan said he was a cheese. He said the best of them all, better than Fulton even, was Gunboat Smith, who had the frog, Carpentier, licked that time in London or Paris or wherever they fought. They wondered what they would do, and talked about the heat. Barney suggested seeing the girlies, and they said o. k. Barlowe said he couldn't go. They asked why.

"I still got my dose," he said.

They told him it was tough, and he wanted to take care of it. Coady asked him if it was bad.

"It's started again," he said casually.

"Well, be careful," Coady said.

The other lads piled into a hack, and were off. Studs watched them go, wide-eyed with admiration and envy, and yet quite disappointed. Then he watched Barlowe limp down the street, a big husky guy. He thought of the time when he'd be able to pile into a hack and go with the lads. He thought of Barlowe. He was afraid of things like that, and yet he wished he could stand on the corner and say he had it. Well, it wouldn't be long now before he'd be the big-time stuff.

Davey Cohen, Tommy Doyle, Haggerty, Red Kelly and Killarney happened along. Killarney had a pepper cellar, and they went over to the park to look for Jews and throw pepper in their eyes. Over in the park, Studs saw a pretty nurse, and he started objecting that molls like that should walk around and not have guys taking care of them; it was a lot of good stuff gone to waste, he repeated, and the kids all laughed, because it was a good wisecrack.

III

Studs and Paulie walked south along Prairie Avenue, eating the last of the candy. The candy came from the famous raid on Schreiber's ice cream parlor. Schreiber's place was between Prairie and Indiana on Fifty-eighth. Schreiber was a good guy, but you know he liked his nooky, and he was always mixed up with some woman or other. They caught up with him. One day when Studs was walking down Fifty-eighth Street, he saw two dicks taking the guy away. The bunch found out, through Red Kelly, whose old man was a police sergeant, that Schreiber was in on a white slavery rap. Three-Star Hennessey discovered that the back door of the candy store wasn't locked, and all the kids in the neighborhood raided the place. For five days they were filling up on sodas, having fights with ice cream and whipped cream, carting away candy. They stole wagons from little kids, and bikes, and carted the stuff to George Kahler's basement. It was a swell feed they had. Most of them couldn't eat supper for a week. But with so many hogging it, the loot didn't last as long as it should have. Anyway, it was a time to remember for your grandchildren. They talked about it, and laughed.

"Well, it's August already," Paulie said.

"Yeh, Goddamn it!"

"I wonder what school I'll go to next year?" Paulie said.

"Can't you go back to St. Patrick's?" asked Studs.

"Jesus, I don't think so. And if I did get back, they probably wouldn't pass me anyway . . . Say, why in hell is school?" asked Paulie.

Studs shrugged his shoulders and cursed school.

"Say, why don't you bring your old lady up to see Bernadette," said Studs.

"Maybe I will. Hell, St. Patrick's gets more holidays and is out sooner in June than the public schools. Only I got bounced out of there three times already," said Paulie.

"Well, maybe you can break the record," said Studs.

"That's something," said Paulie.

They walked along. Paulie sniped a butt and lit it.

"Doesn't Iris live here?" said Studs, pointing at a red brick, three-story building.

"Yeh, and I'd like to bump into her," Paulie said.

"Me, too," said Studs.

Studs suddenly resented Paulie. Paulie couldn't fight as well as he but got more girls, and knew what it was all about.

Iris, fourteen, bobbed-haired, blue-eyed, innocent with a sunny smile, walked out of the building. She had a body too old for her years; the legs were nice and her breasts were already well-formed.

Iris was glad to see them. Paulie asked her how was

tricks. She said what tricks. Paulie said just tricks. She said
he was naughty-naughty. She flung lascivious looks at
them, and Studs was thrilled as he had never been thrilled
by Lucy. He shifted his weight from foot to foot, and studied the sky. Then he became absorbed in his shoes. They
were high ones, scuffed and dirty, very much like army
shoes. Paulie asked how about it. She said her mother was
home. Paulie said they could go over to the park. She said
no, because she had to help her old woman clean house.
She cursed her mother, glibly. Hearing a girl call her
mother names was different from hearing a guy, and it
shocked Studs. Paulie asked how about it. She said some
other afternoon. She told Studs she especially wanted him
to come and see her some time, because she had never met
him before and everybody said nice things about him. She
looked at him in that way of hers, and said she'd be nice to
him. Then she tripped toward Fifty-fifth Street, and they
watched her wriggle along. They had a discussion about
the way girls wriggled along. Studs said the one who had
them all beat at wriggling was Helen Borax. Paulie said Iris
was no slouch though. Studs wondered if girls wriggled on
purpose, and how about decent ones. He told this to Paulie,
and added that he hadn't ever noticed if his sister did or
not. Paulie said all girls had to wriggle when they walked,
and he guessed there was nothing wrong with it. He said
that anything a girl did was o.k. with him, as long as she
was good-looking.

They met Weary at Fifty-eighth Street. Weary had his
long jeans on. He looked at Studs; Studs sort of glowered
back. Paulie suggested that it was foolish not to shake
hands and settle old scores. They shook.

Studs tried to be a little friendly. He asked:

"What you been doing?"

"Workin' in an office downtown," said Weary.

"Off today?" asked Paulie.

"I took the day off, and my old lady got sore and yelled

at me. I had a big scrap with the family. The gaffer was home and he tried to pitch in, too, and my sister Fran, she got wise. They noticed that my hip pocket was bulgin' a little. And when I leaned down to pick somethin' up, they saw my twenty-two. They shot their gabs off till I got sick of listenin' to them, and I got sore and cursed them out. I told them just what they could do without mincing my words, and they all gaped at me like I was a circus. The ole lady jerked on the tears, and started blessing herself, and Fran got snotty, like she never heard the words before, and she bawled, and the old man said he'd bust my snoot, but he knew better than try it. So I tells them they could all take a fast and furious, flyin', leapin' jump at Sandy Claus, and I walks out, and I'll be damned if I go home. Maybe I might try stickin' somebody up," he said.

They were shocked, but they admired Weary tremendously. They acted casual and gave him some advice. He showed them his rusty twenty-two, and said he needed bullets. Paulie said it might be a little dangerous carrying a loaded gat around, but Weary didn't care. Studs wished that he could walk dramatically out of the house like Weary did; he told himself that he might some day. Paulie asked Weary what he'd been doing, and Weary said he had been hangin' out at White City; he'd picked up a couple of nice janes there. One of them was eighteen and didn't live at home, and wanted him to live with her. They looked at Weary. Weary was a real adventurous kid, after all was said and done, even if he was something of a bastard. Suddenly Weary left, walking toward Fifty-seventh. They watched him. He met a girl . . . it was Iris . . . and the two of them disappeared in her entrance way.

"Well, I say she's no good," Studs said.

"Well, I'll be damned," said Paulie, scratching his head.

They looked at each other, knowingly, expressing with their faces what even the lousiest words they could think of to call Iris couldn't express.

"Some day I'm gonna up and bust that jane right in her snoot," said Paulie.

"And a guy I licked . . . I ought to hang a couple more on him," Studs said.

"Yeh," said Paulie.

Studs wished to hell there were more swear words in the list so he could use them to curse the world.

IV

Studs had stayed in the bathroom too long, as he was staying most of these days. The old man bellowed that dinner was ready. Studs came out, feeling relieved. He muttered a hasty act of contrition, promising God and the Blessed Virgin that he would try his hardest not to break the sixth commandment by thought, word or deed.

Sunday dinner of roast beef and mashed potatoes was already on the table; the family was seated.

As Studs sat down, the old lady said that they ought to say grace once in a while, thanking God that they were well off and happy and so much better off than most families. The old man agreed, and he said patriarchially:

"Well, Martin, you say grace!"

"Grace!" said Martin.

They laughed. Then Loretta said grace. The two parents insisted that hereafter grace would be said before and after each meal.

"I say this: if you keep God in the home, active and real, you'll have a happier home and can get along better in all you do," the old man said oracularly.

"You say the truth," echoed Mrs. Lonigan.

The old man carved the meat. He spoke to Studs as he sliced. He asked Studs why he was late for dinner. He said Studs was always late for dinner. Everybody else got to the bathroom early enough, so that they could be at the table when dinner was announced. He said that he spent good money for food, and that Studs' mother slaved over a hot stove so that they could have a decent meal. He and the mother both had some right to demand gratitude and respect for this. Studs said that he didn't see nothing wrong in having stopped to wash his hands; and his father, starting into rag-chewing, put Studs in a mood of opposition, made him feel that he was in the right, made him believe that he had delayed only to wash his hands, and that his father was being inconsiderate and un-understanding. The old man said that there had been plenty of time before to wash his hands. Studs said that he didn't see why there was any kicking. He was at the table now, and nothing had happened by his stopping to wash his hands. The old man told him to suppose that the meat had gotten cold. But it didn't get cold, Studs said. Lonigan told him that it might have gotten cold. Frances said that she wished the Sunday quarreling could be stopped. She was tired of sitting down to a Sunday dinner and being forced to listen to this interminable ragging. Old man Lonigan said that there wouldn't be no quarreling if everybody did what was right. He said that he was boss of the household, and that as long as he remained boss of the household there were certain rules that would be observed, and one was that everybody must be at the table on time. It got Studs sore. The old man was always pulling that stuff. Studs said that so far as he was concerned, he wouldn't eat Sunday dinner if there was going to be the same fighting all the time. Frances said that she agreed with Studs. Mrs. Lonigan said that the name was William. The old man said that they could take or leave the rules of the household. Martin asked for meat. Loretta said that the dinner would be cold if it wasn't served soon. She said that there was awful much talking. The old man told her to be more respectful because little children should honor their parents and be seen and not heard. Passing Martin's filled plate down, he assured them that he was a good father. He said he asked very little from them. Frances and Studs looked tiredly at each other, and didn't say anything. They awaited their plates, and then they concentrated on eating.

"This is fine, mama," the old man said, jamming roast beef into his mouth.

"I like it," said Martin.

"Any more for anyone?" said the old man.

"Me," said Martin.

"You got hookworm," the old man said, taking Martin's plate.

Finally, the old boy said, smiling expansively:

"Well, I'm filled. I ate my share."

The others said they had had their fill.

Coffee and ice cream were served, and they talked lazily. The mother changed the stream of conversation, and said:

"William, I wish that you wouldn't be staying out so late."

"Yeh, Bill, we told you about that once before," the old man said.

Bill told himself that he was almost fifteen, and that he ought to have some rights. But what the hell could a guy say to an old man like his? He wished he had an old man like Johnny O'Brien did.

"And, William, I know you don't like me to mention this, but you're still young yet, and can't decide. I do wish you would pray to ask God if you have a vocation or not, and next month start in and make the nine first Fridays. Now that is the least you can do for Almighty God who sacrificed His only begotten Son for you on the cross of Calvary."

"All right," Studs said, knowing the best thing to do with his parents was to agree with them and let it go at that. His mother harped so much on it that he thought maybe he did have a vocation. But he tried not to think of it, when he could do so, without putting the thought out of his head deliberately, because, well, there was . . . Lucy.

"Now, Mary, you know the boy hasn't a vocation. You're putting things in his head, and maybe you'll go and make a priest out of him when I'll be needing him, and then he is not meant for the priesthood, and you know, Mary, it is as bad to send one in that hasn't a vocation as it is to keep away one who really has the call. You know, Mary, there's many the unhappy priest who don't belong in the ranks and is there because his good mother unthinkingly made a priest out of him."

"Patrick, you know I'm not doing anything of the sort. I'm only trying to put the boy in the right spirit, so he can decide whether or not he has the call."

"But, Mary . . ."

It started them off again. This time Loretta interrupted the argument to say that she had seen Studs, she meant *William*, hitching on a motor truck. The old lady shuddered, blessed herself and called on Jesus, Mary and Joseph. The old man said it was dangerous, and that Bill ought to be careful and try and have his fun doing less dangerous things. It might seem brave to hitch on trucks, but it wouldn't if Bill came home with a broken leg. Studs glowered at Loretta, and told her she would do well by minding her own business. He was reprimanded for this. Then Loretta said that she had also seen him taking a puff of that terrible Tommy Doyle's cigarette over in Carter Playground the other day. The old lady cried, and spoke of the proverb: tell me your friends, and I'll tell you who you are. She said William was too well educated to associate with such toughs. She said that smoking was a sin against God. Studs asked why; he said that men smoked. The old man said that smoking stunted a boy's growth, ruined his health, disrupted his moral sense, and was against . . . nature. He lit a long stogy. Frances said smoking was nasty, and Studs said nobody asked her for her two cents. Mrs. Lonigan said

that it might give him TB. Studs kept wishing they would
can the sermon. He asked them to cut it out, and he was re-
minded of the commandment to honor thy father and thy
mother. He said he had some rights. The blah went back
and forth.

When they arose from the table, grace was forgotten.

The old man went into the parlor, and put Cal Stewart's
account of how Uncle Josh joined the Grangers on the Victrola. He listened to it and laughed heartily. Then he made
a decision, and called Studs into the parlor alone.

"Bill, don't you think you ought to keep going to confession regularly?" he said.

"Yeh."

"When's the last time you were there?"

"May," said Studs.

It was April, but he could get away with telling the old
man it was May.

"At St. Patrick's you had your sodality to remind you
and keep you going regular. Now, it's up to you, and you
got to make the effort yourself . . . Now, Bill, I want you to
promise me you'll go next Saturday," the old man said.

Studs promised.

A pause.

The old man's face reddened. He started to speak,
paused, blushed and said:

"Bill, you're gettin' older now, an' . . . well, there's
somethin' I want to tell you. You see, well, it's this way, after a manner of speaking, you see, now the thing is quite
delicate after a manner of speaking but you see, I'm your
father and it's a father's duty to instruct the son, and you
see now if you get a little itch . . . well you don't want to
start . . . rubbin' yourself . . . you know what I mean . . .
because such things are against nature, and they make a
person weak and his mind weak and are liable even to
make him crazy, and they are a sin against God; and then

too, Bill . . . I wish you'd sort of wait a little while before you started in smokin' . . ."

Silence. The boy and the father looking out at the lazy day, which was suddenly robbed of sunlight by a float of clouds. Studs felt self-conscious; he was ashamed of his body; he needed air and sunlight. Maybe if he ran he'd forget his body, or like it again, because running was good.

Studs promised not to smoke. Why the hell not? The old man would maybe give him a little extra spending money. The old man was glad, shook hands with him, as man to man, and gave Studs six bits. Studs pocketed the dough and got his cap. The old man read the Sunday paper. Studs went out. He felt better in the open air, and walked along, snappy; he wasn't so ashamed of his body. He felt the seventy-five cents in his jeans. After a short debate with his conscience he lit a fag, and let it hang from the corner of his mouth. He told himself that he was tough, all right. He arranged his cap at an angle. He thought about Iris, and he wished her old lady was out, and he could go up there this afternoon. He remembered what the old man said about that thing making you crazy, and it bothered him. He tried his shutter trick to get rid of the thoughts, but it was hard. He walked fast and kept thinking his mind was a shutter, closing on these thoughts, until finally he got rid of them. He went over in front of the pool room, and spent the afternoon smoking cigarettes and listening to the lads talking.

V

One afternoon, when Studs missed the guys from Fifty-eighth Street, he wandered back around Indiana Avenue and met Helen Shires. She said hello to him, but he felt self-conscious, and said hello back looking away and watching the clouds. He noticed some iodine on her left hand. He could ask what was the matter, and that would

keep the talk off of himself not being around there any
more. He asked her what had happened.

"Oh, I got a sprained thumb. It was that damn Andy Le
Gare. He got fresh, and one day came up and tickled the
palm of my hand. Well, I'm not letting anybody try and get
dirty around me, so I hauled off on him," she said.

"You hung one on 'im, huh? Good!"

"Yeah, he started to hit me back, but I hit him again, and
he changed his mind. But I sprained my thumb, and it's
pretty sore," she said.

"Gee, that's good, not the thumb, but your hanging a
couple on goofy Andy," said Studs, because he couldn't
think of anything else to say.

She asked him where he had been keeping himself and
how he was getting along. He did not seem as confused
now, and he started bragging about the swell time he had
been having. She invited him to her sister's playhouse,
where it would be cooler and they could sit there and chew
the fat.

"It's been dead around here," she said.

"Yeh!" said Studs, glad that the street was dead, because
it showed that he had been a wise guy in shaking his tail
from Indiana.

"I been having a swell time," he said.

"Well, I been swimming nearly every day. But my
mother keeps naggin'. You know how a kid's old lady is.
They want to do what's right, but they never understand a
kid," she said.

"My old lady wants me to be a priest. Can you imagine
a guy like me bein' a priest?" said Studs as he lit a cigarette, just as Swan lit his cigarettes in front of the pool
room.

Helen said that she wasn't getting on so well with the
family, because they always kicked that she wasn't like
other girls; they said she was too old to go on being a
tomboy. Her old lady wanted her to do like other girls and

give up playing ball, so that she could pay more attention
to other things like studying music, dancing and dramatics.
She said for her part, if she would be allowed to play basketball on the Englewood high school team, music, dramatics and dancing could all go hang. She said she was fed up
on her old lady's nagging.

"But can you imagine a guy like me bein' a priest?" repeated Studs.

"The girls around here are too soft and primpy; they're
cry babies. And they are always talking, talking about boys
and kisses. And some of 'em like Helen Borax are too
damn catty for me," Helen said.

"Well, it seems to me that the whole neighborhood
around here has gone dead. Now aroun' Fifty-eighth and
Prairie we got a real gang," said Studs.

"Well, I don't like them," she said.

Studs shot the butt he'd been smoking. He stocked his
mush with tobacco. She smiled and asked him how long
he'd been chewing. Trying to be matter of fact, he said that
he'd been chewing for a long time. He rose, and walking to
the window he let the brown juice fly. It was a pretty good
performance; he was learning, all right.

He came back and asked her if she could imagine a guy
like him bein' a priest. She said he wasn't such a bad guy
at that.

"But can you imagine a guy like me bein' a priest?" he
said.

They sat. They didn't have much more to say. Studs had
feelings he would have liked to talk about, but he didn't
have words, just those melting feelings that went through
him and made him want Lucy more than he wanted a drink
of water when he was thirsty. Helen would have liked to
talk to him as they used to talk when he hung around Indiana. The words just weren't in either of them any more. After a while she tried to speak, telling him that he was being
a fool hanging around Fifty-eighth Street where the bunch

made a bum out of everybody. She said a guy didn't have
to be a sissy or yellow not to be a bum like those louses
were. She didn't like them, or like the way they picked on
Jews, and beat kids up, and always got in trouble. The
thing the matter with them, she said, was that they thought
every night was Hallowe'en.

Studs said that she just didn't understand them, because
they were great guys, and they had a lot of pep, and
weren't a bunch of mopes. And they always stuck together
and none of them were yellow. They were awake and
lively; they weren't deadnecks.

"If I was you, Studs, I'd can 'em. First thing you know
they'll have you in a jam, and you'll be ridin' in the paddy
wagon."

"Naw," said Studs, letting tobacco juice fly through the
opened window.

He thought about riding in a paddy wagon. It was like
thinking of fighting, a lot of fun; but the real stuff wasn't
always so swell.

"Well, Studs, you'll maybe find out for yourself. I like
you, Studs, and you're a nice kid, but for your own good,
I'd say that you ought to shake them bastards. Red Kelly's
nothin' but a rat, and Tommy Doyle, he's no good. Why, he
used to get drunk when he was only in the sixth grade, and
last summer he used to run for beer for the workmen who
were over at the Prairie Theatre, and he'd drink with them;
and he always goes around with older guys like Jimmy Devlin, getting girls in basements, and not caring at all if they
say yes or not, but just going ahead. No wonder he got
thrown out of St. Patrick's and Carter School. The only
nice kid in the bunch is Paulie, but he won't be long, hanging around with those rats."

"They're all right," insisted Studs.

"And I hear Weary's around again," said she.

"Yeh, him and me made up," said Studs.

"Well, watch him; he's dangerous, and I wouldn't trust him. He's a dirty . . ."

"I don't know. I don't like him particularly, and if he ever gets noisy with me, well, I'll hang a couple more on him, but you gotta admit that he's one guy that don't let nobody run him. He don't even let his old man run him . . . Why, he beat it from home," Studs said.

"Yeh, I heard about it. He lives in basements and generally has peanuts for supper," said she.

"But he's his own boss."

"But that's all boloney. He's going straight for the pen. You mark my word. Then a hell of a lot of bossing himself he'll do," she said.

Studs said he didn't know.

They sat. Silence, and a feeling of artificiality for both of them.

Helen asked him if he had met that Iris that was around.

"I met her on the street with Paulie. That's all," he said.

Studs wanted to say he was going up there, but he didn't know how she'd take it. He remembered the time Iris had given him and Paulie a lot of hot air because she wanted Weary alone. Reilley! He hissed to himself. But maybe Iris didn't know he'd cleaned on Weary. Well, when she did, and she got to know him, she wouldn't have nothing to do with Weary. When she got to know him, well, you just watch his dust. If he had to, he'd take a few more pokes at Reilley . . . only, well, he wasn't afraid of another fight, but then, well, he'd licked the guy once, even if he did get the insides of his face all cut, and a shiner. Iris would . . . understand him. Now that was a discovery. The trouble that always bothered him was that nobody understood him. Well, maybe she would. Maybe that thing was so that fellows and girls could get to understand each other. Maybe there was more to it than just getting girls and doing it because you were curious, and because then you could brag before other guys about it. He wanted to tell Helen about this thought, but he guessed he hadn't better.

"Say, did you find anything more out about that house on Fifty-seventh Street?" asked Studs.

"Lucy's heard something about Iris, and asked me. Lucy still likes you," Helen said.

"Yeh," said Studs, getting quite misty.

A pause.

"Say, do you think there'd be anything doing at that place now? Maybe if we could climb on the porch," said Studs.

Helen shrugged her shoulders.

A pause.

"Is your mother or anybody home?" he asked.

"Why?" Helen asked.

She looked at him; she guessed what was in his mind.

"No," she said. She added, "Lucy really likes you."

Lucy! She seemed quite far away from him now. At times he liked her, and at times he tried to pretend to himself that he didn't. He wanted to tell it all to Helen, and the words choked in his throat. *The time they sat in the tree!* Helen said she could fix things up for him with Lucy. He wanted to say go ahead, but something stopped him, and he told her never mind. He could have kicked himself in the tail all the way around the block for it, but that was what he said and he didn't know why. And it was all on account of that punk, Danny O'Neill. Well, things would turn out all right in the end. Lucy liked him, and it might do her good if she did a little worrying because he acted like he didn't like her. She would come around to him. After all he was STUDS LONI-GAN. He tried to keep Helen talking about Lucy, and he sat there, as if he wasn't interested, spitting tobacco juice like sixty. He told Helen that Lucy was all right, but he didn't think he was interested in girls any more. Helen said, "YEAH!" Silence. Studs tried to explain that he really wasn't, and he got himself all mixed up. Helen didn't answer him. They sat in silence.

"But say, didn't any of the guys find out about that place?" he said.

He looked at her.

She glanced away.

"I don't like to always be talking about those things. Guys always start to talk about them with me, and then, well, they get fresh and start asking me, or scratching the palm of my hand," she said.

She talked to him as if she was talking to Andy Le Gare or somebody else.

Silence. Then she asked him was he going to school. He lied that he wasn't. He guessed he couldn't talk to Helen as he used to. They looked at each other, realizing that they were changed. They looked at each other.

She said he ought to go to high school, because he would be a football star. He said he didn't know.

They sat. He got up, and she said she had to go in and take a bath. He said he'd come in and wait, as long as no-body was home. She gave him a dirty look and said he hadn't better.

She walked out to the front with him. He limped, just like he had seen Barlowe limping. She asked him what was wrong. He said he'd sprained a muscle or something, slid-ing in an indoor game.

He left her, and walked down toward Fifty-eighth. He thought of Lucy, and Iris, and Helen, and . . . then Lucy. He pretended that he was with Lucy over in the park in their tree, with the wind in his hair, and her sitting, swinging her legs, himself watching her, kissing her, her telling him he was a great guy, and she liked him, and was sorry for what had happened, themselves sitting there all afternoon with no one near them, and the air so cool in their hair. And maybe she'd see it was all right for them to . . . well, it might make them understand each other better.

He thought he heard her calling him, and he started his limping again. He turned sharply. There was no one behind him. He dropped his head and walked along. He tried to make himself feel good by telling himself how tough he was.

Lucy, I love you.

VI

"What'll we do?" asked Tommy Doyle.

"I don't know," answered Benny Taite.

"Uh!" muttered Davey Cohen.

"I'm pretty tired of sockin' Jew babies, or we might scout a few," said Red Kelly.

"Me, too," said Davey.

"Well, what I'd like is a glass of beer," said Tommy.

"You always do," said Davey, as he sniped a butt from the curb-edge.

The gang of them were in front of the Fifty-eighth Street elevated station.

"Ope!" laughed Studs Lonigan, pointing to Vinc Curley and Phil Rolfe, who came along Fifty-eighth Street from Calumet.

As they approached, Weary Reilley commanded:

"Commere!"

"Say, goofy, you got any dough?" Studs asked.

"Yeh," said Vinc Curley like an absent-minded dunce.

"Let me see it," said Kenny Killarney.

Vinc said he had made a mistake. He didn't have any money. They ragged him. Weary sneered, grabbed Vinc's arm, and told the guys to frisk him. Studs grabbed Phil, and the gang got six bits out of the two of them. They ran, the victims ran after them, bawling, but they were ditched in an alley.

The group ganged into Joseph's Ice Cream Parlor at Fifty-fifth and Prairie and had sodas. The bill was more

than their six bits, and they didn't see why they should pay
anyway. They figured out how they would make a dash for
the door, and Kenny told them to leave and say he had the
bill. He told Weary to hold the door for him. To stall time,
Kenny fooled around the candy case, took a couple of Her-
shey bars, and ordered some mixed chocolates. While
Joseph was weighing the chocolates Kenny dashed. He and
Weary caught up with the guys, who were crossing the
north drive of Garfield Boulevard. They all tore down
Prairie, and got away easily. They returned toward Fifty-
eighth Street, laughing over it. After a lot of squabbling,
they divided the dough evenly. They wondered what to do.
Kenny and Davey goofed over a cigarette butt. Studs and
Benny Taite sparred. Weary told some new dirty jokes.
Paulie Haggerty then asked Weary about school, but Weary
said the hell with it. He pointed to the objects in the street
that symbolized school for him. He said the family had
taken him back home, and wouldn't make him do what he
didn't want to, because they were scared to hell that he'd
bust out and become a holdup man. Studs thought it would
be a good thing to run away from home, but felt that he
never would. They wondered what they would do. Two
kids came along, and they were stopped and asked where
they came from. The kids said Fifty-ninth and Wentworth.
Red Kelly said it was an Irish neighborhood and all right,
so they let the kids go. They wondered what to do, and
Kenny thought he'd like to play his cat trick. The last time
he had played it, he had caught a couple of cats and
dropped them from a roof, and one cat had almost landed
square on a cop. The cat trick was best, though, when he
could get a dog, and cart the cats to a third floor or a roof
and then sick the dog on them so they'd have to jump.
There were no cats to be found, so Kenny said he'd like to
rob ice boxes. They trailed over to a building at Fifty-
eighth and Michigan, and on the way picked up Johnny
O'Brien. Three buildings stood in a row facing Fifty-eighth

and extending to the Michigan Avenue corner. There was a narrow walk, and a few feet of dirt in the back, and the porches extended all the way along, with no banisters dividing one from another. It was easy for the guys to split up, and for each group to take a floor, while Davey stood downstairs and Johnny O'Brien hung outside in the alley to give jiggs. They got milk, tomatoes, eggs, catsup, and butter. Kenny got most of the loot, because Kenny had a style of his own. Studs got one bottle of milk; he had been a little leery about getting caught, and in a hurry, or he could have hooked some tomatoes. He whewed with relief when they all got safely over to the vacant lot at Fifty-eighth and Indiana. No one was hungry, so they wondered what they would do with their haul. Kenny lammed a bottle of milk against the wall of the three-story gray brick house where O'Connell lived. Red Kelly said it was a shot for the lanky bastard. They flung the other bottles of milk against the wall, and watched the milk trickling into the sandy prairie. Johnny O'Brien saw goofy Andy Le Gare. Johnny flung a tomato, and it smacked Andy square in the mush. Wiping his face with a dirty handkerchief, and stuttering curses, Andy came over. He socked Johnny, who was a year older and bigger than him. They fought and Johnny gave Andy three dirty socks. He was too big for Le Gare, but the fool kept on fighting, getting himself smacked. Benny Taite suddenly gave jiggers. The janitor from the O'Connell building and the one from the building they had looted were coming across the prairie after them.

"The Germans are comin'!" Paulie yelled.

"Boushwah!" Kenny yelled at the janitors.

He flung his last tomato and it caught one of the janitors in the neck. The other guys flung their eggs and tomatoes, and then rocks. They legged it, yelling like a band of movie Indians. They ditched the janitors around Fifty-fifth, and marched on toward Fifty-third. They laughed, and Weary said they could have licked the lousy foreigners anyway, only it was more fun getting shagged. They decided to get the two of them on Hallowe'en. Kenny said every day was Hallowe'en. They laughed. Kenny said they were in little Jewrusalem now, and they could probably catch a couple of Jew babies.

Two hooknoses, about Studs' size, did come along. Andy and Johnny O'Brien, the two youngest in the gang, stopped the shonickers.

"Sock one of 'em, Andy," Studs said.

"Sa-ay, Christ Killer!" Johnny said to his man.

"We ain't done nothin'," the guy pleaded.

"Where you from?" asked Red Kelly.

"Fifty-first and Prairie."

"That's a Jew neighborhood," said Red.

"No!"

Red called him a liar, and said that all Jew neighborhoods were a disgrace, and that was enough.

Andy and Johnny each shoved one of the Jews.

They started to mosey on.

"No you don't, big-nose!" said Red, catching Johnny's man.

Weary grabbed the other.

"You're the guy that got tough with me, ain't you?" said Andy.

"I ain't never seen you before."

"Don't let 'im get out of it, Andy. Take 'im back in the alley," said Davey.

The two Jews were dragged back in the alley.

"Now, if you two sons of Abraham ain't yellow like the rest of your race, fight," said Red Kelly.

They said they didn't want to fight.

Red said they had to.

"Go ahead. These kids are smaller than you and you'll get a fair fight as long as you don't do no dirty work."

They begged to be let off.

"Oh, you don't want to fight. You're yellow. Well, you dirty yellow . . . There, take that," said Andy.

They heard the smack. It was a beaut.

"And this for you, Jewboy," said Johnny.

Johnny's man fell to his knees.

Benny Taite was behind him.

"Take that for killin' Christ," said Benny.

Johnny dragged him to his feet.

"That a boy. One eye's closed, Johnny kid," Davey said, encouraging Johnny.

Johnny's victim was down and wouldn't get up. Kenny got a few yards off, made noises, whistled, and sang:

> *Fire, fire, false alarm*
> *Baby da-dumped*
> *In papa's arm . . .*
> *Fire, fire, false alarm.*

He came up whizzing, snorting, yelling that he was the hose cart.

"House on fire! House on fire! House on fire!"

They laughed.

"Now it's out!" he said.

They laughed.

Johnny's victim tried to wipe his face with his handkerchief. Davey booted him. He rolled back, got up, and ran. Red tore after him, and aimed a good swift kick, but missed and fell on his ear. He cursed the Jew.

Andy's victim had been fighting back all the while. It was a good fight, even, with them trading sock for sock. Then the fellow's weight began to tell. Andy was breathing heavy, and his punches were lumbering ones. Studs laughed, and gave the guy a kick in the pants. The fellow turned, and as he did, Andy got him smack in the eye.

"Jesus, Andy, you got his eye swellin' like a balloon," Benny Taite yelled.

"Hit 'im again, he's only a shonicker," said Davey.

They gave the guy the clouts, and left him moaning in the alley. Kenny ran back, frisked the guy, and took a pearl-handled pocketknife.

They walked on over to the park, and Andy and Johnny gloried in congratulations. Red said they would make Andy their mascot and let him start fights with hebes, because he was small, and then they all could pitch in and finish the job.

"Now it will be a perfect day, if we can only catch a couple of shines," said Weary.

They all wished that.

They passed the duck-pond at Fifty-third, but didn't try any rough stuff there because two cops watched them. Over in the ball field they parked under a massive oak. They played pull-the-peg, and told dirty jokes while the knife passed from left to right.

The park spread away from them in a wide field of grass, shrunken and slowly withering through August, with many spots where the grass was worn down and dirt showed. The baseball diamonds started catercorner from them and rimmed the park, around to the field house that was off toward their left. A scabby line of bushes extended almost completely around the park, and behind the shrubbery the dazzling, shimmering sky fell. Fellows and kids were scattered about playing, some so far away that they seemed like white-shirted dots, and their voices like muffled echoes. About a block to their left, and near the field house, a gang of older fellows lazed under a tree, watching a guy in a sweat shirt lam out flies to four or five guys and a kid. The kid was young Danny O'Neill. For a kid he was a sweet ball player, and it was swell to watch him making cupped catches, spearing drives over his shoulder as if it didn't take any effort, making one-handed running catches, snapping up line drives at his shoestrings. He was a perfect judge of fly balls, and he

never overran the pill. They talked, deciding that Danny
was cracked, but he was a damn good player. Andy said
he wasn't so good. They ragged Andy, because O'Neill
was one of the few punks in the neighborhood who had
beaten Andy up. Kenny halted the knife game while he
mimicked Danny walking along Fifty-eighth Street, un-
conscious, with his goggles stuck in the box scores. They
laughed, because Kenny was a scream when he took
someone off like that. The knife game ended, with Andy
the loser. He squawked when they hammered the burnt
match deeply into the ground, and refused to pull the peg.
They told him he had to, or get his pants taken off and
then dropped in the lagoon at the other end of the park.
Andy bent down and dug his teeth in the ground. He
gnawed around, paused to squawk, and finally came up
with the match and his face smeared with dirt. They kidded Andy because he was of French extraction, and
Kenny punned the word French. Andy missed the pun and
defended the French, and that was funny. Red Kelly said
that Andy wasn't a frog; he was a kike, and his old man
ate kosher, gefilte fish and noodles. Kenny said Andy was
playing a joke on them, because his old man was that
sheeny fox-in-the-bush they always saw on Fifty-eighth
Street. Studs asked Andy when his old man was going to
wash his whiskers. Andy said his old man was the best
old man in the world. Red said he couldn't be, because he
belonged to a labor union. Red said his old man was a police sergeant, and he was always saying labor unions were
a disturbance of the peace, because they destroyed property. "That's what my old man, and what High Collars always says," Studs interrupted. Andy repeated that he had
the best old man in the world. Davey said Andy meant the
best noodle-soup drinker. Andy said he'd get his big
brother after them, and his big brother was tough because
he had been in the ring, and fought a draw with Charlie
White.

Shadows slowly spread and softened over the park, and the scene was like a grass idyll. They sat there talking. Studs watched Danny turn, run with his back to the ball, face around, and catch a fly simply and easily; it was pretty. Studs said Danny was good and that every Sunday he played with men. O'Brien said yeh, but he had a lot of splinters in his roof.

They sat. Kenny said that if Andy was to be their mascot, he'd have to be initiated.

"No! No, I won't have no initiation," Andy protested.

They persuaded him, saying it was an easy initiation. All he had to do was to play letter fly. He said he didn't know nothing about no letter fly, and didn't want to play it. They called him yellow, so he said he'd play.

They all stood around in a circle. The object was for everyone to say some word with fly at the end of it. When you couldn't think of another word, without hesitating, you had to say letter fly. Andy asked what happened then, and Kenny said nothing. The one who said letter fly lost, that was all. But if you didn't play letter fly, you couldn't belong to the Fifty-eighth Street bunch.

"Spanish fly!" Kenny started off.

They laughed because Kenny would always think of something like that to say.

"Shoo fly," said Studs.

"Horse fly," said Johnny.

"Foul fly," said Red.

Andy was slow. They said hurry up.

"You gotta be honest. If you're not and you cheat you can't come around with us," Red said.

"Big fly," said Andy.

The game went around again. By the time it was Andy's turn, the flies were pretty well exhausted. He stood there, his efforts to think plain on his face. They ragged him, and told him to play fair. They gave him thirty to think of some fly. He couldn't. He said:

"Letter fly."

"Come on, guys. Let ur fly!" said Kenny.

The others said let ur fly.

They all let ur fly, and Andy got so many pastes in the mush he was dizzy.

He started to protest.

"You told us to do it, didn'cha?" said Red.

"I didn't neither."

"Didn'cha say let ur fly?"

They had him there. He walked away bawling, and turned to say:

"I'll get my brother after you."

"Go on home, punk, while you're all together," said Weary.

After Andy had gone, Studs pondered and said:

"He's the biggest dumbsock I ever saw."

Red explained why he was so dumb, and Studs glanced aside to blush, because he remembered what his old man had said about going crazy.

They sat. Paulie talked of Iris, and it made Studs restless. They all got that way. Finally they couldn't stand it any longer, so they told Paulie to talk about something else. They said all he ever did was talk that way.

"Some day you'll be ruined right by the molls," Red said to Paulie.

Studs sat, wishing, hoping.

It was almost twilight when they started home, and goofy Danny O'Neill was still shagging flies. They spread out, arms on each other's shoulders, and moved along singing:

> *Hail, hail, the gang's all here!*
> *What the hell do we care,*
> *What the hell do we care*
>
> > *now.*

They walked on along the tennis courts on South Park Avenue, talking away. Studs didn't listen to them. He thought of Iris. He prayed that he would get her soon. He had to, because he couldn't think of anything else these days; and even that shutter trick wouldn't work to get the thought out of his mind.

Chapter Seven

I

AFTER leaving Iris', Davey Cohen walked around the neighborhood, brooding, justifying himself. It hurt, and made a guy pretty goddamn sore, being cut cold by Iris when she didn't bar none of the punks or the dumb Irish in the neighborhood. And she had told him no soap. Jew! All the guys were there now, and punks like Andy with them. She had let him stay there while she showed herself off to the guys. She had let him get all anxious, like the rest. Then, Jew! She wouldn't let a kike touch her. If he didn't leave she had threatened to get Studs and Weary to sock him, and they would have, because she had something to give them. Well, he was glad he hadn't touched her. She'd make him sick. He didn't want the left-overs of the Irish and of degenerates like Three-Star Hennessey. Not him. He didn't want the sweetheart of the pig-Irish.

He walked around and pretended. He pretended that he was Studs Lonigan. Then he pretended that he had long pants on, that he wasn't so bowlegged and that his nose wasn't bent like a fishhook. He pretended that he had cleaned up all the tough guys on Fifty-eighth Street. He saw himself in an imaginary fight with Studs Lonigan, Studs rushing him the way he had rushed Red Kelly, waving his left fist up and down, swinging his right one, him sidestepping and sinking snappy rights into Studs' guts and his jaw, and then hooking lefts around and catching Studs in back of the neck. Himself making a monkey out of Studs.

He had been at Iris', and they had shot craps for turns. Studs had been first; then it was his turn. When Studs came out, MMMMMMMMMMMM, he had jumped up, anxious, and gone in, and she had covered herself and called him a dirty Jew.

He walked around and didn't notice where he was going. He enjoyed hating the micks, the lousy Irish. The Irish were dumb. That was why they always had to fight with their fists. They couldn't use their noodle; they didn't have any to use. All they had up there was bone, hambones and cabbage. He thought of himself, so much cleverer than the Irish. The micks were lousy, all right. A race of beer guzzlers, flatfeets, red mugs and boneheads. Why, they even had to take a Jew Christ, and then what did they do but make a dumb Irishman out of him.

He saw all the Irish race personified in the face of Studs Lonigan, and he imagined himself punching that face, cutting it, bloodying the nose, blackening the eyes, mashing it. He had walked out of Iris', and Studs had yelled ope; he's gotta go and peddle clothes for the old man. And the others had said things: Here's your hat. What's your hurry? Where's the fire? Don't be gone long. He had walked out and hadn't said anything. But the Irish! They were all like Lonigan and that lousy Weary Reilley.

He wanted to outwit the whole goddamn gang. Well, he could do that, but he wanted to bust them one and all. First Lonigan. Bam! Then Reilley. Bam again. Then Doyle, Kelly, all of them one right after the other. He wanted to bust them and he was . . . yellow.

But it was more than being yellow. It wasn't his yellowness, it was his feeling. The Irish didn't have any feeling. They had thick hides and fists like hams. Fighting made him sick. When he went with the guys smacking Jews, he sometimes got so sick he felt as if he'd puke. He didn't like it. He put himself off as a battler, and talked big and hard only because he had to. If you went around with the Irish and didn't make yourself out a scrapper, you had one hell of a time. He had to use his noodle even there, so he could get along with them. They didn't know how to do a damn thing but put up their dukes . . . and look for Iris, the dirty . . .

He knew he was . . . yellow. He had gotten himself a rep as a tough guy by using his mouth and getting in with the guys that were tough. He had gotten in with Doyle and Kelly, then with Studs after Studs had taken on the redhead over at Carter Playground, and now that Reilley was coming around he was nosing in with him, too. Well, he could lick some of the guys like Bob Stole, who was heavier than he was, or Benny Taite, or goofy Kenny Killarney. But if anybody ever leaned on Kenny the whole gang would pile on him and send him to the hospital. He was supposed to be as tough as they were; but, well, it was just because a Jew had more gray matter in one little corner of his nut than an Irishman, or a whole gang of them, had in their whole damn heads. Yes, sir, if Studs ever let him have one, it would be curtains. But he had the rep for being as hard as Studs or any of them. And Iris had threatened to put her dress on and call the party off if he didn't get out; and he had walked out like a whipped dog with its tail between its legs.

He walked around and sniped a butt. He smoked and brooded. He felt that he was different from the guys. All they ever wanted to do was to roughhouse around, make noise, give guys the clouts, raid ice boxes and have gang-shags with girls like Iris, the dirty . . .

He was different. He liked to read books. He thought of the books he read when he got a chance, late at night, after his goddamned old man was in bed, snoring. He thought of the characters, the goddesses of his own pretending, who were like all the nice and fine things in the world. The Lady of the Lake, who had a *breast of snow;* Guinevere, who was *the fairest of all flesh on earth;* Elaine, *the lily maid of Astolat.* He was their champion, their knight; and he roamed through a wild world of his own imaginings . . . all for them. They were his, and none of the Irish bastards could know them, touch them, think of them, see them all white and fine and beautiful and understanding, and like a fine day. They were his. What did he care for fourteen-year-old Iris, the dirty . . . Her age limit was eight to eighty, and maybe she even got kids five and six. He walked and wondered which of the three goddesses he dream-loved the best—or maybe it was Rebecca from *Ivanhoe*? He tried to think of them all as one, and his thoughts got soft and beautiful like music. He wished that he could go home and read about them, imagining himself as their knight, fighting on a white charger to protect their innocence. Then Studs Lonigan and the other dirty micks could have their Iris. But if he went home, his old man would blow his snoot off, calling him a nogoodfornothing loafer, who wouldn't never deliver clothes, but always wanted to be out fighting with the Irish, or else reading books that would never do him no good. It was the sort of crap Davey could remember hearing ever since he could remember hearing anything. He hated like hell delivering clothes for the old man, but he never got any money any other way, unless he stole it. But he got sick of hanging around the tailor shop, listening to his old man nag as bad as if he was an Irish hag.

He wondered. He sniped another butt. He got chilly with fear, thinking of what might have happened if he hadn't cleared out of Iris', and she had got Studs, maybe Studs and Weary, to bust him. He kept feeling more and more sorry for himself, and making dream resolves that he would get even with them all some day. Maybe he would get rid of all yellowness and become a great fighter like Benny

Leonard, who was one smart hebe that could beat the Irish
at their own game; and when Benny got in the ring with
Freddy Welsh, the champ, well, he'd kill Welsh. He would
be a champ as scientific as Benny. They would see then. Or
he would write a great poem about someone like Elaine or
Ellen or Rebecca, with himself the knight, and Iris, the
dirty . . . as the woman who cleaned out the chamber pots.
Dirty Iris made him sore as hell. He hoped to hell she'd
have a baby that looked like Studs Lonigan, only uglier, or
that her old lady would come home and catch the bunch
and call the police, and get them all a jolt in reform school.
Then it would be his turn to laugh. She was so low that she
wouldn't even bar a cockroach, a nigger, or a flea. She was
nearer the ground than a snake.

He wished that he had a nickel for an ice cream cone.
Studs and the other guys generally had spending money,
and he always had to cadge off them. Himself with a
chocolate ice cream cone, licking it with his tongue, slow.
He thought of this until he passed a pretty girl, and that
brought the scene at Iris' back to him. It made him sick and
sore with wanting, and it cut him again, when he thought of
her calling him a kike, and a Jew, and ordering him out after she had let him hang around, see her, shoot craps for his
turn, and all that. And the ice cream cone. Himself and an
ice cream cone, and a jane, like the one that passed, over
on the wooded island at night, when the sky was choked
with stars, like diamonds on the head of Elaine, and the
moon was cool and blue, and the air nice, with the smell of
the trees hitting you, and . . . the jane there . . . and . . . The
goddamn Irish! Goddamn 'em! Goddamn Studs Lonigan
and the whole race of 'em! They got everything and de-
served nothing. They were thickheaded. The dumbest Jew
was smarter than the smartest Irishman. Well, some day!

He met Vinc Curley.

"Hello, Vinc," said Davey.

"Hello! Say!"

"Yeh?"

"Say!"

"What?"

"Say, Davey! Say!"

"What in hell do you want?"

"Say, did you see Andy?"

"Yeh. Why?"

"Oh, I just wondered where he was, 'cause he said he'd
see me aroun' this afternoon."

Davey said that Andy was with the older guys at Iris',
where they were all having a gang-shag.

"What's that?"

"You're too young to know."

Vinc slowly realized what it was, and his feelings
seemed hurt.

"What did he do a thing like that for?" Vinc asked,
speaking in that slow sort of drawl he had.

"He wanted to. What do you suppose?"

Davey was impatient with the idiot.

"I didn't think Andy was like that," said Vinc sadly.

"You'll be the same some day, only don't pick 'em like
Iris."

Vinc asked if Davey had seen Danny O'Neill, Paulie,
Studs, Red and others. And he sadly said he didn't think
that Paulie would do a thing like that. Davey started to
walk away. Vinc rushed up to him, tapped his shoulder, and
said:

"Say! say!"

"Yeh!"

"Did you see Johnny O'Brien?"

"No, nuts!" said Davey.

"I was supposed to see him, too . . . Gee, I wonder why
none of the guys came around this afternoon?"

"Say, Vinc, let me take a nickel, will you?" asked Davey.

"You say you ain't seen any of the guys? Gee, that's

funny. All of them said they were gonna be around," said
Vinc.

"They shoulda been, if they said they would; it was a
dirty trick, them tellin' you they'd be around when they
knew they wouldn't be," said Davey.

"Well, I just wondered," said Vinc.

"Well, what do you say, Vinc? You'll let me take a jit,
won't you? I'll give it back to you tonight. My old man is
gonna give me a couple of bucks for deliverin' clothes for
him. I'll give you the jit back with a nickel interest,"
coaxed Davey.

There was an oblivious look in Vinc's eye. He still wondered why none of the guys were around.

"But how about leavin' me take that jit?" said Davey.

Vinc watched a kid pass on a bike. He exclaimed:
"Oh!"

Davey asked again. Vinc said that he couldn't. He didn't
have any money. He wondered why no one was around.

Davey walked down the street, deciding that Vinc was
another Irish bastard. Davey suddenly turned around and
saw Vinc coming out of the drug store with an ice cream
cone. He said he thought Vinc was broke. Vinc said he'd
found a nickel in his pocket after Davey had gone. Davey
said Vinc was a liar. He said that whenever Vinc got in
trouble, he needn't come around for Davey Cohen to stick
up for him. He'd never stick up for a liar like Vinc Curley.
Vinc said he was sorry. He said: Hones' Dave! He got his
tongue twisted in explanations.

Davey said the guys were coming. Vinc asked where.
Davey pointed in back of Vinc. Vinc turned. Davey
grabbed the cone, and blew, Vinc after him, yelling help,
murder, robber, stop thief. Davey ditched Vinc in the alley
under the elevated tracks.

He walked down Fifty-seventh to South Park, and down
back to Fifty-eighth. At Fifty-eighth and South Park, he
met Stein, an eleven- or twelve-year-old mamma's boy.

Davey said hello. So did Stein. Davey got hard-boiled.
Stein nervously moved away. Davey called him back.

"Where's your wrist watch and tennis racket?" Davey
asked.

"I haven't a racket, and I'm going to the store."

"Well, listen!"

"I am."

"Listen!"

Davey made lip-noises.

Stein turned.

"Commere!"

"I have to go to the store for my mother."

Davey dragged Stein back, and was going to sock him.
He felt powerful. Then he let him go on, and felt even
more powerful.

He walked around, and thought how he was going to be
a great guy, when things got different, and he got away
from the Irish. He would then be understood . . . He was
sad . . . He came out of his sadness by imagining himself
going back to Iris', socking Studs and then hanging one on
Iris.

He met Danny O'Neill. Danny asked Davey if he'd seen
anybody. He talked like he wasn't a punk, but was an older
guy. That got Davey a little sore. But even so, he guessed
Danny wasn't such a bad kid. Davey said most of the guys
were having a gang-shag at Iris'.

"Yeah!" said Danny, curious.

"She likes gang-shags," said Davey.

"Yeah!" said Danny, more curious.

"Sure," said Davey.

"How they doin' it?" asked Davey.

"They shot craps for turns, and each guy takes his turn."

"In front of everybody?"

"By yourself!"

"Gee, you think I could go there some time?"

Davey scorned the punk.

"You're too young. You ain't got the stuff of a man."

"Well, I don't know."

"Well, I do."

"Were you there?" asked Danny.

"Oh, yeh," said Davey casually.

"Why didn't you stay?"

"I didn't want to. I don't like bitches," said Davey.

"Who stayed?"

"Oh, Studs, Weary, Tommy, Paulie, Red, Hennessey, a lot of guys."

"Yeh?"

Davey sniped a butt, and stuck it in the corner of his mouth.

They talked of fighting, and Davey told of all the scraps the Fifty-eighth Street gang had, and what a great bunch it was. Danny asked if Davey could lick Studs, and Davey said he wasn't afraid of anybody . . . but then the guys from Fifty-eighth Street stuck together and fought other guys.

After he left Danny, Davey sniped another butt. He thought of Elaine and Ellen. He became proud that he was a Jew. He recalled Chedar, not the beatings, the ugly smells and the dirty rabbi, but the beautiful sing-songed Hebrew, the beautiful-sad history of the Jews. He was proud. The Irish, goddamn them, didn't have anything like that. He hated the Irish. He vowed he'd blow the place, and go on the bum, see the world, make his own way, come back somebody, and leave them all lump it. He thought of Iris. He remembered how white she had been. The dirty . . .

He went home to supper, and the old man started chewing the rag.

After supper, he slunk in a corner and read *The Lady of the Lake*. He read and reread the line:

And Snowdoun's Knight is Scotland's King

It set his imagination ablaze, and Davey Cohen, huddled in a corner of a dirty room in back of the disordered tailor-shop, became Snowdoun's Knight and Scotland's King.

II

After being at Iris', the guys hung around the corner. They started getting hungry, so they split up and went home for supper. Studs, Weary and Paulie walked together.

"Jesus, it woulda been funny if the old lady'd found us," said Studs.

"It would have been a big joke, all right," said Weary.

"It would have been funny, all right," Studs said. "And our old men and old ladies would have found out. It would have been a big joke, all right."

"Well, my old man and old lady can't do nothin' to me. I left home on 'em once, and they're scared I'll do it again. But my old lady would sure get one on. Whew! She'd pray, and sprinkle holy water all over the house, and I'd get drenched with it, and she'd pray and have masses said for my soul, and she might even try to have me exorcised," Weary said.

"Well, there'd have been a stink that I wouldn't have wanted to get mixed in," Studs said.

"But, hell, what's a guy gonna do? If he doesn't get a girl now and then, well, he's liable to put himself in the nut house," said Paulie.

"Yes, I guess a guy does. I guess it's a sin, but . . ." said Studs, shrugging his shoulders.

"But, gee, I don't see why it's a sin if a fellow has to do it. I think the priests and sisters tell us this because they think we're a little too young. Maybe they don't mean it is a sin if you're a little older," said Paulie.

"Maybe," said Studs, who was having a time with his conscience.

"Well, anyway, they don't make machines any better than Iris," said Paulie.

Lucy Scanlan passed them. She smiled sweetly, and they tipped their hats.

"You know, Lucy's nice-looking and she's got pretty good legs," said Weary.

"You know, guys like us are too rotten to go around with girls like her, or your sister, Studs, or Frank's sister, Fran," said Paulie.

"They're goddamn different from Iris, the dirty . . ." said Weary.

They talked about the thing that made some girls, generally Catholic ones, different. Weary and Studs bragged what they'd do if they ever caught guys monkeying around their sisters. That was only half of what Studs told himself he'd do if he caught a fellow getting fresh with Lucy.

"Bet you when Lucy grows up and marries, she's going to be one swell order of pork chops," Paulie said.

Studs felt like socking both of them.

They stood gabbing at the corner of Fifty-eighth and Michigan. Paulie and Studs said it would be hell if Iris ever snitched. Weary said if she did, she knew that he'd smack her teeth down her throat. Then Paulie talked about how Iris had looked, and they compared her with other girls. Weary said Helen Borax had a better figure, but he'd never seen it. Nobody except Weary could touch Helen with a ten-foot pole; and he had gotten what he wanted from her.

"But it would be hell. Mothers get pretty wild about their daughters. I know the punks once had a party at young O'Neill's, and they played kiss-the-pillow, and that young O'Rorty girl told her old lady, and there was hell to pay. The old lady made her wash her mouth out, and then went up to the sisters and raised hell, and Sister Cyrilla gave O'Neill a report card full of zeroes," said Studs.

"I know. I was there. That's when I made a play for

Cabby Devlin, and she got so sore at me she hasn't spoken to me since. She's decent, too," Paulie said.

"Well, here's one gee that's not worried," said Weary.

Studs and Paulie both admired Weary.

At home, Studs' conscience bothered him, and he still worried lest Iris would snitch. But there was nothing to do, unless he wanted to be a damn fool and spill the beans. He tried to pray, promising the Blessed Virgin that he wouldn't never fall into sin like that again, and he'd go to confession, and after this he'd go once a month and make the nine first Fridays. But he couldn't concentrate on his prayers. He had had to do it. All summer he'd been bothered by it, and then, when the guys said they were going to Iris', he couldn't have run out. He'd had to do it. At school, he'd been taught it was the terriblest sin you could commit. In Easter week of his eighth-grade year, he remembered Sister Bertha saying that God tested you with temptations of sins of the flesh, and if you were able to withstand them you needn't worry about not getting into Heaven. Ninety-nine percent of all the souls in Hell were there because of sins of the flesh.

Hell suddenly hissed in Studs' mind like a Chicago fire. It was a sea of dirty, mean, purple flames; a sea so big you couldn't see nothing but it; and the moans from the sea were terrible, more awful and terrible than anything on earth, than the moans of those people who drowned on the Eastland, or than the wind at night when it's zero out and there's snow on the ground. And all the heads of the damned kept bobbing up, bobbing up. And everybody there was damned for eternity, damned to moan and burn, with only their heads now and then bobbing up out of the flames. And if Studs died now, with his soul black from mortal sin, like it was, well, that was where he would go, and he would never see God, and he would never see Lucy, because she was good and would go to heaven, and he would never see Lucy . . . forever.

And Studs was afraid of Old Man Death.

It was a tough break, all right, because you couldn't seem to resist temptations. It was supposed to be your weakness that made you do it. But everybody's father and mother did it. If they didn't nobody but Christ would have ever been born. The newspapers were full of stories about people who did it. Millionaires did it with chorus girls, and got sued. The older guys did it every Saturday night at a can house. Fellows who weren't Catholics said that priests and nuns did it, but that was a lousy lie. Father Shannon, the missionary, had said that he'd seen hospitals full of people who were rotting away in blindness and insanity because of it. It made Barlowe limp. Everybody was always doing it. There were movies about it, and guys in short pants couldn't go, unless they snuck in. ADULTS ONLY. Everybody doing it, doing what . . . not the turkey trot. But you weren't supposed to. It made God sorry, and put a thorn in the side of Jesus. But God was in Heaven where it oughtn't to really bother him. If maybe Adam and Eve hadn't sinned! Studs had once heard his mother say that they were put out of the Garden of Eden because of it, and that the apple story was only a fairy tale told to kids too young to know any better. But it was supposed to be wrong for a guy to do it. It was right for the sisters to warn you, because temptation always got you. But when you didn't do it, well, you couldn't think of anything else, and it made you hot all over, and you couldn't sleep at night. All you did then was to think you were doing it, and to pretend that every woman you saw didn't have nothing on . . . and it wasn't so much, either. It didn't help guys to understand girls any better, and after it Iris didn't understand him any better, and it didn't scarcely last a minute, and it wasn't as much fun as making a clean, hard-flying tackle in a football game, or going swimming like that day he and Kenny had gone; a double chocolate soda had it skinned all hollow.

He was agitated. If Iris should snitch! If he should die

now in a state of mortal sin! If God should get angry with him for sinning, and do something to him! He wasn't even worthy of Lucy now. He remembered that day in the park.

But what could a guy do? It wasn't so much, but it got you. It wasn't so much, and it made you feel dirty, and . . . He was called to supper. He walked into the dining room, acting and feeling like a man.

SECTION FOUR

Chapter Eight

IT WAS a November afternoon. It made Studs happy-sad. He bummed from school and met Weary and Paulie. They went over to Washington Park. The park was bare. The wind rattled through the leaves that were colored with golden decay. The three kids strolled around, crunching leaves as they walked. Almost nobody was in the park, and their echoes traveled far. Just walking around and talking made them feel different.

They moved, lazily, over toward the wooded island with its trees gaunt and ugly. They talked a little.

As they walked along, Studs started to laugh to himself. They asked him what he was laughing about. He said:

"I was just thinking about the guy in the drug store out near school. Every time a gang of us guys come in, he laughs, and says to his clerk: 'Ope lookat! Hey, Charlie, here comes the higher Catholic education! Lock up the candy cases.' "

"That's a good one. Here comes the higher Catholic education. Lock up the candy cases," said Paulie.

They stood gazing at the chilled-looking lagoon that was tremulous with low waves. Leaves drifted, feebly and willy-nilly, on its wrinkled surface, and there was no sun. They wandered on along the shore line, and Weary broke off a branch from the shrubbery. He whittled a point on it and stopped to poke some ooze out of a dead fish.

"Ugh!" muttered Paulie.

"Dead as a door nail," said Studs.

"Death's a funny thing," said Paulie.

"I ain't afraid of it," said Weary.

"Well, it's a funny thing," said Paulie.

"It's different with a fish. A fish don't count anyway. It ain't got any soul," Studs said.

"Nothing counts enough to make me afraid of it," Weary said.

"How about you, Studs?" asked Paulie.

"Well, I ain't gonna die for a while," Studs said, his voice a little strained.

"None of us know when we're gonna kick the bucket," said Paulie.

"Come on, crepe hanger," said Weary.

"Yeah, Paulie, you sound like your old man was in the undertaking business," Studs said.

Nothing in particular happened; and the day seemed so different from other days. Nothing happened, and it wasn't dull. The three kids felt something in common, a communion of spirit, given to them by the swooning, cloudy, Indian summer day that was rich and good and belonged only to them.

They stopped at the squat stone bridge and looked down into the water, watching the movement of the current, noticing the leaves and branches swimming on its surface.

"How's it going today, Paulie?" asked Studs.

"Oh, the athlete is still running," Paulie said.

"Still running?" said Studs.

"Yeh, he's a good track man," said Paulie.

"If I was you, I'd get the jane that did it to you, and paste the living hell out of her," said Weary.

"So would I, if I could find her. She was a pickup," said Paulie.

"What did she look like?" asked Weary.

"I don't know much. It was at night. I know she was young; she couldn't have been more than sixteen. I guess she had dark hair. She had a voice that was kinda shrill and sharp. I might remember it, but it would be hard to pick her out of a crowd in full daylight," said Paulie.

"Janes like that are no good, and they ought to be smacked," said Weary.

"You better go to a doctor," said Studs.

"I ain't got the jack," said Paulie.

"How about telling your old man?" asked Studs.

"Hell, I can't. He'd get too sore. He's sore enough about school, and keeps yelping about me only being in seventh grade now when I shoulda been graduated," said Paulie.

"Ain't you doin' nothin' for it?" said Studs.

"I got some stuff at the drug store, but they ain't done no good," said Paulie.

"I'd look for that jane and bust her," said Weary.

"Well, you ought to do something for it," said Studs.

Studs wanted to ask Paulie questions about it, but he could see that Paulie didn't want to talk further.

They walked on and stopped at the denuded oak tree where Studs and Lucy had sat. It stirred memories in him that were sharp with poignancy and a sense of loss. Seeing the tree, all stripped like it was dying, made him doubly sad. And Lucy didn't even speak to him any more when she saw him on the street, and she had sat in the tree with him, swinging her legs. . . . He leaned against the trunk and said:

"Well, tomorrow is Saturday!"

"Yeh, and you guys won't have to take the trouble to bum from school," laughed Weary.

"That's a tough break for us," said Studs.

"Yeh, we ought to kick. Studs'll write a letter of complaint to old Father Mahin, ain't that his name, at Loyola, and I'll up and see Battling Bertha, and ask her why is Saturday," said Paulie.

"How is Bertha?" asked Studs.

"Oh, she's as big a crab as ever," said Paulie.

"You ain't seen her, have you?" asked Weary, ironically.

"Yeh, I was to school two weeks ago," said Paulie.

They talked. Paulie wondered out loud about when he would return to school, and if he would get back in class. The sisters said they were giving him his last chance when his mother went up in September and begged that he be let in. Studs said that he ought to have George Kahler write him an excuse, because George was a bearcat at forging handwriting. If Paulie got a sample of his old lady's handwriting, the trick could be turned. Then he wouldn't get canned. Studs and Paulie talked of how they hated school. Weary stood there, whittling.

Suddenly, Studs said:

"Gee, I wonder where Davey Cohen is by now."

"He hasn't written anybody, has he?" said Paulie.

"No, he blew out right after that first time we were at Iris', went on the bum like a damn fool. You wouldn't catch me doing that. I know where I get my pork chops," said Studs.

"He was a kike, and kikes are no good," said Weary.

"Well, with an old man like his, I don't blame the guy for taking to the road," said Paulie.

"He was a kike, and kikes are yellow. If a gee is yellow, I ain't got no use for him, and I ain't never seen a hebe that didn't have yellow all over his back," said Weary.

"Well, Davey's gone," said Paulie.

They wished they had cigarettes.

"And Iris. They didn't make machines better than she was," said Paulie.

"And she never snitched on you, did she, Weary?" said Studs.

"She knew better," said Weary.

"The old lady caught you with her, didn't she," said Paulie.

"And she acted like all old ladies. She went up in the air, threw a faint, cried and hollered. She went to sock me, and I told her hands off, and walked out," said Weary.

"Well, she's in a boarding school, where she can't see any guys now," said Studs.

"And she was good stuff, too, even if she was a little young," said Paulie.

Studs sat down in the leaves by his tree.

Weary said his old man still wanted him to go to school, but he wouldn't go because it was all the bunk.

They hung around Studs' tree a while. Then they walked on in silence. Finally, Paulie said:

"Gee, it's nice here!"

They said yeh, and they walked around. Studs thought of Lucy and how far away last summer was. He wanted to talk about her to the guys, but felt he hadn't better, and anyway, he couldn't hit upon words that would say what he wanted to say. He wished he could go back to that afternoon.

Paulie asked Studs about football.

Studs didn't hear him, but after Paulie repeated the question, Studs said:

"Oh, I was out for the freshman team, and the coach liked my stuff, but he finally canned me. Said it was discipline, because I didn't show up every day. Hell, if I showed up every day, that meant I'd have to go to school. And they raise hell with you for not having homework and that stuff. You can't fake knowing Latin and algebra, and, Jesus, you have to write compositions for English. None of that for me," said Studs.

"Well, you'd make good if you went out regularly," said Paulie.

"It ain't worth it," said Studs.

They walked on. Paulie got soft, and told about how he

liked Cabby Devlin, but he couldn't get to first base with
her since he'd been such a damn fool at young O'Neill's
party. Weary said love was the bunk.

They sat down in leaves by the stepping stones. They
talked a while. Then they were silent. Finally Weary said:

"It's swell here."

"Yeh," they answered.

Darkness came, feather-soft. The park grew lonely, and
the wind beat more steadily, until its wail sounded upon
Studs' ears like that of many souls forever damned. It
ripped through the empty branches. It curved through the
dead leaves on the ground, whipped bunches of them,
rolled them across bare stretches of earth, until they resem-
bled droves of frightened, scurrying animals. Studs wanted
to get out of the park now.

They said so long, and each trooped moodily home. As
he was leaving the park, Studs saw a tin can. He commenced kicking it, and stopped. He was wearing his long
pants every day now, and only kids, punks, kicked tin cans
along. He started walking on. He turned. He looked at the
tin can. He came back and kicked it. He walked on. No one
saw him. He thought about the day. He wondered about
other days, and wished he had a lot of them back. He
wished that he was back at St. Patrick's, instead of being in
high school and in dutch for bumming. He wished that he
and Lucy were together, instead of being like strangers. He
guessed she knew about Iris.

At supper they had a quarrel, as usual. And his mother
asked him to pray so he could decide about his vocation.
And the old man told him he ought to go to confession, because he hadn't been there since June. Then they kicked at
Martin not having his finger nails cleaned and Loretta and
Frances squabbled. After supper, he went to sit by the parlor window. Frances sat down to do her homework. The old
man asked him didn't he have homework. Studs said he
had done it in a study period at school. The old man said it

would be good to get ahead. Studs said he didn't know what homework they'd have ahead. Frances called in to ask him if he knew what declension "socius" belonged to. He said he didn't. The mother said she guessed the girls learned more rapidly than boys did, and they went ahead faster in their lessons. The old man put on his house slippers. He listened to *Uncle Josh Joins the Grangers* on the Vic. Then he opened his *Chicago Evening Journal.* Looking over his paper once, he said:

"Well, Mary, now that the kids are coming along, we'll have to take more time to ourselves, and next summer we'll have to do a little gallivantin' of our own, and go out and make a night of it at Riverview Park."

Studs sat looking out of the parlor window, listening to night sounds, to the wind in the empty tree outside. He told himself that he felt like he was a sad song. He sat there, and hummed over and over to himself . . . *The Blue Ridge Mountains of Virginia.*

1929–1931

SELECTED BIBLIOGRAPHY

Works by James T. Farrell

THE STUDS LONIGAN TRILOGY

Young Lonigan 1932
The Young Manhood of Studs Lonigan 1934
Judgment Day 1935

THE DANNY O'NEILL PENTALOGY

A World I Never Made 1936
No Star Is Lost 1938
Father and Son 1940
My Days of Anger 1943
The Face of Time 1953

THE BERNARD CARR TRILOGY

Bernard Claer 1946
The Road Between 1949
Yet Other Waters 1952

Gas-House McGinty 1933 Novel
A Note on Literary Criticism 1936 Essays
Tommy Gallagher's Crusade 1939 Novel
Ellen Rogers 1941 Novel

Literature and Morality 1947 Essays
Reflections at Fifty 1954 Essays
My Baseball Diary 1957 Memoir
Boarding House Blues 1961 Novel
Collected Poems 1965 Poems
A Universe of Time 1963–68 Stories
Invisible Swords 1971 Novel
The Dunne Family 1976 Novel
The Death of Nora Ryan 1978 Novel

Biography and Criticism

Aldridge, John W. *In Search of Heresy: American Literature in an Age of Conformity*. Westport, CT: Greenwood Publishing Group, 1982.

Branch, Edgar Marquess, ed. *A Paris Year: Dorothy and James T. Farrell, 1931–1932*. Athens: Ohio University Press, 1998.

Farrell, Kathleen. *Literary Integrity and Political Action: The Public Argument of James T. Farrell*. Boulder, CO: Westview Press, 2000.

Flynn, Dennis. *On Irish Themes: James T. Farrell*. Philadelphia: University of Pennsylvania Press, 1982.

Landers, Robert K. *An Honest Writer: The Life and Times of James T. Farrell*. San Francisco: Encounter Books, 2004.

Pizer, Donald. *Documents of American Realism and Naturalism*. Carbondale: Southern Illinois University Press, 1998.

Walcutt, Charles Child. *American Literary Naturalism: A Divided Stream*. Westport, CT: Greenwood Publishing Group, 1974.

Wald, Alan M. *James T. Farrell: The Revolutionary Socialist Years*. New York: New York University Press, 1978.